THE LEGACY SERIES

SERIES TITLES

These Are My People
Steve Fox

We Should Be Somewhere by Now
Stephen Tuttle

Burner and Other Stories
Katrina Denza

The Plan of Chicago
Barry Pearce

The Caged Man
Calvin Mills

A Day Doesn't Go By When I Don't Have Regrets
J. Malcolm Garcia

Trust Issues
K.P. Davis

Adult Children
Laurence Klavan

Guardians & Saints
Diane Josefowicz

Western Terminus: Stories and A Novella
Michael Keefe

Like Human
Janet Goldberg

The Hopefuls
Elizabeth Oness

Never Stop Exiting
Michael Hopkins

Broken Heart Syndrome
Anne Colwell

The Mexican Messiah: A Novella & Stories
Jay Kauffmann

Close to a Flame
Colleen Alles

American Animism
Jamey Gallagher

Keeping What's Best Left Kept Secret
David Ricchiute

Soaked
Toby LeBlanc

The Path of Totality
Marie Zhuikov

Shocker in Gloomtown
Dan Libman

The Continental Divide
Bob Johnson

The Three Devils and Other Stories
William Luvaas

The Correct Response
Manfred Gabriel

Welcome Back to the World: A Novella & Stories
Rob Davidson

Greyhound Cowboy and Other Stories
Ken Post

Close Call
Kim Suhr

The Waterman
Gary Schanbacher

Signs of the Imminent Apocalypse and Other Stories
Heidi Bell

What We Might Become
Sara Reish Desmond

The Silver State Stories
Michael Darcher

An Instinct for Movement
Michael Mattes

The Machine We Trust
Tim Conrad

Gridlock
Brett Biebel

Salt Folk
Ryan Habermeyer

The Commission of Inquiry
Patrick Nevins

Maximum Speed
Kevin Clouther

Reach Her in This Light
Jane Curtis

The Spirit in My Shoes
John Michael Cummings

The Effects of Urban Renewal on Mid-Century America and Other Crime Stories
Jeff Esterholm

What Makes You Think You're Supposed to Feel Better
Jody Hobbs Hesler

Fugitive Daydreams
Leah McCormack

Hoist House: A Novella & Stories
Jenny Robertson

Finding the Bones: Stories & A Novella
Nikki Kallio

These Are My People is a completely engrossing deep-dive into the messy psyches and eccentric behaviors of a wide-ranging group of outcasts and misfits whose company I cherished. Which makes them my people too. And yours. These exquisitely-crafted stories move with great energy and grace, and Steve Fox is equipped with the kind of courage and imagination that forces us to face ourselves and each other with hard-earned forgiveness. I'm grateful that these very real people have survived to share their stories.

—MATT CASHION
author of *Our 13th Divorce*
Winner of the Edna Ferber Fiction Award

Steve Fox writes people. It's as simple (and complicated) as that. In *These Are My People*, his people become ours, become us. Identifiable. Ordinary. Quixotodian. Recovering. Dimensional. Fallible. Falling. Rising. Watching their lives flash before their eyes as readers see Fox's stories do the same. Details from oak trees to beef jerky to baseball to cats are skillfully woven together with Fox's award-winning and approachable words. In his memorable second book, Fox redefines a collection of individuals and their stories into community.

—AMY CIPOLLA BARNES
author of *Child Craft*

Steve Fox's characters are the awkward sort of Midwesterners who don't know what to do with their hands—or their feelings. But when they blurt their weird truth anyway, to strangers, or else let it spiral to deeper mystery inside their own minds, something tremendous happens. Witty but lyrical, absurd yet distressingly grim, these are stories of death, grief, deep childhood trauma, and isolation. Together, they create an interwoven tapestry in which human reaches for human—across the bitter Wisconsin winter, across disassociation and fugue, across a circle of frozen cats, across apple pie with a slice of cheddar—and the characters find (we find) connection. Because "These Are My People."

—ALLISON WYSS
author of *Splendid Anatomies*

Steve Fox's interconnected tales remind us how entwined we are in each other's lives, whether we know it or not. He shows us with microscopic precision that despite our differences, we all encounter grief, loss and mortality, and thousands of ways in which we shatter and recover. A bit like finding lost treasure under the sea, Steve's stories take us on a deep dive into his character's minds, where we discover lost truths about human emotion and experience.

—NIKKI KALLIO
author of *Finding the Bone*
Edna Ferber Fiction Award Finalist

These Are My People is a powerful collection of dark stories that grabs you and doesn't let go. Not without hope, but certainly staying in the shadows. A gripping read.

—RICHARD THOMAS
Bram Stoker Award Finalist

The experience of reading Steve Fox's tender yet chilling collection, his second, is eviscerating as you come to realize that one selection joins with another, a dark piece that snaps with engineered precision into the circular puzzle of each character's life. Be aware, the characters that inhabit *These Are My People* ultimately are not only his people. By the time you finish reading the collection—and you'll want to reread it—you will find that these are your people too.

—JEFF ESTERHOLM
author of *The Effects of Urban Renewal
On Mid-Century America & Other Crime Stories*
Wisconsin Library Association Finalist

Nuanced and thought-provoking, *These Are My People* creates an interconnected universe of high vibrational energy, showing us a myriad of insightful and surprising perspectives.

—MICHAEL HOPKINS
author of *Never Stop Exiting*

The characters inhabiting *These Are My People* may seem to lead conventional lives in cozy settings, but beware! A wrong turn of the wheel leads to a freefalling demise. A faux pas delivered over apple pie reveals a somewhat rotten core. The news of a friend's fatal disease sparks a deeper rumination of one's own mortality. These stories are stuffed to the gills with glorious derailments and emotional avalanches. With both gimlet eye and true compassion, Steve Fox presents a unique view of Americana. It is safe to say these truly are his people. He knows them deeply. Dive into this book and you will know them too.

—ALICE KALTMAN
author of *Almost Deadly, Almost Good*

Each story in this book feels like its own planet orbiting the fictional Wisconsin town of Noisy Creek, with its "cat occurrences," tavern culture, and a bakery whose bread ends seem enchanted. Fox is a master of the short story, plunging us into the lives of his characters who are as noble as they are flawed.

—KIM SUHR
author of *Close Call*

Steve Fox's stories brim with imagination. They'll captivate you with engaging characters in situations that blend the familiar with the unexpected.

—MANFRED GABRIEL
author of *The Correct Response*

These tales are laced with eloquent descriptions of the people and places that make anyone from the Midwest part of "my people." Filled with interesting twists and impeccable dark humor, the stories tell us who we are and sometimes warn us of who we might become.

—JIM LANDWEHR
author of *At the Lake*

THESE ARE MY PEOPLE

stories

STEVE FOX

CORNERSTONE PRESS
UNIVERSITY OF WISCONSIN-STEVENS POINT

Cornerstone Press, Stevens Point, Wisconsin 54481
Copyright © 2025 Steve Fox
www.uwsp.edu/cornerstone

Printed in the United States of America by
Point Print and Design Studio, Stevens Point, Wisconsin

Library of Congress Control Number: 2025944901
ISBN: 978-1-968148-17-1

Cornerstone Press titles are produced in courses and internships offered by the Department of English at the University of Wisconsin–Stevens Point.

DIRECTOR & PUBLISHER
Dr. Ross K. Tangedal

EXECUTIVE EDITORS
Jeff Snowbarger, Freesia McKee

EDITORIAL DIRECTOR
Brett Hill

SENIOR EDITORS
Paige Biever, Eva Nielsen, Reilly Crous

PRESS STAFF
Karlie Harpold, Lilly Kulbeck, Gwen Goetter, Kimberly Janesch, Samantha Bjork, Sophie McPherson, Madison Schultz, Autumn Vine

for Stephanie

ALSO BY STEVE FOX:

Sometimes Creek

STORIES

for all PTSD stumblers and zombie slayers out there
everywhere, doing a Quixote in the same nowhere as me
—just somewhere else.

RISE

Turbulence, panicked hands, panicked feet, and manly shrieking as Robert's 3,500-pound pickup truck skips onto the median, vaults the overpass, and roars straight down and smashes on the highway fifty feet below. The truck breaks apart like a toy. Then silence.

Rewind.

He wants an ejection seat. And a parachute. Bad. But strapped inside his pickup truck, Robert has neither. He was the driver but now he's the faller. Robert the faller. Falling fast through an interstate highway overpass. Falling. Really fast, but rotating slowly, knowing soon enough everything is about to end.

His head whirls. This isn't normal. Trucks are not supposed to fly. And even the passing birds can concur: this is not normal.

But he and Craig aren't flying. They are falling. Quicker and faster and heavier by the blink. Interstate highway. Brutally cold evening. Snowless winter. Ground harder than the highway. Down, down, down, tumbling and twirling downward gasping like a flushed spider. Falling, falling, heavily weightless.

Robert's life isn't flashing before his eyes, though. Well, it is, but it isn't. Contrary to that old cliché, for now, Robert's already skipped to the end of this mess and his thoughts scramble toward his near future. At what lies hours and days and weeks ahead that he'll no longer be a part of.

A glimpse of the moon, aromas of the tender pork stewed in black beer and carrots and onions and potatoes, drifting nude into the welcoming, steamy shower. His son's talented voice he'll never again hear perform, and his Marcie he'll never again smell. All of his possible near-futures.

The roadway below races up and seems to be the thing moving, not them. A ribbon of starlings packing it in for the night twists, folds, and bolts out of the way. Metal filings drawn to a magnet. Robert blinks, right foot still on the brake, hands on the wheel, pressing and pressing in vain to stop their plummet mid-air. Or steer out of their fall, like a skid. But they never covered evasive maneuvers for soaring nosedives in Drivers' Ed. Soaring, falling, slipping through the air like sliding across a sheet of wet ice.

Minutes before, the radio advised of a nearby traffic accident and suggested alternate routes. "Looks like a confirmed fatality," the broadcaster declared, voice dripping with relish. "And gonna be a huge delay." Falling. Another imminent accident. Falling, radio plays Gogol Bordello's "To Rise Above."

Twirling end over end now, faster yet slower and heavier and twistier. Hoarse manly throatiness on the radio. "To Rise Above." Irony. And it should be to *raise* above anyway. Wait. No, to *rise* is fine. *To lend vs. to loan.* Manly squeals in the seat next to him, down toward the speeding highway about to claim their futures.

Will it hurt? Will they die instantly? How long, exactly, does it take to bleed to death? This should not be happening. He is a good driver. Respects speed limits (mostly), yields to pedestrians, always checks his blind spot, and never merges into anyone else's lane. He follows all the rules of the road. And yet one moment they are minding their own business in the passing lane, the next they're zipping atop the median of

Eastbound Interstate 94 at 70 mph, then launched mid-air over the guardrail. Falling. Fifty feet straight down inside a heavy pickup truck. Marcie's soft, perfect, warm mouth, sweet tongue, spot where the curl of her ear becomes neck. Children shouting. Split-pea soup. Warm, fresh, crusty bread. Unpaid bills. Her every angle, curve, dimple. Parted lips. The inside of her forearm. That one spot above her ankle, and the one behind her knee... So many secrets untold. Her crazy, insane eyes and that adorable laugh and roaring sneezes and curiously strong grip. All screaming to an end beneath a silent, snowless winter moon.

So. After decades of banging metaphorical mud from his cleats between pitches, ducking curveballs that never really curved, glares at home-plate umpires, line drives, banter with catchers, toeing the ruts in batters' boxes, and drinking beers with the opponents, after so much of this, *this* is what strike three looks like? Hah, at long last. He always thought that when Death arrived, he wouldn't be there. That Death would find him gone for the day. He'd just stepped out: Sorry, *{your name here}*, please leave a message, and I'll get right back to ya. Or that he was simply just too busy to die that day or, even, say, just standing out there on second base, hands on hips and squinting in for the next pitch.

But there were at least two big strikes against him in his lifetime of staring down opposing pitchers, plus innumerable, lucky foul balls that allowed him to face another pitch. Perhaps his prolonged and charmed at-bat will now end with a swinging strike. He *has* to go down swinging.

Strike one should have done him in back in '87. Got into an argument with his girlfriend and tore off in his car only to hit some loose gravel on a winding county road and roll nine times down the side of a bluff along the St. Croix. Nine times. He should have died then. Twice. And yet he walked away with just a few nicks and a sore neck. *Seat belt!* Entire car destroyed, except for a miracle bubble above and around him. German engineering. Almost made him believe in God again.

Well, at least he won't wind up in a nursing home to rot in his own piss and dementia, stressing the kids out by only vaguely recognizing them, if at all—or even himself, for that matter—and waiting for him simply to pass. Snowless winter. People constantly writing "please RSVP." Resentful, but helpful senior home crew acting happy to clip his toenails, change his squishy adult diapers, and wipe his ass.

No, he'll soon be spared all that.

Highway closing in now. Will they land in traffic or on the shoulder? Looks like the shoulder. Robert hopes as much so no one else gets hurt. Bad enough *they're* going to die. Could have made a change in his job, maybe even gone back to school. Finish his degree in architectural design. Why plumbing? Ah, that's right: it pays well. He learned that rather quickly. People will pay you dearly to stop the river of shit when the sewer backs up into their basement. Craig next to him screaming too loud to hear the radio now. Here comes the ground.

Sleepless nights. Worry about kids. Under the gun again. Trouble always finding him. Will they say that in his eulogy? Will he get one? Apt ending—fifty-eight years of bullshit sleepless nights boil down to an obligatory ten minutes on a lectern by some dude in some church in some place in some town chosen by some people in some other place in some where somewhere else. No control. His family will probably try to do an open casket. Oh, Christ—does anyone really truly know him really truly? That he's lied all along about so many little things? Like knowing how to play the guitar? Or completing the Sunday *Times* crossword each weekend? Or his college G.P.A.? Do they even know that he wants to be cremated? And that to him it's a small miracle that he does not burst into flames on the rare occasion in which he *does* set foot in a church?

Now he's hungry again. Once this is all over, he's got to let that one rattle around his brains for a little while: How, after all, in the process of dying could one possibly contemplate anything other than the *dying* part of one's death? A sandwich? A slab of meatloaf or a wedge of cheese? Jesus. But as absurd as it may seem, Robert realizes that is exactly what's happening now while falling in an upside-down pickup truck: thinking about food. And eating it of course. And knowing now that all that slice of pie he ate on a break really accomplished was to make him hungry. Was supposed to have the opposite effect. And . . . what was it that waitress said that left a grin on his face? Oh yeah: *If yer not drivin round with your windows rolled down, yer just drivin around . . . Jus driiiiivin around . . .* As if giving him a broader message to enjoy the minus-seventeen wind in his hair for a moment while he still could. She rolled her eyes, laughed and spun away to pour more creamer into a loud old lady's cup near the end of the counter.

Strike two was a blast from a twelve-gauge shotgun that managed only to tear up his jacket and shoulder a bit. Actually that was strike one since it happened way before totaling his GTI, but it doesn't really matter—he should have died then, too. But, lucky for him, he was standing too close to the shooter for the buckshot to fully spread and rip off his head. While pheasant "hunting" (no dog, lots of shitty beer) with his teenage friends, they'd tired of fighting the waist-high weeds in semi-drunken pursuit of game out in some farmer's frozen scrub. And, chatting in a circle up on a rise in the field, one of his fellow idiot friends decided to experiment with his own version of Russian Roulette. He stood in the middle of them and spun around and pulled the trigger at random. That moment unfolded itself into the shotgun's recoil and blast, the pellets stretching infinitely long between the barrel of the gun and the small gap between Robert and his buddy Will.

He decided in that moment, even before the twelve-gauge's boom split the sky, even before the pellets hit, barely after the trigger was squeezed, to start telling his parents the truth again. And, despite his tired, washed-up teachers, he'd start trying harder in typing and biology class. He would. He flinched, twisting at the waist to avoid the pellets, all academic at this point of the firing of the weapon, the shot roaring by, catching on his thick hunting jacket, and he would, he decided, feeling the fiery pellets penetrate and lift bits of flesh from his shoulder, fess up and tell his parents that he and his buddies did not, in fact, even bother to cut a hole in the ice that last time they went ice fishing. They got drunk on the lake and slept, passed out sprawled flat on their backs in their snow angels until one of them awoke hours later and declared himself sober enough to drive off the lake. Problem was, they were still too young, still too naïve, still too new at everything. And still too drunk. They climbed into the backseat of a wood-paneled station wagon, all of them, just like the kids they were, piling in and waiting for an adult to slip in behind the wheel up front and cart them away to hockey practice or church. Oh, yeah, Mark finally said, laying on the floor of the backseat, fishing around in his jacket pockets for the car keys.

Robert would tell them all that. And this gun-and-nearly-blown-off-head thing wasn't worth making up a story over, either. It wasn't. He and Will walked away alive, each forever after with one less gleam in their eye, the shock compelling Robert to be a bit more honest, even if only for a little while. Promises made during a panic rarely last.

Newlywed Craig next to him in the upside-down truck and soon father-to-be going to die. That Craig kid, who didn't even need to tag along for this job. Falling. Truck getting heavier, falling faster. Robert just wanted the company. Poor bastard. Shit—here comes the road. Uncaring cold moon.

He ended up much shorter than everyone had expected. Shorter than his sisters, even. Always spelled out his numbers under one hundred: ninety-seven, twenty-three, forty-two. Number vs. numeral. *Eleven* is a number; 11 is a *numeral*. And there exists a distinct difference. Actually understood and could relate to the metric system, able to picture 524 ml, 31 km, 93 kg, and -19 C.

Craig rasps, and there's that one retired couple on the Interstate Highway in the middle of Wisconsin asking for directions to Alaska. As if it were just down the road a piece, like a gas station or a truck stop. So sweet—they had started out in Georgia. But Robert, being the Robert he was, didn't hesitate. He turned and faced west, and explained the way with long sweeps of his huge hands: *Take 94 West here to Fargo, then go North to Winnipeg. Then take a left about nine hundred miles to Edmonton, then a right for about twelve hundred miles more. It'll be on yer left. Give yerself a few days.* They thanked him.

The figurative foul balls of his fifty-eight years now seem infinite, and Robert wishes this current pitch could be yet another. But he knows. He's going to swing and miss this one. Clearly he will not tip this one over the catcher's head, not send it down onto his toe, not pull it foul, nor launch a souvenir up into the bleachers behind him. Not this pitch.

Although, a very long literal at-bat during a game against a team from Santa Fe, New Mexico, comes to mind: quarter-finals of the Men's National Fastpitch Softball Tournament. And somehow the count never did go full, despite fouling off a stunning forty-four pitches. He missed five home runs, clearing the fence just foul down each line. Hit himself in the ankle once, hit the umpire's mask four times, caught the catcher on the shoulder twice, sent two into his own team's dugout, scattering his buddies, almost hit the third base coach twice, and sizzled over one dozen straight back into the backstop. And, gasping at each delivered pitch, the crowd went dead silent. Forty-four foul balls. For a sublime while there it was just Robert, the pitcher, and the catcher out on that dusty infield. And, too worn out to muster any other pitch from his repertoire, the guy finally just threw him a knuckle ball. Robert lunged and missed what should have been ball three, walked back to the bench, found his hat and glove, and sat down, arms folded and legs crossed. Strike three, one down. Easily the most awesome and productive strike-out of his career: His team promptly scored four runs during the remainder of that same inning, and by the middle of the next, Santa Fe's ace was done.

It wasn't until after the game someone told him how long he'd been up there batting—twenty-five minutes. For one at-bat. Longer than most innings last. Probably longer, since no one bothered to check their watch until about ten minutes into it all, and Robert tends to step out after every other pitch to stretch and reset his vision by focusing on the horizon for a moment.

An hour later, the two teams found themselves seeking refreshment at the same tavern down the road. Santa Fe's ace joked over beers and icepacks that it would have been another twenty minutes had Robert let that pitch go for ball three—*it was in the dirt!* Robert laughed and said the catcher should have just called that knuckler when count first got to one and two and have done with him straight away.

But this falling-upside-down-inside-a-truck deal is indeed a whole other type of at-bat, a whole different pitch, and not one in the dirt. And now his twenty-five minutes in the batter's box are about up.

Debacles from his past. How his life could have forked. Surely in a parallel universe he's not screaming toward the planet's surface upside down in a pickup truck. Shoulda woulda coulda didn't. So many little decisions and tiny acts never made that could have re-routed his life entirely. Smiles refused. Poems carefully written on the shore of a sandy beach gentle waves pulled away, forever, stanza by stanza, into the Pacific depths. Small kindnesses spurned or ignored. So busy. So fucking tired. And that one kiss he never risked.

How many hours of his life spent on hold? Hours? Days? *Weeks*. Ugh. Muzak interspersed with explanations of how very important his call was to whoever it was who held him on hold.

County highway racing up from below. Why did they rename it? He liked the old name, whatever it was. Shrieking Craig next to him, wailing like a newborn. Going to die. Very soon. Truck completely upside down now. Large objects with sharp edges tossing about inside the truck, hitting them. Cups. Cans. Bottles. Friends. Forgotten passwords. Stiffed waitresses. Crappy PCs. Pretty, young downtown girl with *Nice Tits* inscribed impeccably across the ample bust of her t-shirt. Couldn't argue with that one at the time. So much energy. And life. Pain. Laughter. Joy. Truck a mess. Winter moon. Approaching road. Falling straight down now, heavier and upside down. Panicked hands, pressing pressing steering stomping grabbing steering pressing. Nothing. They won't see this.

Falling. Upside down. Marcie's clear eyes, perfect neck, warm breath, parted lips, their secrets and wry looks. Concurring birds. Giggling kids. Approaching road. All of Marcie. All of her all. Moonflash.

No ejection seat. No parachute. No time. Robert reaches for the volume.

RINGS

Love is a many splendored, murderous thing, as you will soon see. Harriet Boslem understood this. Which is why she murdered her husband, Emmet. It was what he wanted and what a good wife would do for the man she loved. And Harriet Boslem, nationally renowned professor of chemistry at University of Wisconsin-Noisy Creek, was a very, very good wife, indeed.

ANOTHER CAT CAME TO DIE on the frozen turf outside Harriet Boslem's window twenty minutes after dawn. By now she'd come to expect the sight of one or two newly dead cats around sun-up in the backyard of her yellow house on Vincent Street. And by now, after so many cats, the entire thing had gotten old. She watched this last one walk into the yard and trace a large ring around the pile of other dead cats—now numbering too many to quickly count—before selecting a spot to settle in to die, fused to the bare earth, in fresh, dead, livor mortis.

"Here we go again," Harriet cawed, tearing at a wedge of dried venison with her teeth. She looked across the room in the direction of the hallway and announced with a sigh, "I'm gonna go have a look." She cleared her throat of a large amount of viscid mucus. "Ya never know," she grunted, pressing a palm into her lower back as she raised herself into a standing stretch. "This one might be tagged, honey."

"Ja. Ya never know . . ." a much younger woman's voice echoed back through the house.

"Makes you wonder," Harriet said, again. She first muttered this remark to herself three weeks prior while observing Cat No. 7 arrive, coil up, and die minutes later out there in her yard, connecting itself, end to end, to two other frozen, dead cats. It propped its chin upon the haunches of the cat to the front and curled its tail around behind to touch the snout of another, deliberately filling a gap between the two others, completing the perimeter of a rough circle approximately eight feet in diameter. Cat No. 7 promptly froze directly to the ground, as unmovable as a protruding oak root. She couldn't even budge it with a spade.

"Lends to their mystique, perhaps," the voice said. "Don't forget some people think cats are people spirits on the inside."

Harriet loosed a derisive snort, chewing her morning jerky hungrily and in chunks. She stopped abruptly when a sharp fragment jammed up along the gum-line between a pair of teeth.

"Ja, ja," she called out, rolling her eyes and moving the tip of her tongue to the jerky sliver. "Ask a dog person. 'Dogs are people, too,' they all say." She coughed noisily. "Bollocks. Dogs and cats are mere mammals." With some effort she swallowed the dried meat and raised her teacup. "Just like us."

The source of the younger woman's voice stared out, alarmed, from behind the looking glass in the back hallway.

"Oh, my," she said, watching her hands touch one, then the other bare shoulder. "What does that make me?"

Harriet looked over at the reflection of the much younger woman behind the framed glass on the wall. "Gorgeous." She smiled, tugging at a tooth, and looked back out the window at the latest cat.

HARRIET SLIPPED HER FEET into a pair of sandals and pulled on Emmet's heavy leather Air Force jacket over her nightgown and stepped out into the very cold, still morning to examine the newest dead arrival. Naked blades of crystalized grass snapped and shattered beneath each step. Her breath hung in stiff plumes in the calm morning air as she eased toward the woods on the west end of her city lot. Beyond the woods Noisy Creek chattered cold and swift and loud over rocks and boulders in its rush to join the St. Croix River a few miles to the south and west. She rested a bare foot on the back of the newest cat, dead on its side and still warm to the touch. Her toes glided through soft tufts of fur and pressed down on its ribcage. Ectoplasmic threads of gossamer steam looped up from the cat's nostrils, and slowly coiled and glided toward the house, knifing through the winter air and finally dissipating near the slender trunk of a young maple tree near her back porch.

Beyond the young maple a man and woman on the sidewalk exchanged much livelier breaths as they conversed in cold, poofy dialogue bubbles. Harriet penciled an imagined conversation into their translucent plumes, framing the couple onto the page of a Sunday morning comic strip, with one bare foot still resting on the fleeting heat of the cat's furry ribcage.

```
woman: Got one at the Walgreen's, then.
man: A flu shot?
woman: No. A palm-reading.
man: Oh! Geez.
```

Her gaze returned to the cat beneath her foot. Cold, still morning. January. Noisy Creek, Wisconsin. She wiggled the toes of her other foot, bare beneath the straps of the slip-on sandal. *A Walgreen's palm-reading,* she chuckled. *Of all things.*

She glanced at Cat No. 1, its hazel eyes now long frozen solid, two freezer-burned ice orbs peering, stunned, across the lawn through the spindly winter shrubbery toward Vinny Street.

She wasn't sure about Cat No. 2, when it came, and how it acted or behaved prior to hooking up with cat No. 1 to die with its nose on No. 1's rump. Cat No. 2 had appeared in the middle of the night, and Harriet wouldn't have noticed it at all if it weren't for the jeering blue jays calling out in distress (or delight) at the sight of the new dead thing at first light.

Cat No. 3 had wandered into Harriet's yard practically lost, like some stoned, adolescent boy. The cat stopped mid-stride, and looked directly at Harriet, who was reading inside at the kitchen table, as if to ask, *So . . . Is this, like, the right place? I'm looking for, like, a string of dead cats?* to which Harriet calmly indicated with a slight tilt of her head, channeling her brainwaves down an invisible conduit, *Yep, it's over there.* The cat moved on and finally saw the other two sprawled out end to end to form the beginning of a crescent. No. 3 glanced back toward Harriet as if to say, *Looks like I found it? Thanks?* and continued. It lay down and connected to cat No. 2, completing a perfect half-moon of felines. Minutes later, she set down her book, slipped on her sandals and threw a coat over her shoulders and walked outside to check it for a tag.

"No one ever lays claim to the damn things," she said, giving the cat a solid punt. It didn't budge, having already adhered so firmly to the ground as to practically become part of the earth itself. Harriet rubbed her foot and cussed.

The next group of cats settled inside the first seven, forming a concentric circle within. Then the next grouping coiled inside those, and so on, until the entire area of the circle filled with dead, frozen cats.

"Rings," Harriet croaked, shaking her head in the café across the street. The waitress poured coffee. "They're coming," she said to the waitress, casually, as if noticing that the leaves were clinging to the branches a week or so longer than expected this fall, "to die in rings." Harriet drank coffee from a cup fashioned after Elvis Presley. The waitress asked about waiting for spring to bury them. Harriet nodded. She liked the waitress. "Thankfully, it's been so mercifully cold," Harriet told her. "So they won't stink up the place."

Everything else about the cat occurrence was unexplainable so it was nice to have something, some sort of pattern, to cling to in the middle of what had become a bit of a curious situation and posed something of a logistics problem for a woman living alone now retired. Rings. Rings of dead cats. In her backyard. All of which would have been highly unusual for anyone were it not for the fact that it had happened in nearly identical fashion in Harriet's backyard the previous year, except with dogs. All cleaned, groomed, and well-cared-for dogs. One short-haired runt had even worn a green doggie-sweater-vest the day it decided to wander in.

"But it's *not* the same as the dogs," Harriet sighed, now pacing through her house. She paused, hands on hips, looking into the looking glass hung on the wall connecting the piano room to the library.

"I know," her reflection said. She twisted the ends of a length of her copper-colored hair between a thumb and forefinger. "The dogs made connecting rings, not concentric ones, by those two ash trees where the woods get thick. About twenty-five, all ... connected." She glanced out from her side of the mirror toward the cat stack and folded her arms. "I was here for that. Remember, Harriet?"

Harriet laughed like a raven. "Of course, honey." She glanced quickly back at her reflection and smiled. She liked how she looked thirty or so years ago. Her reflection smiled back at her, liking what she saw thirty or so years later.

HARRIET HAD HOPED this winter would be different. She glanced off to her right where the 'dog ditch,' as she called it, had been dug and subsequently filled with dead dogs, all of which came for their final nap during the dead of winter, too.

She hired a college kid to bury them once the weather broke. Same kid who painted her house the summer before. The quality of his work was adequate, she supposed. Though it took him the entire summer to finish painting. Harriet knew he was simply showing off for the passing college girls who'd hung around for the summer session. He—Lance— would strip down to his cut-off jeans to ripple and flex in the sun as he "painted." And ripple and flex and glisten in the sun he indeed did. Strapping, gleaming lad with wavy, sun-bleached blonde hair and dark, walnut eyes. Harriet's reflection practically leapt out from behind her frame to accost the boy. But that wasn't necessary. Lance clambered in through the frame of the looking glass eagerly enough each day during his lengthy lunch break.

A couple years before the dogs it was herds of bunnies that came to her yard to die, and then prior to that it had been squirrels, though she believed that case to be logically explained easily enough.

The squirrels dying en masse in her yard was merely coincidental to losing an enormous oak tree to a powerful storm that hit exactly on the Summer Solstice. Once the fallen tree was cleared, each adult squirrel continued to leap from tree to tree, as its years of developed muscle memory and the habit of daily routine had trained it, only to leap out and grasp at a sudden nothingness where a connect- ing tree should have sprawled out across the back yard to receive it. One by one, each squirrel fell straight down to the ground, dead in one thump on her rock-hard yard forty feet below, dying hard like an old habit. Took about a week. That season's new kits seemed to be the only recipients of the That-one-enormous-oak-tree-connecting-the-woods-to- the-other-side-of-the-house-is-gone memo, and managed to circumvent the new chasm and therefore a premature and ugly end.

That year Harriet simply threw each dead squirrel into Noisy Creek behind her house. Done. Unlike the squirrels, however, the dogs eventually required burial once the weather broke a few months later.

So did her husband, who died in her yard, the winter many years before the squirrels. The dogs, very mysterious. They stumped her. The squirrels, easily explainable by the missing oak limbs, the broken bridge that had once spanned her backyard. The occasional, infrequent bird, which she'd until now discounted completely as a thing that had come to die in her back lot, Harriet chalked up to her very old and very protected window cleaning elixir involving lemons, vinegar, and newspapers. Harriet was a chemist, after all, and had insisted if she couldn't manage a decent window cleaning solution, she'd demand the Regents at UW-Madison rescind her degrees. Bunnies? Well, who knows. Bunnies are just dumb. Could have been some city-wide bunny blight or brain malaise that got into them. These cats, though, she was still unsure. This felt a lot—too much—like the dogs, and nothing like Emmet, who died before all of them out in her yard, and for good reason. Emmet was the easiest to explain of all. Harriet poisoned him.

HARRIET REMOVED HER BARE FOOT from the back of today's cat, Cat No. 22 or No. 23, and placed it back inside her leather sandal. She clutched Emmet's Air Force jacket to her body and wondered again just what the hell exactly happened to Emmet, what permanent change came over him so quickly to drive Harriet, in the end, to murder.

She had known him all her life, going back to early child-hood when they took baths together while their parents socialized outside beneath a gazebo or downstairs at a bridge table. Their marriage was practically pre-arranged, and they knew it, managing to avoid a romantic encounter of any sort until their mid-twenties when Emmet finally called up Harriet for a date.

"Uh . . . Hi, Hare. Emm here."

"Yes, I know it's you, Emmet," Harriet said, already impatient. Harriet's mother, Georgia, had declared Harriet, as early as age nine, *world's youngest curmudgeon.* She wasn't wrong. "What is it?" she said.

"Well, I was just talking to Mom . . . and . . . well—"

"Oh for heaven's sake, Emmet!" Harriet snapped, "Just ask me out and let's be done with it, then."

And he did. Classic walk in the park, dinner, and a movie.

"Did you have a nice time?" Emmet asked her, the following day, over the phone.

"I suppose so," Harriet sighed, leafing through a chemistry textbook. "About as enjoyable as could be expected, I imagine." She flipped a page.

Emmet would eventually come to understand that this was about as much as Harriet would gush over anything. Harriet was dry yet easy to please, one who remained forever and continuously unimpressed. An extraordinarily prepared crème brûlée begat about the same *oh, that's nice* or *of course* reaction as Emmet's attempts at tuna salad or meatloaf. Never any malice, simply a perpetual state of ho-hum underwhelment.

Until after Emmet changed. Harriet never did understand what it was that changed in him, and she suspected Emmet didn't know, either. Or notice. Or care. No real warning signs, no easy explanation such as a slip into alcoholism or other chemical abuse or dependency or even some tawdry affair (or one gone horribly awry). Nothing. He simply woke up one morning with a personality completely changed for the worse. As though he'd suffered some deep cerebral trauma in his sleep.

She shook her head and turned away from her pile of dead cats and tightened his jacket around her and trod back to the house, shattering the frozen grass, delicate blades bursting into fine crystal shards that tinkled in her wake back to the patio. She kicked off her sandals and hung Emmet's thick jacket on a hook. She grabbed a grapefruit and stirred the logs in the fireplace and sat down next to the book she'd been reading near the fire.

Harriet looked around, then pulled the skin back from her morning grapefruit, exposing the flesh of the ruby red meat beneath. She carefully tore off another palm-sized piece of peel, then another, and again, until all that remained in her hands was the juicy, raw grapefruit, naked and fresh. She glanced out the window at the stark morning and brushed the peelings aside. A pair of dog-walkers on the sidewalk paused to chat. Harriet added dialogue to their fleeting plumes:

    Man 1: But, then . . . What about the moon?
    Man 2: Oh, easy—that's also flat.
    Man 1: Ah, of course.

She watched the two men and the two dogs separate and resume their paths—

    Dog 1: Later.
    Dog 2: Yup.

—moving in opposite directions, Man 1 crouched at a steep angle as he practically tumbled down the sidewalk toward the Vinny Street bridge.

The wind must be gusting over there, she thought. She blinked. Harriet frequently divined the passing conversations of others, and enjoyed the challenge of stenciling the dialogue into the ethereal winter dialogue vapor plume-bubbles. Made for more entertaining, impromptu and often, in her mind at least, amusing exchanges. But never once did any conversation contain mention of all the animals that had traversed the town to die in her back lot or comment on a missing pet. Nor, for that matter, did the subject of Emmet ever make its way into any passing plume.

She looked down at the dripping grapefruit she turned over in her hands, and sighed. Her thoughts, though, began to drift toward Emmet, like they often did, when the woman beyond the looking glass interrupted her.

"Can you open today's crossword?"

Harriet blinked, and looked around as if recalling where she was. "Certainly, honey." She opened the newspaper carefully with wet fingertips.

"How's it lookin?" her reflection asked.

"Let's see . . ." She pressed the paper flat on the table with the side of her fist. "Want one?"

"Sure," her reflection said quickly. "What's, uh . . . three-down?"

Harriet adjusted her 'cheaters' and located the clue. "Hanging Garden River," she called out. "Six letters. Probably starts with a—"

"Tigris," her reflection said.

Harriet eyed the page, shook her head, and curled her lips into a very satisfied smirk. She reached for a pen. "Very good." She paused to write, still smirking as each letter filled its corresponding square. She looked up. "Another?"

"Naw," her reflection said. "Think I'll quit while I'm ahead." She looked around. "Need to use the loo anyway. Excuse m—"

"Hang on," Harriet said. "While you're back there . . . Could you grab me a book, honey?"

Her reflection stopped and turned. "Which one?"

"The Pierre Menard one."

Beyond the looking glass her reflection tossed her hair aside while she tapped her lips with her fingertips and thought about where the book may be located. "Oh," she said, and raised her eyes brightly and nodded. "Right. Sure, Harriet. No problem." She reached out and picked through a pile of magazines on an end table. "On my way back, though, if you don't mind." She smiled and selected a magazine.

"Thanks," Harriet said. "No rush. A footnote in the book I'm currently reading makes reference to a footnote in that one. Both fiction." She smiled. "Can you believe that? Like a ring of about a hundred books that one after another connects to and leads back to the first."

The woman behind the mirror smiled and faded away down the hallway on the other side of the looking glass frame, long copper hair swishing behind her.

Harriet pulled a section from her grapefruit and eased it methodically over her lips and pulled it into her mouth with her tongue and pressed her molars slowly upon it, closing her eyes, tender fruit flesh tearing and breaking, juices oozing forth, flowing across her tongue and moistening her lips. She removed another dripping section and licked her lips as she reached for a napkin. All this wonderful, delicious grapefruit mess used to be Emmet's job. And there was never a 'mess' when he did it. No mess that she ever knew of, anyway—Harriet was always still in bed when Emmet tended to this portion of their mornings.

WHATEVER HAD HAPPENED to change Emmet so dramatically did so permanently. Until finally after more than three years of his attempts to drown Harriet's spirit, Emmet crossed a line, and Harriet poisoned him outright. He fell over dead minutes later, out in the yard.

The final straw happened during a Boslem Christmas. Traditionally, Harriet and Emmet had never exchanged gifts during the holidays, even before they were married. It was a good arrangement. No expectations to crush, no obligations to fulfill, no metaphorical bar to surpass the following holiday season.

Though they occasionally did pick up an impromptu gift of flowers, a piece of jewelry, a small piece of art that caught the eye. Little things that in the moment made them think of the other. These gestures and exchanges were always spontaneous, and never obligatory nor spendy for the sake of spendiness. Such as the demands of the Christmas season.

Then one day Emmet woke up with that horrible new personality and rapidly became the withdrawn, changed man she would later kill. The spontaneous gifts stopped. There were no treats of milkshakes, ice creams, flowers, morning grapefruit. Nothing. And the comments and remarks and notes he left behind became less humorous and sharper and more harsh as the year ground to a close. Occasionally downright mean, then more frequently mean, until eventually Emmet spewed very confidently nothing but downright cruelty and aspersions.

That was a long year. And Emmet showed little sign of letting up the next. Harriet also became withdrawn, mostly kept to herself when at home. Their house was old enough and large enough to allow for that sort of living. And she found herself spending more time at her labs and the YMCA. She invented a couple of time-consuming projects and assembled teams of young researchers who needed the experience; meanwhile maybe more time at the Y could help her drop a few pounds. Maybe that's all this was? She was a little older and a little heavier?

About Halloween the next year, though, Emmet showed signs of turning back to his old self. She almost couldn't bear to open the note he'd left taped to the seat of her bicycle one morning. And she may not have pained herself to read it at all were it not for the very awkward (for Emmet) appeal to
PLEASE READ!!!
on the outside. So unlike Emmet to punctuate in a manner he generally derided, even in his new-found otherness. Perhaps he was mocking one of their friends? Gloria, possibly. Harriet herself even had a thing or two to say about Gloria's holiday cards. She looked at the folded note again. Such a small square of paper, Harriet thought. Yet no square is too small for the pain of his pen.

Harriet opened the note.

All of this . . . <u>this</u> . . . I promise, I will make up to you. There's no excuse for how I've been behaving. And for so long at that.

She slipped the note into her shorts and pedaled off to Hypatia Hall.

THE HOLIDAYS CAME. Thanksgiving was a delightful feast with friends and some family. Seventeen guests. Emmet stayed up all night making the final preparations and started the last stages of malt-brined turkeys (one oven-roasted, one charcoal-grilled) early that morning for the mid-afternoon meal. He assembled and baked a vegetarian lasagna with a very patiently prepared homemade ragù sauce, cut vegetables and readied cheeses for appetizers and stewed sides and warmed other sauces and marinades days in the making and rolled pie crusts and kneaded bread; meanwhile, he brewed an exotic civet coffee served in a warmed cup with a rich cream for Harriet as she slept in. She later enjoyed an in-house massage followed by a leisurely effervescent bath while he continued to prepare the meal and finished readying for guests.

It was the return of Emmet's sweet gestures Harriet had come to expect over the years. Small kindnesses. Flowers, short love notes, and breakfast in bed—grapefruit painstakingly peeled, separated, trimmed and arranged upon a crescent-shaped platter, homemade yogurt and homemade granola nestled within and dotted with berries, kiwi slices, or pieces of other nice fruit. Often he'd retain the rinds of mango or orange peels to make a special afternoon tea to share before the hearth or out on the porch or patio. For years he'd been so effusively good to Harriet and cozied her on an embarrassing level. It made her feel guilty to the extent that she never mentioned it to any of her friends until it all stopped abruptly, then bent into the exact opposite, barbed direction.

Saturday after Thanksgiving he rolled onto his side in their bed and touched her face. Harriet opened her eyes while he covered her shoulder with the bedsheet. He pressed a hand into her back. "I've put you through so much, Hare," he said. He stroked each eyebrow above her light green eyes, then brushed the backs of his fingertips along a high cheekbone.

Harriet snuggled in closer to him and began a quiet curmudgeon chuckle but stopped when Emmet pulled away. There was a chill in his eyes.

"Promise me something, Hare," he said. He looked deeply into her eyes, though his voice seemed unsteady.

"Of course." Harriet felt her heart thud.

"Promise me that if I ever go back to—if I'm ever like that again—that you'll put a gun to my head."

Harriet gasped and backed away to look at him. To take him all in. And she could see was completely serious. "Emmet," she breathed. "That's the stuff of movies. Not—"

"And pull the trigger."

"Emmet! No! I—"

"I mean it," he said. "I desperately do *not* want to be remembered like that."

"Emmet," she said, still laying on her side. She placed a palm on the side of his face. "Emmet, we could consult a—"

"NO—Please, Harriet," he said, voice wavering. "Promise me. No doctors. No shrinks. No meds. Promise me you'll just end it yourself."

With a dry throat, Harriet promised.

WEEKS PASSED. They celebrated Christmas at her sister Velora's home in Raleigh that year. Emmet's mood felt different Christmas morning, but Harriet, wary only for a moment, brushed it aside and went to sit with her mother for coffee while Emmet came to life, grumbling around the guest bath.

And she'd forgotten about his morning moodiness until after the evening meal, when he pulled out a small, ornate chest bearing a hand-tied red bow in front of Harriet's entire family and placed it in her lap. She was seated on the floor laughing and enjoying a cognac, resting her back against a davenport.

She looked up at him and recalled he seemed off earlier in the day.

"It's a special gift," he announced, looking around to make sure the entire family heard.

"Oh, Emmet," she exclaimed. "Here? For heaven's sake." Her heart sank, and she flushed with embarrassment. She glanced away and looked around the room, then did a double take as her gaze caught Emmet's, and with a jolt of dread, knew he was very serious. Whatever lurked inside the chest, she'd have to act as surprised and demonstrably appreciative as a sub-forty curmudgeon could. And possibly she wouldn't have to act at all. He may well have hit this one out of the park. Possibly Emmet would indeed take her breath away. Possibly. But after so many years of no Christmastime gifts whatsoever ... Well, she just had no way of knowing. From that little chest she was as likely to pull out something horribly gaudy and tacky as she was an elegant string of pearls. She'd actually wanted one of those. Harriet sighed inside and looked around again. She'd have to wing it.

"Yes," Emmet said, "Open it here, please. I want the whole family to see this, darling."

Harriet lowered her head and stared at the lid. Traced the edge of an embedded glass gemstone with her thumb. She was out of ideas for what to do, other than open the thing and get it over with. She looked up and explained, breathless, around the room—there certainly were a *lot* of family here—that she and Emmet had made a point of never exchanging Christmas gifts. And that this little chest was the first gift since, well, ever.

Family members glanced around at one another, grinning with confusion and intrigue. They closed in. She removed the bow and lifted the lid carefully to reveal folded gold tissue paper that matched the trim on the chest. Something solid and hard beneath.

"Go on!" Emmet urged, rocking on his knees. "Unwrap it."

Harriet hesitated as hushed family edged closer still, completely silent, as if peering over a railing that separates the public from a panda exhibit at the zoo. Someone sniffed from above her shoulder.

"Okay."

Harriet pulled away the tissue paper. A gasp echoed around the room.

"It's . . ." she started, and caught herself. "Emmet. It's . . ."

"Yep!" Emmet cried, like a TV game-show host, "Gold! It's gold! Gold, Harriet, gold!"

"I—" Harriet started, but couldn't speak. She stared into the trunk.

"Gold coins! Like a pirate's booty" he roared. "Ten quarter-ounce Gold Eagle coins!"

Harriet lifted a coin from the neat row. The gleaming head of a bald eagle on one side, Lady Liberty bearing a torch on the other.

"Gold coi—" Velora blurted, and clamped a hand over her mouth. An uncomfortable silence spread through the room like a gas leak.

"How . . . wonderful," her mother finally said, and looked at Emmet, who had also gone very quiet. "Emmet?"

"Yep," Emmet said, eyes blazing, "Worth about thousand bucks a pop! But timeless and priceless, really." His head swung around at the roomful of folded arms and agape jaws. Harriet's brother set down his cognac and clasped his hands behind his back and stared.

"And, best of all," Emmet said, taking the coin from Harriet and flashing it around the room. He squatted down beside her and continued. "She gets to keep it *all*," he hissed, and snatched the trunk from her lap and stood up straight in one motion. "Once she finally loses some weight!"

Harriet fell back on her hands. She'd been seated on the floor, leaning against that davenport, and now in a blink felt far too fat to be sitting on a floor, legs folded and crammed into a pair of blue jeans. Or sitting cross-legged, anywhere, any longer. Every ounce of every pound of fat she'd slowly and very agonizingly lost during the blinding, mindless stream of jumping jacks, treadmills, jogging, swimming, pretending to care about inane cul-de-sac yakety-yak at the Y, food deprivation and outright hunger—twenty-five pounds over the course of eighty-seven (yes, she'd kept count) weeks—returned from an unknown underworld, the afterlife of fat, or wherever it is fat disappears to when you lose it, and pulled and cloyed at her heavily, fleshily, and sweatily. Harriet parted her lips to speak, but her mouth, her voice, all time folded into an invisible, static-free, void.

She was only aware of her painfully dry mouth, her wooden tongue, perhaps of a fly buzzing above the horrified silence, then the creak of the floorboards that sagged beneath her weight, and the wide-eyed heads of family members disintegrating into tiny dots, buttons, and beads, all spinning more and more rapidly all around her.

FAT AND AFRAID, Harriet never did recover from that gift of Gold Eagles. Nor would Emmet. Within a week he fell over dead in the backyard of their yellow house following a mango tea. A mango tea stirred with a lethal dose of a potassium chloride (KCl) concoction that masked his murder as a massive heart attack.

Emmet had requested a bullet. But Harriet was a non-violent person. She avoided swatting mosquitoes, shooed houseflies from her home with an eerie, nearly supernatural ease, and even trapped spiders with a napkin and paper cup, once they'd grown to a certain size, and released them outside. She didn't own a gun and, besides, as she explained to her reflection, "A gun would make a horrible mess."

"And a horrible noise," her reflection said.

No, Harriet was not prone to violence. But she was a chemist. So a KCl elixir it was.

This compound breaks down into both potassium and chlorine, in which the chlorine (Cl) binds with the human body's naturally occurring sodium (Na) to create NaCl—sodium chloride—common table salt. The resultant heart attack is found to have no known cause—as all that is found in the body is a slightly elevated level of NaCl. Too much potassium in the body causes tachycardia (fast heart rate), which then leads to something known as ventricular fibrillation, one of many possible causes of cardiac arrest. During Emmet's elevated state of otherness he was known to function at a relatively high level of stress and on insufficient amounts of sleep. And given his so-so health, a certain amount of weight gain—that so-called 'family paunch'—plus the fact he'd already lost colleagues who'd also fallen over dead the past few years, heart failure didn't come as much of a surprise to anyone. No questions asked.

Harriet melted the earth with pots of boiling water and dug a knee-deep hole near a pair of ash trees at the edge of the woods. She placed the clay urn bearing Emmet's remains and swept the wet earth over it and went back into the house. She prepared a snack and went for a long walk through the winter woods where the creek parts the UW-NC commons. There, Harriet rested on a large stone near the creek. She held a tissue to her mouth and stared, vacantly, at the razor-thin plates of ice that formed and cracked and occasionally broke way along the bank of the loud little river.

Harriet encountered her permanent reflection in the looking glass for the first time the next afternoon, still wearing the previous day's outfit.

HARRIET SLOWLY DID RECOVER, mostly, thanks in great part to Velora's visits and continued conversation with the woman beyond the looking glass. And she clung to the image of Emmet, the man she'd married. Emmet, the man who made her quiver with excitement beneath the sheets while he peeled the grapefruit, gently, so meticulously working the tips of his fingers, gradually, along the delicate flesh beneath the barrier of skin, so carefully separating each fragile slice, then spooning up small, measured dollops of homemade yogurt. Emmet, the man she'd known her entire life. This had been a wonderful man. He was all she had and all she could have asked for and the only one who could handle the likes of her. 'The Harriet,' Emmet had called her, affectionately. He didn't want anything to do with the sort of person he'd become, and neither did she. There had been a decades-old Emmet who loved Harriet desperately. And so she chose the man she loved and killed the one she didn't. She killed him and she was happy about it. Emmet would have been, too. She wore the wedding band he'd slipped onto her finger when they said their vows. It came from the Emmet she'd fallen in love with, married, and eventually grew to love enough to murder in cold blood. Harriet Boslem, self-made widow-maker. And she knew that from somewhere out there, perhaps just beyond where all those squirrels and cats and dogs and bunnies had come to die, Emmet thanked her.

"GET THAT LANCE BOY ON THE PHONE," Harriet called out in the direction of the looking glass. But her reflection was nowhere to be seen. Probably still using the loo. Her eyes returned to the crossword puzzle and her mess of a grapefruit. She sniffed.

"Lance?" she heard the looking glass call out, excited, from around the corner. Harriet could hear her hastened approach on the hardwood flooring.

"Yes, *Laaaance.* That boy who painted our house and did the dogs." She looked back down at the crossword, then gave her a side-eyed smirk.

"Okay." Her reflection smiled, and said quietly, touching her bare arms, "I'll call him." She paused and raised herself onto the balls of her feet briefly to see what Harriet was working on. "Here's that Menard book, by the way. I'll just drop it here." She pointed at the narrow hall table resting against the wall just beneath the mirror. Cream with a light green Japanese Ivy pattern looping up the legs sprawled across the top. "The last of your ring of books." She shook her head. "Pretty cool, Harriet."

Harriet laughed and snorted. "Bah. It's just reading. Anyone half-wit can manage that. And—" she pulled at the tooth near where the jerky had wedged—"I could be wrong." She raised her eyebrows and closed her eyes slowly. "Could be two hundred books. I don't remember now . . ." she said, looking at her reflection. Harriet stretched and rubbed her neck and watched her young and comely self push the book through the surface of the old mercury looking glass, spine first. The glass hummed then loosed a hollow *pop* when the book rippled through to settle onto the table below the frame of the mirror. The surface of the mirror stilled and regained its form as the book landed with a voiceless *thomp.* Her reflection smiled at Harriet.

"Done with the crossword yet?"

"Almost," Harriet said, wiping her fingers. "Tell that boy he must bury those cats as soon as the weather breaks. Aprilish, I'm guessing." She looked outside and back. "Like the dogs." She was quiet for a moment, then added, "Maybe Lance can come over and have a look later this week?"

"Okay . . ." Her reflection hinted at a grin and nodded, watching Harriet gaze up at the ceiling, then out the window, and wondered what else was on her mind, apart from dead cats and Lance. She saw Harriet look back at the crossword.

"Which one are you stuck on?" she asked, raising up on the tips of her toes again, straining to see.

"17-Across," Harriet said loudly, shaking her head. She pulled at another wet section of grapefruit and looked outside. A rafter of a half-dozen wild turkeys bobbed their heads and moseyed through the yard toward the creek without a second glance at the cats. A hushed murder of crows shuddered in the naked elms above and gleamed black in the rising sun. And a slender jogger in greenish-gray running skins breezed past on the sidewalk out front, toes of her silent strides scarcely touching, a thin veil of intermittent thought-bubble breath plumes—which Harriet filled with ellipses—trailing behind. Harriet glanced at her reflection in the hall, and picked up the last slice of grapefruit and looked down at the table, patting the tip of her pen repeatedly on the newspaper, *pat, pat, pat*. She looked up at her reflection again and smiled. 17-Across was a long one, but they had all day.

GIRAFFES

The newly arrived giraffe dioramas towered above the ivy garden on Walnut Street in a woven embrace of wrought iron rods. The name Helen ascended the neck of one giraffe, and Raewyn descended the other in an elegant, welded script.

The moving trucks hadn't even pulled away from the drive before the gray-haired homeowners had planted the sculptures with careful blows from a rubber mallet. From my vantage point, walking up the sidewalk on Walnut, I could hear one of the women call out instructions for proper positioning of the Helen. There was one more tap to finish the job, and the new neighbors quickly retreated hand in hand into their new home. I didn't see them again until I showed up on their stoop a week later.

The entwined giraffes made a bold statement that reverberated quickly with ripples of gossip and speculation throughout our quiet little Wisconsin neighborhood. These giraffes were a far cry from the outbreaks of concrete gnomes and other attempts at landscape art that mar our yards here, and I could sense onlookers, who just *happened to be meandering* by Helen and Raewyn's new home, stiffen at first sight of the quite literally necking giraffes.

I, for one, exhaled tremendous relief to finally have some different and interesting neighbors around here, albeit rather senior ones. They seemed energetic and spry, though, and I quickly found myself eager to meet the women who had chosen to call our small town home. And I intended to be the first to extend a warm welcome amid what almost certainly had been a chilly if not hostile reception from the Jilkes and Issackson families next door and just across the street, respectively.

The Jilkeses and Issacksons could kiss my fat, gay ass as far as I was concerned. Nearly anyone would have been an improvement over the Grivets, who lived there before Helen and Raewyn moved in. Messy people. Loud and heavy drinkers. But just so like those Jilkeses to fret over the lifestyle choices of folks minding their own business, and for Mary Issackson to race over there right away clutching a stack of church pamphlets and bludgeon them with a crucifix.

No, these decent people had bestowed us with their presence and deserved a respectful welcome, and that was that. And I was not about to let anyone make these poor folks feel uncomfortable or turned away. A proper pie was therefore in order.

A pie, yes. But a pie of what kind? It was early September and fresh blueberries, my favorite, were no longer an option.

My mother's famous five-layer chocolate came to mind, but that was fraught with allergen perils. Her dazzling pecan pie, along with several others, quickly fell victim to the same fate. Pumpkins were still at least a month out from harvest, but peaches, I was reminded, happened to be in mid-season form, so I quickly opted for that. I had a fantastic recipe that could make a cactus cry. And it would have been perfect except for the fact that it would take two solid days to make. Peeling and slicing and roasting that many peaches for one or two pies alone takes the better part of a day. It's a demanding recipe, one that precludes shortcuts, and in this case I simply didn't have two days to spare. I had to get to Helen and Raewyn before any of my busy-nosy-busy neighbors could.

So I paced around, growing steadily uneasy as around town I overheard murmurs and whispered snippets about "that new, uh . . . *couple* . . . with the giraffes." Crude code for what they really meant to say, yet I had no doubt they were also busy plotting to claim first intros, all of us now entangled in a sort of weary merit-badge-earning competition.

It didn't take long before I could sense the tension coming to a boil up and down the intersecting streets that formed Helen and Raewyn's corner lot. Who would be the first to offer these women a proper welcome? It only took a moment to rule out the non-competitors, those responsible for troweling out the icy silence and steely glances and—yes, I mean you, Meredith—guilty shrugs. That left a relatively small number of folks. But competent folks easily as eager as me to say they were first to *be there* and who, thanks to early retirement, had an exhausting surplus of time and energy on their hands. The new residents with the tall, engaging, entwined things soaring high in their side ivy garden on Walnut Street provided a perfect remedy for the locals' idleness and—dare I say it?—otherwise empty lives.

Rhoda would make a straight-up zucchini bread—that is, no walnuts—using the enormous, woody things she lugged up from her garden. She'd been dropping them on my stoop for over a week and I finally had to ask her to please stop. How much zucchini, after all, could a guy like me eat, freeze, grill, or make bread from? The next day she dutifully plunked down a load of fresh carrots, also yanked from the orderly rows of her little Eden, onto my steps. Of course this made me consider carrot cake. And perhaps Rhoda was already busy at making one. Or maybe she was trying to divert my plan by making a zucchini-for-carrots-on-my-stoop-swap, thereby adding to my list of potential baked-goods candidates and thus delaying my eventual course of action. I wouldn't put it past her.

But it didn't matter. I had to hurry. I ticked off the remaining competitors. Tom: Blueberry jam. He returns annually from some heroic trek (to hear him tell it) along the Michigan coast of Lake Superior with the bed of his S-10 filled with the things. He freezes upwards of twenty quarts of berries each summer, and cranks out around a case of preserves with the rest. He'd flatten a used Christmas bow onto the lid and call it done. Betsy: Dal. She's a smart one, that Bets. Always using the noodle. She'd have picked something that could be used both as a side yet had the legs to survive as a main, and for days at that. Perfect for someone who's just moved in and far too busy with unpacking and organizing and painting to cook.

I sighed and strode over to the front window to peer down the street to Helen and Raewyn's yard, where the dark metal frames rose from the lush ivy, Helen's neck so perfectly and gracefully woven—touching her partner, but not—around Raewyn's neck. I smiled.

Randy would probably make brownies. A dirt-dry chocolate slab charred to the core and buried in a drift of powdered sugar. James Velure, some terrifying Jell-O salad or tuna chow mein casserole. He always cooks as though someone has just died. Every occasion a funeral or a wake, and folks pick through whatever he blops on their plate as if fearing to find a severed finger or scattered toenail clippings in there. Jell-O salad doesn't even count as cooking anyway. If I were smart, I'd let Velure's toenail savories arrive slightly before mine. But there was no time for that sort of strategizing. I needed to get on with it.

Marian, well, who knows what she'd come up with. Probably just buy a cake from the bakery on her way home one night. Masterful stuff from that place, but *buying* a baked item would be cheating. Plus I can't stand that Elspaith girl. She runs the place now. Humble yet smug. Pretentious about her humility. I don't know how she does it. A distracting amount of blue hair, and this disarming mouth of teeth … I swear talking to her is like conversing with a pike, though most male patrons find Elspaith wildly intriguing. And speaking of Elspaith, she'd breeze over to Helen and Raewyn's with something plain and simple like one of her burly bread rounds. Unsliced, of course.

But anyway, it would be nothing store-bought from me, thank you. These women, this senior couple now living here with a permanent address right in our neighborhood in our town, these interesting folks who chose to live here, deserved better. Something hand-made with accepting, neighborly hands. They had staked tasteful and dignified hand-welded giraffes proclaiming their love for one another into their yard, for Christ's sake.

I eventually decided to make a pawpaw pie. Something original, something made with a local, lesser-known Wisconsin fruit to introduce them to this part of the country (I'd noticed the South Carolina license plates on the cars parked in their driveway). Pawpaw fruit may quite possibly be the most delicious American fruit no one has ever heard of. How, is beyond me. Crazy good. Just ask Thomas Jefferson. (Yes, *Thomas Jefferson*. The architect-scholar-thinker-author-of-our-Declaration-and-first-ever-secretary-of-state-and-third-President one.) But then I looked at the ingredient listing again and noticed that the recipe calls for an *entire can* of condensed milk. Drat. I'd forgotten about that. It's hard to sub out for condensed milk. And with my luck these newcomers were super lactose-intolerant and would find themselves made to feel uncomfortable for faking graciousness in accepting a gift that would either give them horrible stomach cramps or a turbulent case of the runs.

So, I consulted my cookbooks again, now a day later, and I could sense another rise in the competitive tension among my neighborhood rivals. For days it seemed no one had left their home, and I imagined them all bent over kitchen counters, wielding rolling pins, sifting flower, boiling marshmallows, and melting chocolate, all plotting to get to Helen and Raewyn first, and set them straight about what's what with who's who around the neighborhood.

I pulled out my mom's *Joy of Cooking*, my go-to tome for sturdy Americana cuisine. *Joy* also happened to contain a sporadic accounting of my childhood. Mom jotted notes about the goings-on at our place in the margins of a given recipe as she prepared it. She cooked constantly, and thus there were many notes scattered throughout many cookbooks, snapshots of our lives sprinkled over the years like the herbs that graced Mom's linguines, salads, stews, and roasts. And apparently the day she consulted *Joy* for apple pie happened to be my birthday, part of which, she noted, I'd celebrated by gopher hunting with my Dachshund, Gretchen. No comment on my success afield nor how Gretchen had held up. Actually she wasn't my dog as much as I was her human, and Gretchen knew it. I was eleven. She was fourteen.

And there it was. Apple pie. Boom. A fresh and pastoral gem lifted directly from Mom's annotations of simpler and softer times. Simple, yet elegant and sophisticated for these newly arrived lovers with the magnificent giraffes rising from their gardens.

A hand-crafted apple pie is actually harder work than the person on the other end of the fork may understand, and I concluded that the rather involved process may explain Mom's terse marginalia commentary about my gopher hunting expedition. But then again, like the pie, Mom kept her verse pretty simple, at times so achingly plain and clear, each word seemingly cut into the page with tears:

Yesterday, in the produce aisle, a man looked my way.

I smiled.

He looked away.

Or tragically funny, such as randomly adding ½ c. *Wild Turkey* to a recipe's ingredients.

I decided to make three pies. One for Helen, one for Raewyn, and one for me. What the heck. I figured for all the mess and heating up of my kitchen, why not?

As I fitted the top crusts I got an idea, and rather than etching cutesy little bird tracks into the crusts for venting, I took my fillet knife and carved a very slick cursive H into one pie, and a large, looping R into another. Then I slid the pies into the oven and dashed a quick note of my own in the margin of *Joy*: *I've lost 35 lbs! only 50 to go!!—Phillip.*

I walked over to Helen and Raewyn's house, carrying a pie on the flattened palm of each hand, elbows held high like a waiter hoisting platters of champagne flutes, gliding them above the heads of seated diners. The giraffes were gone but Helen and Raewyn's cars were home. For all my fretting, my moment had finally come. I glanced around again for the giraffes—Where had they gone?—and puffed up their front steps where I set down the pies, tucked my shirt back into my pants, took a deep breath, and rapped on their door. An enviably fit woman in her late sixties or early seventies flitted to the door and swung it open.

"Hello," she sang, snow-white teeth flashing behind a liberal application of crimson lipstick. She wore a saffron blouse with a string of golfball-sized beads that matched her lips and clattered around her neck. Her medium-length, grayed auburn hair was parted along one side, and pulled neatly back. She smelled faintly of a fresh bite of dark chocolate.

"Hello," I replied, and swallowed. "I'd like to welcome you to the neighborhood. My name is Phillip—"

"Oh! How lovely!" she exclaimed. She clasped her jeweled hands and pitched forward over the pies, inhaling deeply. "Mmmmmmm!" she moaned, then slowly straightened up, her bluish eyelids squeezed tightly shut, preened eyebrows arced upward. A pair of dark coal eyes flashed back at me.

"My name is Joyce," she said. "Wait here—I'll get Roger!" She turned and vanished without a sound, disappeared as if by a magic snap of the fingers, leaving me alone on their stoop in the middle of an idyllic Saturday afternoon wondering, *Roger?* and holding up a pair of pies inscribed H and R. I turned and scanned their yard and gardens, then the driveway. Subaru, Volvo. Joyce, Roger. Helen … Raewyn? I looked back into the house to see an older man thud deliberately across the polished hardwood flooring. Roger, I presumed. He walked like a knee or a hip caused him quite a lot of pain.

"Howdy!" he called out, the way people who are hard of hearing do. "I'm Roger." He offered his hand to shake, then stopped himself when he saw the pies and shook his head and cawed. "Here," he yelled, "I'll take those. C'mon in."

He smiled and asked my name and thudded every other step through the front room into a gleaming kitchen, where he grunted loudly and slid the pie tins onto a granite counter. He sat down and winced. He smelled warm and dusky, like outdoorsy morning sweat. It occurred to me that I'd never been inside this house before, and that somehow the Grivets had lived here for over ten years and I'd never actually spoken more than three words to them. Seemed indecent, despite my strong desire to never have anything to do with them. And here I was in their former house now owned by this married couple who seemed as likely to scream at a ballgame on the TV as the Grivets were to uncork a chilled Albariño.

"Coffee?" Joyce asked, and curved up her eyebrows again.

"Sure," I said, though unsure and confused. And it may have showed. I glanced around, noticing a loaf of what had to be Rhoda bread on a cutting board resting near a tray of blizzard brownies and a large pan of partially eaten Rice Krispie bars, beyond which lurked a dark Mason jar adorned with a dulled greenish-red bow. I glanced at the crimped edges of my golden-brown pie crusts, and how nice the flakey H and R turned out.

"Everyone here has been so hospitable. We didn't know what to expect, you know," she said. She spoke in undulating tones the way some wished they could sing. "Considering how 'cold' we heard everyone up here in the North was."

Roger laughed, massaging a hip. "I'd say things here are quite the opposite," he said. "In fact," he called out, nearly shouting, "we should move to Wisconsin more often!" He patted his belly appreciatively and smiled and scratched at his chin. Roger spoke with cat-gray eyes and a caramel drawl that could hail from anywhere south of however far south you need to travel for grits to show up on a breakfast menu. He slid a cup of coffee my way and when he nodded, I realized I'd been staring.

"Sorry," I said, and shook my head, feeling ridiculous. "I thought," I started, wondering how, exactly, to explain that I'd believed these nice, straight Southern white married people to be lesbian lovers named Helen and Raewyn. Finally I decided to just come out with it. "I thought your names were Helen," I said, pointing to one pie, "and Raewyn," and gestured toward the other, nearest Roger. (At least I got the R right.)

They looked at each of the pies, following my lead, in turn, then at each other, and frowned. Maybe the H and R didn't turn out quite as clearly as my wishful thinking had presumed. Then again, a lot of my thinking turned out to be not as clear as I'd presumed. There I was, still alone, still the lone gay person here on Straight Street, with its clean rectangular blocks and crisp corners forming perfect right angles. I sighed, frustrated, disgusted, devastated, and marooned in their vast, yet suddenly crowded kitchen. My new neighbors had moved here from such a different and far away place only to turn out to be the same as everyone else around here. Same people, different accent.

"You know," I said, searching. "The names on the giraffes in your garden?" I'm not certain why I felt compelled to spell this out, but I did. Even waved vaguely in the direction I'd last seen the sculptures, wondering again where they could have wandered off to. "I thought those were *your* names. And that you and Roger . . ."

I gulped coffee instead of continuing.

"Oh, that—" Joyce said, with a full stop. She bristled. Clearly others had asked about the indeed very interesting sculptures. But no one, I could tell now, had connected the dots in the same manner as me.

"Those," she said, now raising her voice and erecting a guarded perimeter, "were giraffes we adopted from Africa." She sniffed. "Chad, actually. You sponsor a giraffe and you receive updates on how"—and she paused here for a moment to glance away from me to Roger. I saw her jaw tighten—"on how they're getting along. And all that. Some man in a nearby village welds their likeness and they"—she sighed—"ship them to you." She looked back at me, refolded her arms.

"Oh." I dared not look away. I could blink, though. So I did. I blinked.

"Nearby village my ass," Roger grumbled. "More like made in some Chinese sweatshop. Damn things fell apart—barely survived the move," he said, cranky. "Some kinda shitty solder. Dragged 'em around back just this morning . . . Maybe I'll fix 'em up . . . They'd look good in this here winda," he said, drawling out *window* in a way no dialog coach ever could, "with some Christmas lights strung through their necks!"

"Oh, Roger!" Joyce snorted into her coffee. They both watched me, each with different intent. Roger seemed to evaluate my level of appreciation of his take on how to repurpose the things, as well as the shoddy state of Chinese workmanship, apparently. Meanwhile an awareness of who—what?—I was crept into Joyce's gaze, which for now seemed more resentful than welcoming, with an added layer of how anyone could possibly mistake *her* for a lesbian.

I sat in a silent panic, sipping at my coffee. It was only a matter of time before she ran the whole I-thought-the-two-of-you-were-lesbians angle through her head again. But to her credit, Joyce picked up the slack. This was her house now, after all. And I was the guest.

"Would you like some pie?" Her mouth formed more of a jagged line than the crimson curl that greeted me at the door. I saw my slack-jawed face, reflected minutely back at myself, clear and inverted in her black eyes, and knew the worst. I'd forced her into the position of negotiating strained cordial civility and good neighborliness with the naïve and presumptuous fag down the street.

"Yes! Let's try some of this *lovely* pie!" Joyce insisted, her accent flush with Southern coziness, the convexity of her etched eyebrows nice and smooth and round again. "We've been sharing whatever anyone brings over right as they drop it off."

I shrugged off my giraffe gaffe and considered the pie. "Certainly," I said. My only other option at this point being to gnaw off my paw and make a run for it. And here was Joyce, making nice. I sighed inside. Okay, so maybe we wouldn't wind up being *friends,* these new neighbors and me. But we could at least be friend*ly* from here out.

We ate, and after a few approving and appreciative nods and murmurs from both Joyce and Roger, I brought up the matter of the giraffes again, desperate to put it to bed and move on. Move on to the being-friend*ly* part of afternoon coffee and pie and . . . cheese. I'd forgotten to bring along the nine-year-old cheddar! "What is apple pie without a cheddar that bites?" Mom used to say. I decided not to call attention to the oversight, and stuck to lawn ornaments instead.

"That's really interesting about the giraffes," I said, lowering my coffee cup. "How long have you been doing that? Sponsoring them, that is."

"About three years," Roger said, chewing.

"They were a gift from our eldest daughter," Joyce said. "Apparently, it's becoming a bit of a 'thing.'"

Okay, then. So not lesbians but a pair of Southern breeders, and prolific ones at that. Possibly on the order of Catholic breeders. Prolific enough, at least, to parade an "eldest" among their litter of puppies. I looked around Joyce and Roger's front room again.

"They're really quite lovely," I said. "So regal."

And here was my opportunity to let the whole giraffe matter lay at that, and simply stop talking. The tactful Midwestern thing to do would have been to remain silent, eating pie and drinking coffee, until an appropriate amount of time had passed and someone else either politely changed the subject or disrupted the silence with the clank of a coffee cup on a saucer or a fork on a plate. I'm not certain about the Southern thing to do in these situations, but I do know that across the rest of the world we Americans have a reputation for filling any silence with words. Lots of them. Wordsy wordsy word words. And I rushed to fill the void.

"And," I asked, still with time to stop or veer, "how are they doing, then? Your adopted giraffes."

This question hit Joyce mid-swallow, and she choked and snorted. Roger looked at me and answered, curtly. "Dead."

Joyce coughed, suppressing a guffaw, and coughed again and stood up to keep from choking.

"Oh, no!" I yelped, my voice bouncing against each of the bare walls. I glanced around. Not a cross or religious icon of any sort in sight. Just books and art awaiting shelves and hooks and pegs. So saying I'd keep their dead giraffes in my thoughts and prayers may not be so apt here.

I settled on, "How awful."

"Oh . . ." Joyce said, looking up. Her eyes had remained narrow, the arc of her eyebrows now pinched. "They had a good life." She wiped her eyes, still smiling. "Sorry," she said. "Some virus," she shook her head. "They just . . . fell over dead one day, I guess. Before we moved here." She set down her cup.

"Jesus," I murmured, imagining the sight of two toppling giraffes, visualizing it all in agonizing slow-motion. The gorgeous things, their deliberate tipping, then sickening thuds upon a dusty savanna, both dead before they hit the ground from some giraffe cough or fast-moving prairie pox. I struggled for a moment to remember what part of Africa they are native to. Chad, I thought. She'd said Chad. Where else? I wondered.

We finished our pie and coffee in a silence broken only by the sound of swallowing and dishware touching. Soon enough I had things to get back to and they had bookshelves to arrange and they thanked me and I left.

The next spring the Issacksons, across the street from Joyce and Roger, put their house up for sale and moved to Arizona a week before it sold. A new straight couple and their twin three-year-old girls moved in. And days later, there I was walking past Joyce and Roger working in their yard as I toted two pies. Apart from cordial conversation with Roger when he returned the pie tins—I invited him in, he declined—I had seen them only in passing all winter long.

Now here was Roger stooped in the fresh, sprouting ivy of the side garden, busy with spring clean-up. He raised a hand spade to me and nodded howdy. Joyce stood near the sidewalk and called out instructions.

The sound of her voice was triggering. As if the waves of my brain spun together with the sound waves of her voice and transported me to a place beside Helen and Raewyn. Those two dead giraffes, laid out flat and dead on some Chad savanna, days after tipping and hitting the earth.

The greasy drone of unrelenting flies, Raewyn's swollen tongue, Helen's dried eyes, the squalid sun. My breath went cold. I took another step. Joyce spoke again, breaking the spell, the dusty rope connecting me to that savanna quickly dissipating to reveal her standing in front of me on a warm spring morning.

She'd wintered well, seemed somehow taller. And when she turned to look in my direction, prettier. Like a television version of herself. Beyond her shoulder, at the corner, my eyes fell upon a pea-green garbage bin, stuffed to the brim, a pair of black wrought-iron snouts jutting from beneath the lid. Joyce nodded to me as a wry grin twitched a slim eyebrow upward. I nodded again and she turned to the yard to shout instructions to Roger, and they got back to work. The way long-married couples do.

KEY

Jen winced and extended an arm, pressing her eyelids shut as she slipped a high-tech running shoe onto her left foot, exhaled, and looped the laces into a careful double-knot. She trembled and began to perspire while sitting on the icy tile flooring of the back foyer of her small home. Sunlight angled through the frosted-over windowpanes, and the wide and powerful river, shifting its massive plates of ice, throbbed and beckoned beyond.

She rose to her feet, tightened a glove and pressed a palm into the source of intense pain on her right side. She glanced down at her other shoe. Not tight enough. She removed her gloves and fiddled further with the laces, eyes closed. She took a deep breath, recalling the daily breathing exercises as mandated by the ER doc's discharge orders. Doctor Empath, she thought, and exhaled slowly. And from the moment she walked out of the hospital and tossed his business card into the garbage can by the door, she found herself repeating the same thought over and again: *not crazy after all*.

She'd met another. Finally. It was all she needed to know.

His emotional essence radiated fresh citrus and ginger. And Oreo cookies. All good.

Jen inhaled through her nose as deeply as the pain would permit, then a notch deeper still, and held it for five seconds, thinking and counting: Ripped intercostal muscles . . . and a trio of . . . bruised ribs and exhaled slowly through her nose, leaving her lungs empty for three seconds before repeating. She wiped her brow.

Finally laced up and ready to go, it was time for her run, an entire decade's worth of consecutive daily venture tallied, day by day, mark by mark, upon a gleaming whiteboard located on a wall in that same back foyer. Jen had run through thunder, lightning, floods, tornadoes, heatwaves, illness, heartbreak, and dangerous cold. And she was not about to let something like a bit of pain in her side interrupt her decade-long streak. She smiled.

Nearly time for a larger whiteboard.

She removed her smartphone from a hip pocket and placed it onto the Formica countertop near the utility sink. It rang instantly, displaying the name of her former boss out in Boston. She winced at the sight of his name. The man's wet-dog essence oozed through the phone's gleaming screen. This man was the driving force of the burnout that brought her back home and who now, positioned in whatever the latest workstation furniture craze that happened to be all the rage with the Silicon Valley smarties—what was it now, the Swimming Desk?—had been pestering Jen to fly back out East and give it another shot under his direction.

Jen actually enjoyed Boston, and her work in corporate communications. Though not any longer. Not since the installation of the new wet-dog boss, who had initiated an aggressive *re-engineering* of her practice-area plus the dramatic insertion of a new executive leadership team and their Ivy League business development models. And one day she woke up and she was done. Hit the proverbial wall. Years of fatigue and toiling and ass-kissing and mentoring pet-project hires and passing on taking the credit, all of it, rolled up into the palm of her hand, so obvious, so in front of her, and now so clearly a waste of time and youth.

She reached for her thick woolen cap and running mask. It was cold out, and there was running to do atop a broad, frozen river that waited for her, patiently, just a half-block away.

Jen glanced at her phone, perpetually set in "vibrate" mode. It rang again, the wet-dog ex-boss's name once again elegantly displayed in a sleek, sculpted font upon the countertop, buzzing away as if farting, much like the wet-dog man on the other end placing the call.

It had only taken a few phone calls for Jen to move her craft to a different communications group and into her small house back in Wisconsin, where she worked 100% from home while her mother withered away at a nursing home up the road.

JEN INJURED HER RIBS while performing barbell push-ups at the Y. Her wrist folded, and she crashed onto a thirty-pound weight. She didn't remember the thud of lungs, nor the rush of air that deflated her torso. She only remembered being engulfed in a fast silence, then overhearing the staffer's voice call for an ambulance.

She waited and tried to regain her breath. But dull chisels twisted in her ribcage, spreading her ribs on each attempt at even the shallowest intake of air. Her ears rang. Bright blinking spots and a red halo with black edges closed in.

Don't panic. Breathe with your other side, Jen. Breathe wi—

Over the years, Jen learned pain to be a very capable motivator. Lying. Acquiescence. Poor choices—like the horrible sofa in her mother's front room. There could be no other explanation than Momma's bad back for that. And, in the case of her fall at the Y, for a little while, pain brought her peace.

JEN CAME TO DURING the ambulance ride. Two young male EMTs chatted about their personal lives and referred to Jen in the third person, unaware she was awake.

One of the guys noticed her blank gaze and stopped talking so as to tend to her. Laying at a slight incline, Jen looked into his eyes and got sage. Sage and fresh dandelion leaves. Some spring reeds, too. He moved his hands and wrists with genuine concern. He listened politely to EMT Number Two, who upon a quick scan gave off cinnamon and onion, bemoaning a failed sexual exploit at a local club the night before. Alcohol apparently played a role in the foiling of his ploy.

"It was going good until her friend showed up," cinnamon-and-onion-guy said, and tried to laugh. He shook his head.

Sage-boy nodded but didn't look over at him.

JEN HATED HOSPITALS. Any potentially peopled area, for that matter. She was not agoraphobic, though in general, the ordinary act of going where other humans were known to frequent vexed her. Simple errands like laundry, groceries, the post office. It all meant crowds. And crowds meant distilled despair and woe and rage and dread and sorrow. And anger—so many angry people bounding around out in the wild, she had told a friend online, all of it all, all spun all together so thickly and wound into a throbbing, rotted casserole topped with molded cantaloupe. How no one else seems to perceive this, she wrote, or literally trip over it defies comprehension. But clearly, this is the case: Everyone else out there but me marches merrily along, tra-la-la, tra-la-la, oblivious to the clear, rancid ripples radiating from nearly every single passer-by.

Then you have the hospital. Apart from being a place you go to get sick, you have a distillation of suffering, agony, distress, and grief. Pain from patients and caregivers alike.

And those in pain are incapable of maintaining psychic boundaries of any kind.

This was Jen's superpower. Empathy. The real thing. But she generally considered it more of a burden than anything else. Others' emotions came at her in food aromas in a rather straightforward way: good emotions equaled good smells; bad was bad. And she couldn't always tune it out, which fostered her overall urge to avoid people. Which presented a problem because people liked Jen. They were drawn to her. Like they could sense something special about her. A special ineffable something they often closed in on subconsciously. Which made avoiding them hard.

But she tried. And in the end, she moved away to a house outside her small hometown on the river just north of the University. No lover. No roommate. No commute. No neighbors. Not even a cat or a dog. Just her, her computers, her running gear, and her dead plants. And, of course, the river lumbering and lurking beyond the windowsill, now perfectly frozen. Popping and cracking its hollow, profound snaps with each shift of its powerful plates.

"Hmmm," the doctor hummed, glancing at the questionnaire she'd completed forty minutes before. "Says here you don't smoke or drink."

Jen nodded weakly, staring absently at a mid-air spot between a computer workstation and the door of the examination room. "Destroys muscle tissue and brain cells." She tried to cough but caught herself. "Expensive, too," she rasped.

"I see." The doctor eyed Jen. He nodded. "Well. Let's get an X-ray and some labs and see what's going on. We'll talk after I've had a look."

Jen groaned quietly.

"Good news," he told her an hour later. "Only bruised ribs. And probably some torn intercostal—er, the muscles located between those ribs." He smiled.

"I know what they're called," Jen groaned, annoyed and in pain. "Intercostals."

The doctor looked at her. "Well. Right. You'll be fine, though it will hurt for some time. You'll need to limit physical activity for a few weeks—uh, what is it you do for a living?"

She narrowed her eyes. "It's on the form." Her workout interrupted by a silly injury and now this bullshit. And she still needed to get her run in and catch up on work and research a new project and call that—

"Oh, pardon me." The doctor snapped his gaze down at the clipboard on his lap.

"It's fine. I'm just cranky and I have a lot to do. I work from home on a computer, so not a lot of physical demands when it comes to my job." She pressed her eyelids shut and held them closed, watching a redness throb and drift from side to side upon the innerscape of her mind until after he spoke again.

"You may experience some really distracting discomfort during the next few days. I can write an order to excuse you from your work duties for a day or three if you like."

"Ja, no," she said, opening her eyes. "I'd just end up working anyway. Too much peripheral crap to dig up for clients and I've g—"

"Well, I'll write it anyway in case you change your mind. Those," he pointed at the ripples within her lean torso, "will be very tender come tomorrow morning."

"Probably." She shut an eye. "They're killing me now."

"I can prescribe something for the pain if you like."

"No thanks. Prescription medications and I don't get along so well."

"Oh," he said. "Well, then some ibuprofen as needed." He winked. "And cool it on the workouts for a week or so, Jen."

"Uhhh . . ."

"What is it?"

"My streak," she said.

"Streak?" The doctor hung up his stethoscope.

"Ja. I'm a runner, and I've run at least three miles every day for the past decade. Haven't missed a single day. Workouts, very seldom... but my run? Never."

"I see. Isn't that a tad . . . ?"

"Obsessive?"

"Well, yes." His concern was genuine, and he resonated nothing other than the job at hand. And hunger. He was busy doing the right thing, focusing on what was important, but Jen could tell he'd be en route to the cafeteria as soon as he'd finished with her. So hungry. He must have started the day early. First, she got tarragon from him. Then apple with a touch of cardamom. And peanut butter and Oreo cookies. All good.

"I don't think so, obviously. Keeps my head clear and crap-free."

"Well." He paused. "A day will come when you won't be able to run, Jen. Have you considered that?"

She began to laugh, and snatched herself, acutely unable to speak and briefly fading to starry, spinny, ringing reddish black again.

Christ, she thought. No broken bones? No puncture to the lung or spleen? Really? Are you sure? My God. She winced again and thought, And . . . yes, I have considered that day, Doctor. But let us not put the hearse before the corpse now, shall we?

She nodded minutely, eyes closed. Caught a whiff of fresh blood, listening to the ringing in her ears pitch down to catch up to those drifting stars one by one submerged within that receding blackish red.

Dry tongue. Reach for water bottle. Smile, sort of. Moisten lips. Breathe. Drink.

The ringing eased. And the room stopped looping about on its axis. She wanted to wash her hands and feet. She drank. She swallowed.

"What else is on your mind?" the doctor asked. He blinked and looked at her deeply.

It was not a moment of potential romance. But rather it was a look of recognition that Jen knew. It was a scan.

It took until her mid-twenties for Jen to obtain the vocabulary to describe her abilities and a label to address it by. Abilities some would call *odd*, a condition for herself she had always suspected teetered on the verge of what merited the label *crazy*. Jen was an empath. She looked up at the doctor again. She'd just never met another who was so obvious about it. Then again, it takes one to know one.

Incredible, she thought. She felt a tide of mental relief wash over her.

In some ways, it made sense that the obvious empath would be on full display, such as the case with this physician. Of course they were not all introverted recluses like her. She leaned back on one hand and looked around the examination room. His whole life on display right here: medical degrees and certificates. A community service plaque. A child's sketch and watercolor. And a half-dozen framed photos carefully positioned across the walls highlighting a life filled with warm-weather vacations, small-pilot aviation and skydiving, himself posing with attractive family members and friends.

Then there was *him*. His tanned January skin, heavy rings gilding fine fingers, and a blocky jeweled watch dangling from his wrist.

"What happened at the gym?" he finally asked, taking a seat.

Ah, what happened indeed? Not like her to slip. At anything, ever.

They each paused. Mutual scan.

"Can I just leave, please?"

"I'm simply concerned just how this happened in the first place. Doesn't seem to fit your profile . . ." He tapped a temple with his pen.

"Profile? Please. You didn't even know where I work."

"You know what I mean."

Jen exhaled. Fine, she thought.

"I've been off kilter since my mom died," she croaked, and flinched. She held up a hand to prevent him from interrupting, and continued, following a short, labored breath. "She was in a home with dementia and died recently. And I haven't been myself, whoever that is . . . was. So much stress dealing with her decline and my brother totally losing it coupled with the avalanche of what can only be called 'the business of death.' People…" She held back a flush of tears. "So fucking frail. So angry and worried and depressed and sad and fatigued and smelly and frustrated and stupid and cheating and lying and uncaring and insincere and those vapid, practiced smiles, and—" She paused to catch her breath, then rasped, "Basically just a heap of churning assholes living in their own personal beer commercial, and I can't tune them out. At all. Their mental and emotional buzzing is suffocating and blinding."

The doctor sat back and paused for a long moment. Jen expected him to emit a low whistle. The doctor uncrossed, then recrossed his legs.

"I can recommend someone . . ." he said. He tapped an incisor with the tip of his pen. *Click, click, click.* "Someone who understands all of . . . *this*, Jen," he said, and gestured broadly to indicate the scope and enormity of everything. He wiped his glasses and looked around and back to her again. "She helped me, I know that."

Jen glared at him and winced, reading his obvious benevolence, which infuriated her further. And maybe he was right. Perhaps she needed to see someone, following her mother's lingering death and her brother's brittle mental state. And talk through it all with someone who knows what it's like to constantly smell others' feelings. Even from a photo or over the phone. Give her some mental tools to manage it.

A way to filter it. She nodded. Besides, she thought, there's strength in acknowledging a weakness. Is that what it was? A need. It was a need. She needed help. But she wasn't ready. This much she knew. She smiled faintly.

"I just need to go for my run. And get back to my dead plants," she said.

"Here," he said, "I'll jot down her information on my card." He scribbled and extended a long arm toward her. "Just in case," he said.

She took the card, along with her discharge orders, then recoiled and groaned as she stood up to leave.

He looked at her gently. "Good luck, Jen."

She nodded and flipped his card into the trash bin on her way out of the hospital.

MOMMA WAS TECHNICALLY gone well before she died. The doctors, visitors, hospice staff—everyone but Jen—declared her state of decline to be textbook stuff. But it wasn't. Well, maybe it was, it's just that in her mind, the textbooks weren't entirely correct. Momma was surely not herself, but she was still in there … Somewhere. Jen could feel it. Like the pleasant tug and tension of a guitar string.

A tug and tension that severed and vanished the moment Momma passed. She caught a breath.

She was downtown at a bar with her brother, Mitch, when it happened. But scarcely an hour before they both sat in Momma's room at the nursing home. Jen stared at Momma and half-listened to her brother's occasional remarks.

"Fuck this," she blurted. "I'm going to get a beer."

"You?" Mitch said, snapping from some distant trance. "Are going for a beer?"

"Yes. Me. A Beer." She stood up. "At a bar."

He gave her a long look. This was something his sister would not normally say. Ever.

"Want some company?"

"Not really," she said, and sighed and sniffed the room. Her eyes flicked toward Momma. "But come on." She nodded.

They sat in silence at Ernie's Tap while she tried to shut off the streams of emotions radiating from the bar patrons around her. All their despair, crushed dreams, frustration, bitterness, hostility, and lack of hope. Especially her brother's anguish. She gave him a sideways glance.

They told the bartender and owner, Ernie, an old family friend, about Momma. Jen glanced around. Beer placards, framed Green Bay Packer mirrors, a heavily lacquered wooden State of Wisconsin clock, posters of busty young white women bursting from scant tops, and preserved wild animal heads bolted to the walls. Ernie apparently kept the local taxidermist busy. He looked at Jen and Mitch and slid two fresh lagers across the bar.

She thought of her home, the bare walls. One small painting. Maybe she got this from Momma. The Spartan quarters, her disdain for clutter. The walls at Ernie's glared in confused, crowded, smoky, and mindless disarray.

During the past several months, her brother had slipped into a state of mental decline. Was that the word? Decline? Or was it depression? And it had nothing to do with their dying mother, though that certainly didn't help. No emotional boundaries today. Even without a scan, his depression raged like a neon rose tattooed across his forehead. Jen struggled not to engage in a mental dialog with his feelings and forced her thoughts to drift on to work, the e-mail messages stacking up in her inbox, the noisy ceiling fan, and horrible lighting at the nursing home.

She took a drink from the tall lager glass and tried to remember the last time she had an alcoholic drink of any kind. About a year. Maybe a glass of wine Christmas before last. But Momma was dying, and this felt right. She took another deep swallow. Momma didn't seem to want her and Mitch around anyhow. The near-dead generally don't.

She thought about Momma. Tried to remember good times, and to cling to those rather than her own stifling and strict upbringing. But she couldn't think of a single one. Just a lifetime of *no*. No parties. No school dances. No boys. No travel. No movies. No cookies—except for the ones they baked for care packages shipped overseas. And church: Saturday evening Mass. Sunday Mass. Early Mass. Midnight Mass. Daily morning Mass. Requisite confession. Confessing lying about sins invented for confession. Stringing rosaries for missionaries' trips to Africa. Letters to penitentiary inmates. Was that it? Her entire childhood one long *No*? And church? Was—

Mitch started to speak, probably ramble, but Jen couldn't hear. Her thoughts shifted from Momma to the dark and noisy emotions clanging and banging around the bar that raced like beams of radio waves down a conduit connected directly to her brain. She shook her head and took another swallow and set her lager glass down slowly.

That's when it happened. That tug of a thorny thread that had connected Jen to Momma and persisted like a dull throb inside, despite her advanced state of dementia, vanished in a poof.

Jen cleared her throat suggestively.

Mitch sniffed beside her and flicked his gaze to the NFL highlights thudding away on the high-definition plasma television screen above the bar. He had barely touched his beer, a golden glass column rising from a puddle of condensation on the polished wood.

"She just died."

"Who?" He knew but said it anyway, and blinked up at a millionaire's critical game-changing gaffe: A fumbled punt, laboriously displayed and replayed from multiple angles for the entire planet to relive and comment on, again and again, all in high-def slow-mo. Then a quick pan of the collective groan of a packed Lambeau Field.

"Momma! Just now."

"Huh? How do you know?"

"She's gone. Trust me. She's nowhere now. Not anywhere. Evaporated. I can't feel her anymore, Mitch." She set the glass down with a thump. "Let's go."

They toasted their mother and left for the nursing home to deal with the staff and cadaver and get on with the next phase she'd later tell Doctor Empath about—the business of death.

JEN FOUND HERSELF surprised at how good her ribs felt while running, though leery of how they'd respond the next day. But it's all good for now out here atop the frozen river. No people, no chatter, no emotional clatter. Just a row of bald eagles perched on the ice along the narrow strip of open flowing water. And a fox that had managed to scamper across the ice from Minnesota over a mile at this point—to the sweet shores of Wisconsin. Well, almost. Foxy wasn't quite there yet. Jen laughed, then flinched, though not enough to interrupt her stride nor the flushing of her brain as she wafted, deeper with each stride, into something like the drifting, pre-dream, pre-full-fledged purplish sleep state that rippled her under, fading to white each night.

She listened to her footfalls. Crunch of the snow, the noise of her breath. There was that. Then there was the occasional hollow, rippling sound one gets to hear on occasion when thick ice that spans a large body of water shifts and cracks like tectonic plates in the Earth's crust. It is an intense, humbling sensation to experience and feel beneath one's feet.

So, yes. There was always that humbling moment to add perspective to Jen's daily run. But then there came the very unusual sound that Jen just heard above the landing of her feet atop the river ice, and her cold, reedy breathing. She felt it before she saw or heard it. Sensed what was about to cause the ice to moan with a hollow thud.

The sharp smell of despair and dread, despair and relief, plummeting from the sky struck her before she could turn her head to see and hear a human body land and splat and bleed yards in front of her. Then silence.

She jumped back, snapped her head round and round. She looked up, then back down at the ice around her feet. She stared.

"Dude!" she gasped. "What . . . ?"

After a while, she backed up and raised her chin to glance over at the eagles, now eating gathered prey, and tried to spot Foxy, now since scooted ashore and long gone behind her. Just her and someone else all alone out on the wide ice. Some dead else.

Jen shook her head, folded her arms, staring at the man. The newly perished man, whose remains emanated pure psychic agony.

She caught a breath. This was so unexpected. It really was. And, weirdly, impressive. To absorb such fluid, raw emotion from a corpse. Granted, this happened to be a really recent corpse, but a deceased human being, nonetheless. The man's essence eddied in a pool of pain near her feet and radiated up through the air. She imagined this imparting of emotions to be akin to a radio broadcast that continues to travel across the earth after someone unplugs the radio. The source dies, but the transmission carries on.

She shook her head again, finding herself more swept up in this phenomenon than caring as much as she would expect upon seeing a man fall to his death mere yards away. And she could read it all in his dead, broken and bleeding eyes: He welcomed this. He wanted it. Maybe not at first, but at the end, the very end, he realized all he had to do was let go, and just . . . give in.

She saw it all, all over again, all there so perfectly clear and easy to read, a lifetime of frustration and despair pouring out and spiraling up in front of her. Like black strings of musical notes peeling up and away, all his discord spilling from page upon page of sheet music, popping off note by note, bar upon bar of music spiraling up, drifting off, and fading away overhead.

Jen looked around again and returned her gaze to his sunken eyes. The man also reeked of beer. Not a beer aroma that she was perceiving but rather beer that he'd been drinking. He continued to bleed from the eyes and mouth, blooms of deep red, molten blood steaming and freezing an arm's length from her squat to form a hard, rosy slick.

Who is—*was*—this guy?

She had to know. Something about him felt too, too familiar. But Jen couldn't place him. She quickly but calmly searched his pockets for an ID. Nothing. But she did find a small set of keys. And a pen and a plastic Ziploc bag with a note of some sort inside. She glanced at the writing. Nice script, mostly. Except for the last wobbly bit. Something about . . . frozen fog. She straightened up, flinched in pain, and rumpled her brow, glancing at the inscription again:

> *open frozen fog*
> *across this frozen sheet*
> *creeps up*
> *on bats' wings*

Were you a writer? Or . . . Oh, God—a poet?

She looked up to the top of the bridge and spotted a metallic glint near the railing. A bicycle? His bicycle.

She returned the baggie and pen to their rightful place but took the keys and trotted up to the bridge to find a Trek mountain bike. No saddle pack. Nothing to contain personal items. She'd hoped to find a wallet or another way to identify him. She glanced around. Nothing but busy, speeding commuters and shoppers screaming down the lanes of the Interstate. She scanned them as they zipped past: nausea, fear, delight, confusion, mustard, dachshunds, fatigue, horn-iness, depression, amusement, influenza, sorrow, avocados, pineapple, joy. The last one made her smile.

The key was a perfect fit. She unlocked the bike, strapped on the helmet, pocketed the gloves and super-nifty hat, mounted, and pedaled away. One last look over the ledge at her poet below. The musical dread-notes had all drifted away, leaving only relief and that oozing and freezing red bloom behind.

She glanced down at the frame of the bike again. She smiled and shook her head. He actually bothered to lock the thing up first.

Jen left the bridge. She snaked through town along the river, where soon enough she was stopped by a police officer.

She pulled down her mask and snapped, "What?" at his rolled down window. She didn't intend to snap, but riding a bicycle was proving to be considerably more painful than running. Especially the stopping part.

The officer leaned across the front seat of his squad and motioned her nearer. Jen inched the bike closer. His steamy breath puffed in the cold air. "Just wondering what exactly"—he gasped as a gust took his breath—"you are doing out here. Are you ok, miss?"

She wiped her eyes and scanned and blinked. Ginger-car-rot soup. Whole-grain toast.

"Yes, sir."

"But it's . . . twenty below out here right now. It will be dangerously cold once the wind picks up." He eyed Jen closely, starting with her shoes, and moving slowly up to the jumper's helmet.

"Yes, officer," she said, rolling her grayish-green eyes. They matched her running skins—somewhere between gray and green along with a hue of blue thanks to the empty sky above the bluffs over her shoulder.

She sighed and wanted to yawn. "I am aware of the temperature."

"So, what are you doing?"

"Riding a bicycle." She sighed. "Look, I've got a lot on my mind. And sometimes the weather conditions don't matter so much when you got the busy brains. After all," she said, and paused to allow a chuff of wind to recede. She smiled in appreciation. "It's just wind and cold."

He puffed in the cold air, rubbed his hands, and scooted closer. He grinned. "No such thing as bad weather," he said, reciting the start of the local saying.

Jen finished: "Just bad clothing."

They laughed.

"So . . . what's on your mind?" He smiled.

Not this again. This guy wasn't exactly a doctor, nor a fellow empath, but he was completely transparent and genuine.

"Lots of things." She glanced up at the perfect, minus nineteen sky. Only clear blue vastness lurking beyond the ridge. "Work. Bruised ribs, torn intercostals." She pressed a hand into her side again and panted.

"Torn . . . what?"

"Intercostals. They're the muscles between"—she cringed and pressed the very subject of her sentence—"Your ribs. They are the reason you breathe." She wheezed and clutched herself.

"Isn't that the lungs' job?" He chuckled.

"Yes and no. Intercostals expand your ribcage so as to draw air into your lungs." She groaned. "The lungs take it from there."

"Oh."

"Ja. Very painful when torn." She puffed. "And my brother is a total mess and wails like a newborn. And—" She caught her breath again and wondered why she was telling some small-town cop all this. First, she spills her guts to the doctor and now this guy. "And my mom just died." She wiped frozen snot from her nose and upper lip.

"My god. I am so sorry."

"Oh—don't be." Jen brushed the remark aside with the back of a snot-covered hand. Condolences aren't apologies. "But thanks. She stopped being 'her' long before"—she paused to suck in some cold air and groan and massage her ribs again. The wind was beginning to kick up more steadily. "She wasn't herself for a long time now... But, yeah. Thanks." She looked around again and considered stopping over at Michael's Bistro for a beer and spacing out while watching the line chefs behind the bar flip burgers. Or grill hearts of romaine. She could get used to having a beer once in a while.

A car idled past. Jen nodded at the driver, who responded with a slight smile and an upward flick of his chin. Released remorse. Fading guilt. Relief. Sage. Peaches. Sliced apples. Contentment.

Jen redirected her attention to the police officer. More ginger-carrot soup. "So, you're stopping me because I'm riding a bike on a cold day?" She looked down and toed the strap of a pedal.

A long silence yawned. She pondered her poet again and tilted her head at the handlebars to squeeze the poor guy's brakes, a caring caress extended from the warm, living cold above down into the icy, dead afterlife somewhere yonder. That certain ineffable ether where poets go when they're gone.

Jen glanced at the downtown behind her while pulling a glove taut with her teeth. Cold clutched the city like a planet-sized fist and cloistered all residents within its shadowy mist. Off to her right, dense steam rose from the strip of brick buildings and hovered magically above the main street like a sparkling gray veil. The fallen poet's frozen fog.

"Well, yes. I guess that's the case. Just wondering why on a day like this."

Jen cleared her nose again before the snot could freeze, flickered today's grayish-blue-green eyes at the perfect winter sky, then peered through the ice crystals clinging to her eyelashes to the expanse of the frozen river. A jagged fissure snaked a quarter mile away and faded down into the deep beneath the ice. Tendrils of Momma's frozen fog void eased out and coiled Jen about the middle. Ever present, always absent. A positive void, like a window through which you can only see infinity.

From the tendrils' squeeze came an afternoon spent on Momma's lap. Braiding Jen's hair. Reading with Momma in the big, red wingback chair. The smell of her hair. Helping Momma with knitting. Swinging from her waist in the kitchen.

Jen smiled and blinked her watery eyes. She turned away from the officer and pedaled down the road in the direction of her house, still thinking about maybe having a beer once in a while. She came to a rest on the boardwalk near the old pier. Edges of a sharp fold in the plates snapped in time with a quick, painful stab that pierced her ribcage. Wouldn't kill her to take a day off from running. She straightened and wiped her nose, snot instantly freezing and crackling, then looked downriver to the bridge, the poet's ruby slick.

No more chords, no more discord. Just relief. And a perfect winter sky. She nodded, pulled cold air into her nostrils, and smelled nothing.

LUCK

If they don't shut up, I'm throwing myself out this window!"

"Oh, please, Will," Claara says, looking out the passenger window, almost bored. "You'd be killed."

Will clears his throat. "That's sorta the point."

"Besides," Claara says, and turns in her seat toward Will. "You're driving. Remember?"

"Take the wheel, then."

"Oh, my god."

"They just never . . . Shut. Up . . . Ever."

"I know." Claara reaches over and switches off the radio. "There," she says. "Better?" She smiles. "You just need more coffee." She looks ahead. "Pass this guy," she says, pointing. "Please."

"Coffee . . ." Will rubs at an eye, frowns and changes lanes. "Oh, I suppo—"

"Of course. Funeral . . . Family bullshit, right? It's not like we're taking the kids to the zoo, here."

Sparse purple ditch asters bend in the breeze outside Claara's window. Intermittent billboards skirt passing forests, fields, lakes, and pastures beyond.

"We don't have kids," Will says. "Remember?"

"True enou—"

"And if we *did*, I'd need something stronger—"

"Right! There is that . . . And," she sighs, "I'm not even sure if I want kids." She removes a sandal to fiddle with a strap. "Do you?"

She looks from her toes to Will. Will is silent.

"Uh-huh. I'll take that as a 'no.' For now."

She stretches and looks around while Will turns to her to speak.

"Besides, I—"

A photograph of a coiled human fetus spanning the width of an enormous roadside billboard leaps into view, its image curled and embossed with a splattered red Courier font stamped diagonally across that reads:

I HAD FINGERPRINTS
SEVEN MONTHS . . .
BEFORE I WAS BORN!

A spiraling umbilical cord splits the frame.

Claara shakes her head and watches a mile of stripes flick beneath the wheels of the car. Another similar billboard flashes by.

"My god," she mumbles.

Will squints. "Whazzat?"

"Nothing," Claara says, shaking her head once. "Just the road . . . Anyway . . . I wouldn't know what to do with you dead."

Will looks over at Claara then back at the road ahead. Slabs of highway continue to thrum beneath the wheels. Claara scans the edge of the forest for wildlife. She looks back at Will. "I mean, it's not like we can do a burial at sea here."

Will takes a deep breath. "Well, what about Lake Superior? Just a few hours north of here . . . That's basically an inland sea, now, isn't it?"

"What? You mean you want to be buried at sea?"

"No, I—I never considered it. You're the one who brought it up."

"That was just an example—Look! That one art gallery's coming up. They sell coffee. Stop."

"I don't need a coffee."

"You do."

"Caffeine will have no effect."

"Just stop! We're going to miss the turn!"

"I . . . It's just that—"

"What?"

"This won't just be about coffee." The pleather of the old steering wheel crunches and pops beneath the force of Will's renewed grip. "You'll need to look at every goddamned thing—"

"So?"

"—and pick up each piece to see who made it, where they're from, how they made it, review their technique and artists' statem—"

"Yes. And?"

"Coffee is a by-product."

"Oh, Will. We'll just run in, quick."

"Uh-huh." Will rolls his eyes.

"Besides, we may see something—"

"Here we go!"

"—for a wedding gift. Or whatever," she says, with a single nod. She folds her arms while Will parks on the gravel lot at the Rusted Roof Art Café.

"Can we please just get some coffee and go, please?" He kills the engine. "Funeral . . . Remember? I'm already on your family's shit list. Besides," his gaze travels up the curve of her calf, the hem of her dark organdy dress, then quickly slides through Claara's golden blonde hair to meet her eyes. "You— I—"

He shifts his weight from one side to the other, then back.

Claara groans in murmur and looks askance. "Eyes on the road, Will. Please."

"Uh, we're parked now, Claara." Will raises his eyebrows.

"True, that!" She flashes him a smile and twists the rear-view mirror to check her lipstick. Immediately she spots an eyelash in need of unclogging.

"Uncle Rhonda," she says, pluck, pluck, pull, "will understand."

Will wonders if she'd choose to stop if it were raining. But it isn't. Instead, a perfect July day has favored their trip north to Luck, Wisconsin, for a funeral. Where else would you go to bury the dead? Claara asked.

Claara slips into the gallery as if drawn magnetically inside. A scruffy barista greets her. Will sighs and hesitates at the entrance. Maybe her Uncle Ronny—known affectionately to all as "Uncle Rhonda," a childhood utterance of one of the nieces—would understand if they'd pulled over to fool around and happened to arrive late. He would likely encourage that, actually. But not so much lingering here in some art co-op over pots and quilts and epoxied arrangements of broken glass bits. He blinks.

But Claara is likely right about the coffee. She tends to be right about a lot of things, from every answer on her ACT exam back in high school to proper mid-winter bonsai pruning. She waves him over from across the surprisingly bright and spacious main floor.

Will walks to the counter, where he learns the charcoal-hair guy's name is Crow. Crow has thick forearms and strong hands and wears a clay-soiled apron. A prodigious stainless-steel machine hisses and roars before him, then growls to a more calm and less industrial grumbling purr that ends in an abrupt, muted slurp. Crow slides a coffee drink across the surface of the polished bar toward Claara, and Claara drifts away, soundlessly, over the ceramic flooring. Crow waves a hand casually to scatter a haze of fruit flies that has drifted from a wooden compost bucket nestled into a nearby corner. A decomposing banana peel dangles precariously from its split rim, about to break at a rot point and fall to the floor. Crow leans to a side to look around Will across the room at Claara.

"Breve," Will says, loudly. "For me. Extra shot. Please." He turns to watch Claara read an artist's statement, carefully, near the far wall. She lifts another print-out, examining both sides, and at length, then disappears quietly around a corner, latte in hand, no doubt on her way to some meadow gallery out in the beyond, a display of art landscaped into an apple or pear orchard out back.

"Riiiight," Crow says, with a rasping crackle. He turns to Will again once Claara breezes from sight. He nods and shoos away more of the tiny flies.

Claara returns from the gardens and steps around a collection of tall vases displayed on lone pedestals beneath indirect track lighting near the far wall. Crow eases to her side as she reads. He rasps softly that the four-foot-tall vases with the narrow necks are actually called bottles.

"WELL, I THINK MOTHER WILL LOVE IT," Claara says, placing her bare feet on the dashboard. She considers her toes.

Will glances toward a ten-gallon *bottle* occupying the majority of the back seat of his old Toyota.

"For what? The Second Coming?"

Claara giggles and looks out the window. "Still waiting for the First . . ." She sighs. "I know it's more than you wanted to spend."

"It's exploitation."

"What?"

"Exploitation. You know . . . a pay-off. Hush money."

"Extortion?"

"Yes." Will sighs. "That's what I meant. A . . . bribe. Just one installment toward the enormous price to pay for your mother to look the other way and allow her daughter to promenade arm-in-arm with some brown-eyed troll like me."

"Shut up," Claara laughs, nearly spilling her drink.

"Careful," Will says. "Wouldn't want to soil that lovely dress . . ."

THE MIDDAY SUN PUMMELS Will's old Toyota as they push north, the miles and forests and fields and scary billboards clipping by in rhythm with the center stripes.

"Christ," she breathes. "They're everywhere . . . side of the road, parks, storefronts, t-shirts . . . painted onto trucks, even."

"Tried and true, Claara. God, guns, gays . . ."

"One man, one woman."

A broad cornfield, split by a creek, ends where a pine forest begins.

"There!" Claara lunges forward in her seat. "There is a wayside up ahead there. Pull over," she says quickly. "Please."

"What? Why?" The steering wheel makes a crackling sound in his hands. "Now what?"

She gives Will a slow look.

"I'm about to slop latte all over this dress, silly."

THEY LAY IN THE GRASS near a tree on the bank of a stony creek. Occasionally the surface of the water is broken by trout rising in muffled snaps and slurps for midges that dimple a quiet pool.

One hears the other whisper, "You awake."

After a while, the other responds, "No, not yet. You?"

"Naw. Me neither."

"K."

A cool breeze presses up from tufts of long grass and wet creek stones as a lone cumulus cloud lingers before the sun, casting an enduring shadow. The towering cloud billows an impossible gleaming white at the top, and sags broad and leaden at the base, a stretched cotton ball dipped in dark ink gently rested upon a cerulean summer sky.

"You knew about this place, didn't you?" he says, gently.

There is a pause and the sound of wind and grass and water.

"Yes. But I've never stopped. Except with Mom . . ."

She turns to him, grasps his Achilles tendon between two toes, and squeezes slowly.

There is another pause, and another trout.

"Beer?" she asks.

"Absolutely."

They unhook their legs.

THEY ORDER TWO PINTS and a six-pack at the nearest bar. Yellowed ceiling tiles span the width of the dark and narrow tavern beneath the faint smell of insect repellent, gasoline, and a very hot electric pizza oven. A muffled TV set suspended above the bar airs *The Price is Right*. Tubular fluorescent lightbulbs buzz dimly and mechanically from the low ceiling.

It is hot inside the bar. Will tips and drinks half his pint in one swallow. His eyes widen. "Maybe we get a twelve-pack instead?"

"Lower!" a crouched man seated near the TV set hollers. "Too high!" he yelps. "You'll bust!"

Claara shakes her head. "No cooler in the car, Will. There will be beer at Mom's . . . And we can always stop somewhere on the way back."

They nod and touch glasses.

"Don't bury me in a box," she murmurs.

Will turns his head to face her, conscious of the stare of two men playing cribbage at a nearby table. One of them nods slowly to Will.

"Horrible top she's got on ..." Claara says. Her eyes glance down from the TV set to lock on to Will's. "I don't want to be cremated, either."

The bartender thumps a cold six-pack of bottled beer before Will and drifts down the bar to check on the next contestant on *The Price is Right*. Claara speaks.

"Burned up and incinerated and ground up, bones pulverized into a dusty powder and whisked into some old snuff box and—"

"Okay, okay!" He shudders and raises a hand. "I get it, I get it—no box." He looks around quickly. "No burning." Will swallows. "Do *you* want a burial at sea?" He smiles, vaguely, and flinches when the crouched man yells at the TV again. A chronic skin rash, known for rearing its head during times of stress, ignites above Will's wrist. He rolls up a sleeve to scratch a forearm.

"You kids hungry?" the bartender asks. He smiles and rubs his short white beard. "Or just up to drinkin and drivin around today?" He raises his eyebrows to Will, then turns to Claara. "I could makeya a pizza ..." He gestures toward a freezer chest and nudges a laminated cardboard listing of pizza options tented and teetering atop the bar near Claara.

"No thanks," Claara says, spinning the tent absentmindedly. "We're headed up to a funeral. Almost there ..."

"Ah." He clears his throat and appears to finally take note of just how Claara and Will are dressed, and how incredibly out of place the two of them are here, today, in his little bar. He looks down at his hands, then back up, solemnly. "I—I'm sorry for your loss."

"Thank you," Claara says. "My uncle Rhonda—eh, Ronny."

"Ah, yes." A wave of recognition flashes in his eyes. "Ronald Donald Dolan ... Luck." He perks up for a moment, "Of course! ... say, you *look* like a Dolan girl—" then perks back down when he notices Claara stiffen. He shakes his head. "Forgive me—didn't realize you were a close relation. Heard about that one. Very sad . . . Too young," he says, looking down and picking at a callus.

"Agreed."

"When's the funeral, then?"

"About fifteen minutes ago."

He looks up from his hands.

"I'll get yer change."

WILL PULLS OVER BENEATH the shade of a basswood tree a few streets into Luck.

"OK, Claara," he says. He leans forward to scan the grounds outside the windows on Claara's side of the car. "This is as close as we're going to get to the place, I think." He leans back and thuds the car into Park and kills the engine. "No cremation. Check. What *do* you want?"

She raises and drops her shoulders and checks her lipstick and eyeliner indifferently.

Will taps a beer bottle with an opener and strokes her bare shoulder with the back of a hand. Claara nods and drapes an arm out the window, staring vacantly at the funeral home. Heads of family emerge: an aunt, two uncles, and her mother.

The four surviving Dolan siblings and spouses scatter slowly, settling wide distances apart on the lawn in front of the funeral home. Compact rings of family and friends form, drawn to each nucleus like suds pulled to a basement drain.

Claara looks back at Will and wipes her nose with a tissue. She swivels her gaze out the car window.

Long-sleeve dress shirts intermixed with camouflage button-downs strain over the rotund bellies of the Uncle Bruce group. Their wrists raise as if tethered to a single lead, smoking in unison.

Aunt Christine commands a cadre of thin women bearing sharp, hard features and straight dark hair dressed in funeral ash and black. They pace and move side-to-side in hard shoes where the sidewalk meets the lawn.

The always relaxed, somewhat eccentric Uncle Lloyd leans against a tree, content and, apparently, relieved. Two of Lloyd's friends wear groovy plaid and paisley suits. They press their hands into pants pockets, walk coolly about Lloyd's tree. One of them examines Uncle Rhonda's funeral program. He flips the page over to read the opposite side.

And Claara's mother, blonde hair like Claara's, though cut shorter, stands sentinel farthest away, practically in the next city lot, surrounded by friends touching their faces self-consciously, embarrassed to find themselves returned to a place such as Luck, Wisconsin.

Mourners continue to dribble from the funeral home. Some cling to the very outside near the steps as they clear the way for the flow of more family friends. A young funeral organizer wearing a tight black suit gestures to someone beyond Claara's line of sight. He turns around and looks at his watch, then looks up again, raising an upturned palm. He moves about uncomfortably, looks hot. Claara frowns.

Will stirs and clears his throat.

"And . . . I thought you said you wanted to be cremated? Once upon a time, you said . . ."

"Maybe," Claara says, eyes now allergy dry. She blinks and looks back at Will. "Maybe have me cremated. And make a proper tea of me so that they," she twitches her head at her family, standing in scattered clumps across the lawn, "may drink me in, one and all. Together." She stares out the window. "Together," she repeats, more forcefully. "All of *them* . . . All of *me*."

Will shifts in his seat.

"We should get over there," he says, nodding to where she's staring. He nudges her above the elbow. A pair of Christine's faithful flit back inside the funeral home. Christine nods when one of them darts back with a report of some sort, hard shoes rapping on sidewalk pavers.

A tightness creases Claara's jaw.

"I know . . ." She sighs, eyes downcast, and rubs repetitively at a cuticle.

"What?" Will says, remaining motionless.

Two men about Uncle Rhonda's age hesitate between Claara's mother and Lloyd. These choose Lloyd, the next two split between Christine and Bruce.

"I don't know. Just so—I don't know. All those old people, standing around, shaking their heads. Like they can't . . . believe . . . living the way Uncle Rhonda did . . . for so many years. That his body gave out on him all of a sudden . . ."

A rare, but refreshing breeze sweeps through the old Toyota, tussling Claara's hair and slipping out the half-opened window beyond Will. The gust smells of hot grass, hot sidewalks, hot streets, all of Claara. Will inhales as she runs a hand through her hair and closes her eyes, turning her face into the brief breeze, and speaks.

"I mean . . . You saw him last Christmas, right?" Claara says, vacantly. Her jaw remains tense.

"Ja," Will says quietly, and nods. "Looked terrible."

"I know. And he had this look . . ." Claara opens her eyes and regards the grounds outside her window again, then scoops a handful of hair from her forehead and pulls it to a side. "Just sat there. So . . . broken." She exhales and turns to Will. "Broken, and alone. Looked at me as if to say, 'Well, this has been fun.'"

"Huh. Didn't really notice that . . ." He glances around now, too, then returns to Clara. "Just that he looked like shit, is all . . . That, and he wasn't drinking."

"Right! You saw it. But these guys . . . ? And now here they are, all of Uncle Rhonda's brothers and old buddies . . . All glaring and scowling. Mostly just trying to figure out who it's safe to be seen standing around by. They're like us at Christmas, Will. Remember?"

Will raises his eyebrows and blinks deliberately.

"I just remember they can't stand me and want me out of your life."

Claara catches a breath. "Well . . ."

"You know I'm right. Bruce actually said as much right to my face! Ja, Claara, you'd be best off if I just let you out here with your family, and I kept driving. Head up to Ashland. They got—"

"Will . . ."

"—good beer up there."

"Will," she groans.

"You can get a ride back to your place from someone, I'm sure."

"Will! Stop it. They . . . They're just . . . difficult."

"See? Even you can't deny it. Me, the guy you let see you naked. Completely . . . naked." He pauses, then speaks rapidly. "You, Claara Dolan. *The* Claara Dolan, a.k.a., Miss Planet Earth. a.k.a., Miss Everything. Can't even admit—"

"Will, *please*! God! I *hate* when you do this!" Angry tears load behind Claara's eyes and prepare to launch. "We *have* to do this damn funeral. And I *was* talking about all those sad old people standing around and glaring at every*one*. And every*thing*." She catches her breath, swallows, and lowers her voice. "This isn't about *you*, Will."

"But you know it'll come up. 'Oh, still with that *Will* person, eh, Claara?' Nudge, nudge. 'I can see yer uh, *feeding* him well, there . . . Claara. Heh, heh.'"

Claara quickly raises an open hand and looks away.

Will goes still and remains quiet for a while.

Finally, he says, "Claara."

She looks at him.

"Claara." He gives her a small smile, and nods, then points over her shoulder with his eyes at the gathered family. "It's not glaring, I don't think . . . Just staring, Claara. Which is really just looking. And surprise or no surprise," he takes her hand, "your uncle's death still comes as a shock. I think.

After all, in the end, the End is the End," he says, becoming hesitant, acutely aware he's about to lose whatever recovery or progress he's just made by hopefully sounding remotely insightful, " . . . in the end. I—I'll—I'll shut up." He releases her hand and shakes his head apologetically.

Claara smiles tenderly and cocks her head toward Will. Her eyes soften.

"It's fine," Claara says, slowly making a fist. "Just so much . . . *anger*. Can't you feel it?" Her fist quivers, Will hears the strain return to her voice. "You can practically strum it." She raises her fist and opens her hand outside the window, slender fingers now pliable but curved, like a seer reading ripples of karma, her fingertips prongs of an antenna gathering radio waves bombarding the world outside. A world she feels press in on her, a world in which their everything could evaporate and end at the exact moment they step out of Will's old Toyota.

Will recalls the nature of his relatively stress-free and upbeat family functions.

"I don't know. Pretty sure I can't touch your family's, uh . . . dynasticity. And I don't get how you guys manage feuds, and discord, and family get-togethers, and apparently so consistently well, but . . . going back to my it's-not-glaring theory . . . that's just how their bodies work now." He clears his throat and continues quickly, though speaking with a more measured cadence, "Maybe there's no anger, no malice. And they're just kinda old is all . . . Getting used to how it feels because they're still pretty new at it. New at being old." He sniffs and wipes his nose. "Seeing family they haven't seen in a while looking noticeably older makes them feel even older still. Even you, no longer a kid—all grown up and living your own, independent life . . . Job, grad school." He looks around and takes a swallow. Claara hasn't moved. He continues, "And this, for now, is how this part of getting older works." He looks over her shoulder to nod at the funeral grounds. "For them."

Claara moves her hands and nods and frowns. Her forehead twitches.

Will clears his throat again and swallows. "Reminds me a lot of my family, actually . . . Probably scared shitless, too. Wondering who's next."

"Daddy says that sixty isn't that old anymore. And that sixty is the new forty."

"That's because *he* is sixty." Will looks out the window. "And your father," Will says, nodding at the svelte figure of Claara's father as he glides across the lawn toward the home, "is in better shape than *I* am . . ."

Claara watches her father's effortless stride, the case of his hands' solemn manner and gracious acceptance of condolences. Dignified. And fluid. Claara turns to Will. She notices he's been looking her father's way, too. Will looks in her eyes and takes her hand into his. Claara has her mother's eyes.

Will strokes her fingers with his. "This is your dad's hand," he says, in a gentle, matter-of-fact way.

Claara smiles distantly.

"I just don't want to end up like that," she says, and sighs loudly, as though holding a breath for a long time.

"Dead?"

"No. I mean—Well, yes. But just . . . Just not dead like *that*." She flicks her eyes toward the crowds in front of the funeral home. "All toady and doughy. And in a coffin. Made up to defy death meanwhile everyone you knew needs to take sides and figure out who to avoid."

Claara sighs and then is silent and still for a while. Will stares straight ahead and starts the car and rolls down his window the rest of the way. She opens a beer and drinks a full third in one swallow.

"And the cosmetics!" she groans, all of a sudden. She talks with her hands, one still clutching the bottle of beer, long fingers of the other poised to strum life into a harp.

"All made up, mouth all sewn shut, skin all painted," she says, fingers of her free hand rippling rapidly, "hair tinted, veins drained, and your body pumped full of toxins. No respect for death whatsoever. Death with dignity?" She snorts. "Feh."

She belches quietly and raises a finger. Will knows to be silent, and settles in for one of Claara's classic three-beer paragraphs.

"Ja. Either make me into a tea or slip me into Lake Superior. Or lower me naked into the ground and wrap me in spores and fold me into the soil so come spring I may grow fungus upon the forest floor above . . . From below."

Will takes the bottle. He and Claara have been known to split beers by the twelve-pack for hours, methodically, a long straight line actually a mere segment of one infinitely large circle, one beer at a time.

"Fungus." He drinks. "Okay . . ."

"From beneath." Claara nods at his hand. "Finish that. You know," she says, smiling but perfectly serious and determined. Her hands, opened wide, go motionless before her. "Mushrooms. Beautiful, complex, intricate, infinitely connected, and . . . delicious. Mushrooms, Will!"

They are quiet.

A while later, Will clears his throat. "I don't get it." Will's nose begins to run again. He pats around at his pockets. Claara hands him a tissue.

"But I like it," he says. He wipes his nose and lips and nods. "Thanks . . . And, really, we hardly respect life . . . Why should we be expected to respect death, too?"

She shakes her hair and scratches the back of her neck and glances at the small crowds around the outside of the funeral home. She looks back at Will.

"Oh, we respect life! You saw all those billboards . . ." Her mouth forms a tight line. She takes the bottle.

Will leans back against the headrest and closes his eyes for a moment. He doubts the caffeine had any effect. That, or the depressant effects of the alcohol . . . He could fall sound asleep in under ninety seconds. He summons what remains in his system of Crow's breve, consumed seemingly hours ago by a parallel version of himself, and careens his head forward to speak.

"Are these people here out of love, or obligation, or . . . fear?"

Claara shakes her head and speaks quietly. "All three, guessing."

"Why didn't we just go to the wake instead?"

"Fuck if I know," she says, softly, and takes in a deep breath and exhales it all as she says, "Oh, what am I saying?" and raises her voice, "Of course I know!" She shakes her head, takes another deep breath, and sets it free, resigned, "Let's go, then. Before we miss *all* of it. Here," she swallows and nods and hands the bottle and what little is left of the beer back to Will. "Finish this." She glances out the window and reaches for the door handle. "Please."

AUNT CHRISTINE PARTS her followers on the sidewalk to cut Claara off at the curb.

"You're late, Claara," she says, shaking a funeral program noisily at her. "The service is over."

"Clearly," Claara says, and lowers her eyes.

"Well, *we* have been here since *eight o'clock.*"

"Oh, my!" Claara cries, looking up. "That's early!"

"Had to get ready!" she says, chin first, sweeping an arm broadly at the landscape beyond.

"For a two o'clock service?"

Claara looks around at the gathered crowds. The view was better up the street from Will's old Toyota.

"Excuse us a moment," Will says to Christine, pulling Claara aside. He makes a small show of removing a check-book from a jacket pocket, and comments in a quiet voice, making certain to utter the word *memorial* loudly enough for Christine to hear.

"I thought you said they wouldn't talk to anyone."

"To *others* . . . yes. All cordial and shit. To each other . . . rarely. Wait and see," she whispers, "It'll be a replay of Christmas—all trying to sway us. Aaaaannnd . . ." she lowers her voice further, "probably . . . drop the . . . so-when-are-you-kids-finally-gettin-married question."

They hold a prolonged look. Aunt Christine scuffs a heel on the sidewalk.

"Ja," he says. "Been waitin for that one, too . . . And that's fine." He shifts his weight and makes a fist and scratches at the inside of a forearm. "I should probably get around to popping—"

"Yes!" Claara blurts, then clamps a palm over her mouth, turning and crouching toward the street.

"I—" Will yelps quietly, shaking his head urgently.

Claara straightens herself a moment later, hand still over her mouth, then spreads her fingers to speak. "I mean, no! Wait," she says, barely keeping her voice quiet. "I don't mean that I mean no." She shakes her fists at her sides. "I mean that I don't know!" She pauses and wipes an eye, quickly. "I mean that I didn't mean no. Not yet, anyway." She smiles and scarcely stops herself from stamping a foot on the sidewalk. "I don't know! Just don't ask me today!" she cries in a whisper, fighting a delighted, awkward, squirming urge to explode into laughter or scream in disgust.

Will nods, smiling with pulled lips. He lifts his eyes to see Uncle Bruce, arms folded, dark eyes glaring at a man perfectly bald and tanned on top, bearing a long ponytail and an unbuttoned black leather vest, move slowly toward

Lloyd. They embrace and nod and stand very close. A hand squeezes and remains on Uncle Lloyd's shoulder.

Claara follows Will's line of sight, side-eyes Uncle Bruce. "It's just that when they see us—"

"They wonder what a six like me is doing with a twelve like you."

"Hush." Claara's lips curl, embarrassed in a way that excites Will. She taps his nose with a fingertip and her eyes flick at Aunt Christine, who hasn't budged. "No. It's like we're a reprieve of some sort. Everyone's . . . buff—" Her eyes flare. "Buffer . . . that's all I've ever . . . been good for . . ." She pauses and squints slightly. "Holy shit . . ." she whispers. "That's all I'm ever good for at these things!" Claara looks around, then pushes the checkbook back at Will, making a small show of handing him a pen, nodding sincerely at Will, indicating in a rising mumble something about a sizable memorial. She sniffs and nods again. "Besides," she chirps, "you're a five anyway."

Will starts to laugh. Aunt Christine clicks her tongue and steps forward to interrupt.

"Two o'clock, *yes*," she says. "But there were *arrangements* to be made, Claara, and—"

"Thought those would have been taken care of by now? Mom said—"

"Yes! But there was still— Well. It doesn't matter now, does it? Two o'clock p.m. in the goddamn afternoon, Claara . . . and you're *still late*."

Claara raises her chin. "You're not my mother, Aunt Christine."

"Aunt Chris*tine*." She scoffs and scrapes a shoe on the concrete. "Well, look at you. Not so long ago I was 'Auntie Chrissy.'"

Claara blinks. "I'm going to find Mom," she mutters. She releases Will's hand and steps around Christine brusquely, eyes avoiding her glare.

Aunt Christine's glower follows Claara's lithe stride and flowing dress, then turns on Will. She folds her arms across the chest of her black blouse. A polished stone necklace rattles, her eyes form sharp, dark slits.

"You could have at least gotten her here on time ..." she says, in an ascending voice that could leave blisters. She shakes her head with a tic, abandoning a brief struggle to recall Will's name. "... young man."

"I ... Have you ever traveled—"

"The disrespect!"

"—with Claara?"

"And drinking!"

ACROSS THE SHADY LAWN, Claara inhales her mother's embrace. She feels her chest rise and fall in shallow breaths and smells her hair. Flax, clothes on the line, sliced cucumber, cool summer rain. Her mother nods. She looks tired, but good. Claara senses relief there, somewhere in the back of her mother's eyes. Yet a wary tension remains in her embrace. It's over, mostly. Her brother's sharp decline, the blur and slow drip of hospice, is now at an end. This, at last, is good-bye.

Almost.

Claara embraces her mother again, glancing at her nearby support circle, established a significant distance from each of her brothers' and sister's isolated encampments. Separate compact factions, all maintaining a hostile silence, all there for Uncle Rhonda yet divided. All standing, arms folded, in split solidarity.

Claara holds her mother's hands, her thumb pausing on the thin wedding band. They touch foreheads, nodding together, brushing noses. She slides her head to the side as her mother presses a warm cheek into hers.

When she opens her eyes, Claara sees Aunt Christine on the other side of the yard thrust an open palm up to Will's face. Will flinches. Claara catches a breath and stiffens and leans back from her mother and raises her eyebrows as Christine shrieks.

"STOP! I said STOP! Just SHUT! UP! Who*ever* you are!"

The family clusters rupture and scatter, though only briefly. Distinct pockets reform on the yard, friends and family like electrons resuming atomic orbit, pulled magnetically to their respective nuclei of Aunt Christine, Uncle Lloyd, Uncle Bruce, and Claara's mother.

The murmurers, smokers, groovy jacket-wearers, and small-town admonishers stop their quiet chatter and banter and lower their cigarettes to share a moment of levity amid their mutual animosity to partake in a satisfied, collective nod of understanding, as well as a shared scoff, here, today, upon the shady lawn of a funeral home during a gorgeous summer's day in Luck, Wisconsin, where they've gathered to bid Ronald Donald Dolan the final farewell.

Christine continues to mutter as Will grasps a wrist behind his waist. He's gone pale and starts to scratch at a forearm awkwardly, hands still behind his back. A friend touches Christine on the shoulder, she turns her head. Others pace and flit.

The Bruce group raise their cigarettes as one, the Lloyds in jackets regard one another and blink, eyebrows raised, and the Moms turn at the hips to look alternately between Claara's mom and Claara, hands clasped before their waists. Two women and one man cough dryly. Claara's father reemerges from the funeral home. He tugs at the lapels of his suitcoat. His line of sight shifts calmly from group to cluster, his eyes resting on, then sliding from each. He blinks and reaches for the railing and starts down the steps.

Claara replaces her cheek against the warmth of her mother's. She lifts a lock of her mother's hair to her nose and closes her eyes, reliving a preschool morning where she's pulling off her shirt, about to take her daily 'mommy-hair' bath. Claara pressed and spread and wrapped her mother's wavy mane of long golden hair over every surface of her bare skin so as to "always forever remember" her while away all day at Miss Elaine's room.

Claara opens her eyes.

THE OLD TOYOTA NEEDS GAS. They stop to fill up and buy microwave burritos from the Kwik Trip on the edge of Luck.

Claara stretches, places a bare foot on the dash. "So whaddya say?" she says, absently chewing a burrito. "To her."

Will starts the truck. He turns his head and leans forward to look for oncoming traffic.

"Tea. Mushrooms. No make-up. No burned bones . . ." He glances back at her. "No box."

Claara looks into Will's eyes. They are clear and stark white and dark brown.

"I mean after."

There is a gap in traffic and Will floors it.

MILES SOUTH OF LUCK, the terrain changes and the roadway hugs bluffs and parts the cover of a dense forest.

A different art gallery and café passes silently at sixty-two mph.

Claara snakes an arm into the back seat and raps a knuckle on the large piece of pottery behind her. For a moment the car is filled with the echo of kiln-fired clay, and with the same hand, she reaches to Will, traces the edge of his ear with a fingertip, and strokes the three-day scruff along his jawline.

Will shudders and quickly scratches at his jaw where she stroked it. The rest of his body is quiet and driving. The highway thrums hypnotically beneath the car.

"Will we . . . be back?"

Claara nods, strokes his scruff again.

"Shave this," she says, softly, then looks ahead to where the highway disappears into the face of a deep green bluff. "Please."

JSUT

It doesn't creep over you.

Actually, it does. But you don't know that. For you, it's a sledgehammer flung straight down from the sky. For others looking in, your decline spirals and crumples and bends and folds upon itself slowly, like a spinning top giving in to fatigue. It wobbles and finally tips onto a side and becomes a flopping carp on a grassy riverbank. But you only feel some of that. And see even less. Everyone else sees it all and marvels at how you, twitching and gasping for life, cannot.

Mitch eyes the perspiring glass of beer placed before him by the tavern owner's meaty left hand. The bartender looks somberly at Mitch, nods, and pushes the five-dollar bill back across the surface of the polished walnut bar. Mitch lowers his head, blinks a silent thank you to Ernie, and trades out the five-spot for a one. A tip. He expected as much from Ernie but felt compelled to undergo the formality of at least offering *to pay for his own beer, despite his grim news of Momma's health now in rapid decline.*

He stretches both arms over his head. Long, cold drive from Oregon to get to Momma here in Wisconsin. His sister, Jen, called with the news while he was eating lunch. He set down his sandwich and drove in one shot to meet her. Got real-deal cold as God intended the second he hit Montana. The grinding cold tightened and darkened beneath a disintegrating sky, his car a dull blade gradually sinking, gradually pressing into the frozen earth, numbly gnawing ever deeper, ever eastward.

Thirty hours later, Mitch coasted into Noisy Creek. He pulled over atop the bluffs along the north ridge of town and stepped out of his car. He bent in the cold and looked down upon a hoary layer of sparkling steam suspended and glittering above the treetops of his hometown. Two water towers and a handful of church steeples poked up through the shroud and gleamed with purpose in the brilliant sunshine and pale blue January sky. He blinked and recalled Jen had told him over the phone it was as if the whole town had the light squeezed right out of it by a massive fist.

A lake of frozen steam, she said, pressing down upon the town below. Keeping it dark all day long. And no snow. Brutal winter drought. Dry as a beetle-eaten dog-bone, and as Jen explained—

He's doing it again, Mitch is. Narrating about himself from afar. As though he were someone else. Why, he isn't exactly certain, though he indeed harbors a few suspicions. It's been happening ever since a fugue clutched his psyche with a prolonged case of mental vapor-lock. Months later, Mitch now considers himself fortunate to have avoided a complete personal catastrophe.

The fugue arrived with no warning signs. And ever since that day he pulled out of that deep and dark lapse, this self-narrative phenomenon lurks mostly out of Mitch's control, pulsing involuntarily like your breathing which you can stop, but only for a relatively short time, resulting in all of Mitch's mental meanderings converting into a repeated hybrid of third person, then first, and back again, frequently during the same span of thought. "Fird Person," he recently joked with his shrink. Or, "Thirst Person," he said. Something of an out-of-body experience, or an extra-personal awareness with the catch that it's viewed from deep within a cavity, a vacuous space your body suddenly becomes. From very, very far inside yourself. From places you never knew existed. Which is to say for Mitch, at least, it's as though he's watching it all happen to himself through a very thick sheet of ice, pinned between that impossibly narrow space on a frozen lake where the surface of the liquid meets the underside of the layer of ice. Forever enormous, forever deafening, forever quiet, forever cold, forever alone, forever always, forever.

MY SHRINK CALLS what happened to me, my mental collapse, *Dissociation*. It's one possible side-effect of Post-Traumatic Stress Disorder. With PTSD, it's normal to feel distressed and fearful for yourself and those around you. What's not as common is to completely disassociate, or detach entirely, and exist in some mammalian state of survival mode. It's your brain's attempt to protect you from re-experiencing your own personal horrors. And I have a hard time accepting this is what happened to me, yet I find it very hard to deny the days-long memory gaps of the last year, the longest and most recent bout spanning a duration of approximately nineteen weeks, possibly more.

Nineteen *weeks*.

That's a long time to be so totally and completely gone. Come to think of it, that's a long time to do anything, really. But total darkness? No memory, no sight, no sound for nineteen weeks?

Gone, yes. But where, Mitch couldn't be certain. All he recalls now is that somewhere in there he missed out on a rare Pacific spring blizzard, a dramatic change of seasons, a son growing nearly four inches, every holiday from Halloween to Easter and whatever it was I did that caused me to spend my daughter's birthday a few weeks later in the hospital with off-the-rails, crash-and-burn vertigo once I came to. No idea how I got there. All I know is I spun out of the pitchy mire and into a thudding vortex hammer, in a lot of pain but very alert, and very me, though still oddly removed from myself lying in a hospital bed with squishy IV bags dangling on either side.

But now I feel I should have known the shit was going to hit the fan. All the clues were there, I just didn't have the insight nor the tools to recognize them at the time. I slept more and more poorly, experienced vivid nightmares with greater and more precise detail, and constantly feared for the well-being of anyone within my sight, especially my family. Impending doom. Classic symptoms, now viewed through that 20-20 lens of hindsight. It's like the mouse that dies or the potato that rots in the back of your pantry. After a few days, you become aware that something is wrong in there, but you can't quite identify just what. Life is busy, you have things to do, and time takes its toll. Meanwhile the stench intensifies until one random day it jolts you into an awareness that your pantry has become nothing but the stench.

So, gone from my dreams were most any nuance and dreamland magic and convolution. You know, the stuff that can make dreams goofy and fun. Instead, I got full-blown episodic replays of me as a kid choking and puking down by the river with a man named Todd, me coming home day after day of "fishing" on the creek always sick and a mess. And Momma promptly saying, "No fish again?" wielding a wooden spoon quizzically. "You usually catch a limit of trout, Mitchell," she'd add, suspecting, no doubt, I was sneaking treats someplace or otherwise up to some harmless no good.

If only.

Trout? No. Todd was never very interested in trout but rather more preoccupied with me sucking his cock. A lot. Usually right away when we first got there, and at least one more time before we left. And making me stroke and fondle myself while he snapped God knows how many photos, over and over for as long as it took him to get hard again. It was generally the same, though there was a set rotation of specific props for each photo session: an old football helmet with dangling chinstrap, a raincoat and matching plaid umbrella, rhinestone-studded sunglasses, and Batman boots and cape. I think Batman was his favorite.

The space between was filled mostly with me pretending to fish, me praying, me puking, me posing, and me playing with myself on camera. Until he finally called me over to remind me that I couldn't tell anyone, that he'd let all my friends know and convince them the whole thing was all my idea, that he'd tell the priest about what I'd been doing while supposedly fishing and how much I liked it, and, yes, Mitch, that's it . . . just . . . like . . . that, he'd say, wrapping a hand around the back of my head, else he'd tell Momma, that's it . . . Mitch . . . Mitch . . . *there*, then shudder and pull me all the way down onto him.

Momma liked Todd. Todd was a respected man in the neighborhood. Todd put on a suit every day and Todd wore a crisp dress shirt and smart tie to work. Todd was important. Todd was solemn and stoic. Todd read in church, Todd rumpled his forehead and knit his eyebrows on cue, and Todd shrugged with piety. People would believe him over me. I was just a kid with an over-active imagination who swore an eight-pound trout lived under the stump at Halcy's Hole. He said he'd tell my friends. He said he'd tell our priest. And he said he'd tell my parents.

Fear and pain—particularly of the eternal, afterlife sort awaiting naughty little mortal boys—compel. Especially at age seven. And I had my priest every Sunday to remind me persistently in his shuddering, sweaty voice of such post-death miseries that surely, without fail—the blowjobs and on-camera self-abuse aside—lay ahead.

So, doomed, I choked it all down, often puking it all back up, doing what I was told summer after summer, year after year, praying for mercy, praying for an end, praying for winter to come, praying for winter to come and never leave, praying for a winter without end. Amen.

And some years spring came mercifully late. Other years spring was more cruel and showed up miserably early. But mostly spring always came right about on time, year upon year, until by the time I'd reached the ripe old age of eleven I'd given more head than most men get in a lifetime.

DISSOCIATIVE FUGUE. You're there, yet you're so clearly not. Sort of like "going through the motions," though even more distant. Adrenaline overdrive. It throbs and flows steadily, makes your ears all hot, and fuels the leaping flames of your fears, pushing you away, keeping you aloof.

I carried on totally lucid throughout the entire ordeal of my dissociative mess: I drove cars, ran errands for myself and the kids, picked up speeding tickets, and argued with cops. I cooked dinner for everyone, shopped for groceries, wrote out Christmas cards, met my wife out for dinner, even made new friends (as well as some new enemies). Always so interesting to bump into an acquaintance "I" made during vapor-lock, have them pat me on the back to ask how I've been, what I've been up to of late, and even recall a joke I shared, as well as learn I said *many bizarre things Mitch now deeply regrets. Which was worse—the messy fugue's morass itself, or the post-fugue aftermath—he now finds himself uncertain, glimpsing a fellow's cigarette smolder idly in an ashtray a couple stools down the bar, the widening coils climbing to form a powerful tornado that rises and skips out of town, sucking up trailer parks along the way.*

I look back at my beer. *Mitch still hasn't touched it despite the beckoning condensation puddling at its base.* I turn to Jen, seated at the bar beside me to my left. She is about to say something I don't want to hear. *Mitch can tell. He knows that coming voice all too well.*

But whatever it is she's about to tell me shortly . . . I can handle it. I can. After re-living what I lived so vividly and so clearly, and reconciling my life after that wicked blackout, images of it coming and going in flashes like someone else's Quixotic acid trip, how could I not be able to cope with some of Jen's not-so-great news?

The guy with the tornado sprouting from his ashtray points at the local newspaper atop the bar between us. "There, but for the grace of God . . ." he murmurs. He shakes his head solemnly and taps the paper. All I can see is the partial headline:

SHERIFF: PLUMBERS' PLUMM

There, but for the grace of God . . . *the expression echoes in Mitch's head, and* I know you're supposed to reflect upon your own blessings, then complete that refrain with the requisite "... go I," but it always seems to me what's actually implied, with a certain sense of guilty relief, is "... *goes someone else.*"

But that headline stirs something within me, and connects me, for now, to this older guy here at the bar whose name I probably should know. A noticeably dimmer, unkempt, and swollen version of the same pinched face I once knew as a boy. He was an adult then, too, when I was a kid, an acquaintance of my parents. It's hard to remember now. There were so many, and everyone seems so big and so old when you're little. And, now that I'm an adult, his face brightens when he recognizes my strong family resemblance. And as such I can tell he'd be hurt on some level that I cannot remember his name. So, I fake it and hope Ernie does me a favor and calls out to ask if he'd like another beer. Schultzie? *No.* Kelbo? *No.* Chelbs? *That's it! Wait. No, that isn't it. Shit.*

I blink at the mirrors above the bottles across the bar and consider asking Jen if she knows tornado-guy's name. She'd know, probably. She must. But I don't feel like putting her on the spot right now. She's tense enough, and for good reason. Momma's dying.

I give the room a quick scan, then look at tornado-in-an-ashtray guy again, whatever his name is—I'd re-introduce myself, but that feels like a lot of work right now—and pull the newspaper closer to me and unfold it to reveal the entire headline:

SHERIFF: PLUMBERS' PLUMMET
DUAL-SUICIDE

Double suicide. Whoa. Apparently, these two guys drove off an overpass and crashed onto the highway below. The story depicts two men, both smiling straight ahead from within printed black frames. One face is familiar. That'd be my buddy Robert from back in the day. For a while there, before his family moved away, the two of us were inseparable, sharing a life of siblings. Almost. The sort of best-friendship you only get a shot at a few times in life, and when it happens you may not even be aware of it. But everyone else is. You never have friends like you do when you're a kid.

Robert. Mitch catches a breath.

Jesus of all things Christ, Mitch murmurs half-aloud. Suicide? Robert? No. Not Robert. Never.

On more than one occasion, Mitch took refuge from Todd within Robert's house.

Mitch, age seven, arrived in a crying rush the first time, fall-ing through the screen door and landing on a wicker chair on the enclosed porch at Robert's house, startling Robert's mother, who was canning tomatoes in the kitchen. She was always up to her elbows in some sort of kitchen magic. She swung the porch door wide and said nothing as she curled Mitch in her arms. She touched his burning cheek and he cried even harder. He sobbed into her housecoat and buried his head in her bosom. Deep, choking cries of Mitch desperately trying but unable to disappear.

In the end, once his voice returned, he explained he simply felt sick to his stomach and had worried about vomiting on the floor of his first-best-friend's porch. Actually, he said 'puking.'

YOU WANT TO SCREAM but there's not even space for noise inside where you are, pressed between that sheet of ice and the surface of the lake. You want to scream and stop yourself, but you can't. So, you watch yourself move in torpid staggers. Torpidly not eating. Torpidly not sleeping, torpidly torpid and manic and aloof all at once. You've finally caught a fly with a pair of chopsticks and, to celebrate, you drop it down, your precious victory, down into the deep and narrow neck of a soda pop bottle for safe keeping. You watch yourself—now the fly—struggle atop the carbonated syrupy soda, gossamer wings all sticky, heavy, and wet and slowly sinking like a black crow tricked into believing a tar pit is a refreshing oasis until you drink yourself down and belch yourself back out.

So, I watched fugue-me gradually move into the stone cellar of our home. First it was just a few of my things like books, extra pairs of shoes and boots. Or sweatshirts that were in Bren's way because I felt myself feel like I was always in Bren's way, always. Then it was more and more of me until quickly it became all of my things, all of me, packed away downstairs. I watched myself watch her watch me pull our closet apart to give her more space, suit coat by suit coat, pairs and pairs of pants, and shirt upon shirt until finally nearly everything that you could call 'me' had been trans-ferred, hanging and folded and boxed and put away   neatly, I might add—downstairs. I felt myself feel like I was crowding her, and I felt myself feeling like I was doing her a favor by getting out of her way. Maybe I was. I saw myself wonder what it was like to live with me. I didn't like what I saw, but torpid fugue-me guy trudged stubbornly on.

Who was this fugue-me guy? I'm glad he's gone, but he was like tornado-in-ashtray guy here at the bar, actually—Cernie? *No.* Kooz? Jantzy? *No, no. Dammit.* That is, I looked familiar enough to myself at the time, but I had no clue. I watched myself tell someone at the store about a homeless person who'd been living surreptitiously in our old basement for an unknown length of time now. Racks of clothing and shoes, I said. Boxes of all kinds of shit. Must be getting in through the old coal chute, I heard myself tell someone else. Some homeless guy, I said. Harmless, I'm sure, but creepy, nonetheless. Homeless basement barnacles happen a lot more than people realize, I saw myself confidently explain, in cities all across America. But especially here, where they're everywhere in Portland, those homeless. Guys just move in from off the streets and hang in basements that receive only a few visits per year to check a water heater or furnace and that's about it.

Until I discovered myself catch the transient in the basement of my house. I witnessed myself call the police to report it. And they came, in two squad cars, all keyed up for vagrancy and trespassing. Relieved, I watched them come. I called from behind a ratty old couch downstairs so he wouldn't see me as I saw and heard myself talk the police into my home and guide them down the back stairs until I could see them apprehend me and view them drag me outside. I told them how happy I was they were finally getting the guy as I saw them press my head under the roof of the squad, feeling how it felt to be handcuffed for the first time ever, wondering what would become of that guy, and seeing myself suddenly ask if being homeless is a crime for Chrissake.

Some time later—Hours? Days? A week?—I watched myself get freed by Bren who later told me she had to play the PTSD card to get me outta there, arrested and jailed for trespassing and loitering in my own home.

DISCONNECT. MISALIGNMENT. Disjoint. Disorder. Out of order. Jsut.

I found that word the other day, *jsut*. It appeared in a book I discovered under a panel of a dresser I picked up off the street. You know, one of those things like a chair or a stroller people leave outside near the street in front of their house hoping someone who may need it will take it away. And while restoring the thing (a relatively safe, trigger-free activity for the PTSD-plagued, I thought), I discovered taped to the underside of a drawer an old journal belonging to a man named Jonas. And on page 27—he numbered each of the handwritten pages—he details, in his precise script:

The following words (typed) died today: teh, smoe, tjamls, and jsut. Brutal, beautiful, and harsh is the editing process of typography. And what a shame. Teh and jsut may be the most aesthetically perfect words I've ever written, especially now, having just drawn them. Beautiful mistakes, rapped out by metal arms. Words that would have never come to the light of day by hand, never flowed from the tip of any pen. Pity they're completely meaningless.

Meaningless? There it was. I sat and stared at it, mouthing it over and over: *Jsut.* Suspended from the bottom of Jonas's drawer all these years, all written out intentionally and waiting for me to finally come along and open up to the correct page silently calling out to me from across the decades: *Ahoy, Mitchell. Herein this binder lies the key to the universe of thy manic aloofness.*

Jsut. *It idles alongside that persistent, driving beat that rolls around in the back of Mitch's mind, and throbs along to accompany his thoughts like a prolonged guitar chord. Sometimes he could blur his focus and picture that sturdy, rhythmic beat, thump, a bass drum, thump, the stretch of a bass guitar's string, thruuuumb, along with his clutter of thoughts, all in and out of order like a common misspelled word anyone else can at first glance understand, yet knows, too, that something, somehow, is seriously wrong.*

Mitch stretches again and rubs an eye and finds himself wondering where his car may be parked.

Outside.

Outside? Yes, of course it's outside. But *where* outside? That is the question.

In the street.

Fine, be that way. Asshole.

I suppose if I can't find it right away I can just fire off my car alarm and follow the honking. That usually does the trick.

Usually, he says. As though there are times when things that should reliably happen do not.

THE OPPORTUNITY FOR your PTSD to pounce can take the form of anything ranging from a mild spark of in-the-moment stress—junk mail, job loss, minor injury, and so on—to something major like paralysis, death, or divorce that your Disorder is waiting patiently for you to be distracted by. Because your Disorder is always there, and follows you everywhere, ready and waiting. Like Camus's plague bacillus, it never dies, and never entirely disappears, calmly biding its time all cozy and dozy in a bolt of wool folded inside a dresser drawer. And it strikes while your psychological armor is disturbed and you, always and unknowingly keeping those starship *Enterprise* shields up, let your amazing force field down, even if only for a moment, to recharge.

I'd never experienced psychological fugue on such a profound level before. Though I'm now starting to think that I may have experienced some minor cases of it over the years. Short bouts not lasting more than a few minutes. But now, over a year later, I'm still recovering from that blackout, and wonder with every day, just like today before I went to meet Jen at Momma's room at the Home and came to the bar here, a dying Momma staring me in the face topping off that long-ass drive from Portland, if today would be the day it would happen all over again, if the bottom would fall out yet another time. For all I know, it could hit me now when standing up from this barstool, or an hour from now while pumping gas on the edge of some little ass-crack of a town down the road. Or it may have already started, and I'm already falling forever away, fluttering down a frigid void. Never pausing, never stopping, never landing.

JEN STIRS BESIDE MITCH. Her muscular legs grip the stool upon which she sits and twist it to obey her will to squeak around toward him. She is closer to saying that certain something. He continues to ignore his beer and looks away and stares at the enormous television screen above the bar. Mitch has no interest in the NFL, its existence a mere reminder that the Roman Col-iseum gore and glory worship will never leave us. But for now, for Jen's sake, he pretends to care, allowing his eyes to glaze over and reflect highlights and miscues of a recent Packer game. Her chin raises, a hand smooths back elegant loops of honey-colored hair, and the small of her back straightens as she uncoils to speak.

"She just died."

Ernie looks up, agape mouth an ebony hole between chapped gray lips.

"Who?" Mitch blinks up at the game-changing gaffe: a fumbled punt, laboriously displayed and replayed for the entire planet to relive in high-def slow-mo.

"Momma! Just now."

"Huh? How do you know?" *The question is a formality. Mitch knows exactly what she means.*

"She's gone. Trust me. She's nowhere now. Not anywhere. Evaporated. I can't feel her anymore, Mitch."

Jen takes a long swallow.

"Let's go," she says.

IT'S ALL WRAPPED UP smartly at the nursing home. Staff so clinical and detached, standing and waiting for us and our final goodbyes. Body removal then a mere checkbox item on a listing of chores to strike through: toilet, linens, floor, cadaver. My breath went cold. Jen waited for me to lose it.

SO, I GET DONE SHOPPING. Picked up lots of stuff for Jen and me but mostly for her as sort of a thank-you for letting me stay at her place for so long since Momma. I gotta get back to Portland anyway, and so I got two shopping carts loaded with goodies to drop off on my way outta town. She'll be surprised, I'm sure—she's only ever got enough to eat there for about a day it seems. I check the time on my phone and see I got an email. I decide to scan it quick before heading outside—probably just work again, and I can likely answer it fast while standing here and get it off my plate.

I'd like to get back and have all these groceries put away before she returns from her daily run along the river. I look at that email and there's a name I haven't seen or heard in a very, very long time. The email hails from the *indifferent moon of his childhood. Something about how good it was to see Mitch at Evan's the other day after so many years, and perhaps meeting again for a drink or three? Minutes pass. A boot on one cart, fingertips of his free hand on the other. Mitch sniffs and wipes his nose with the back of his gloved hand and looks up and sees that it's snowing outside. Snow. Finally. Mitch can't believe how much, in fact, it's snowed since he first walked into the store. He taps at his phone, dials Jen. She answers on the first ring.*

Distance.

Mitch tells her he's going to wait for it to quit snowing or at least for the snowplows to come through so he can get out of the lot because holy shit has it ever snowed a lot since he got here.

Jen goes quiet on the other end.

"Mitch," she says, her voice an echo. "Where are you?"

"I'm at the supermarket. Got groceries. Leaving town soon so I thought I'd load ya up—Two shopping carts-full! So weird to shop without the kids for once!" He laughs with exuberance.

"Which supermarket?"

"That one huge new one up in the bluffs."

Mitch can hear Jen moving around inside her house. "It's snowing in the bluffs?"

"Yeah. Just getting hammered, too. Can you believe it? Finally . . . at long last. Anyway. I'm gonna lay low here for a while, I think, Jen."

"Mitchell." Jen pauses and steps over to a window. "It's not snowing outside. Please come home." She sounds scared. But why? It's just snow. In Wisconsin. During winter. "Come to think of it, Mitch," she says quickly, "Stay there. I'll come get you."

"What? No, no, Jen. I'm fine. Really. I have a car. Once I find it, that is. Then I'll just head back."

Jen is quiet for a few seconds.

"Mitch." Her voice seems measured. "I think maybe living in Portland has dulled your ability to deal with winter driving. I'll come pick ya up. Please just stay put."

"But the snow . . ."

Mitch can tell she's moving around quickly on the other end. She hangs up.

Mitch glances out the tall storefront windows. Jen doesn't understand. Must not be snowing down there by the river. She shouldn't come—getting up the slope of the bluff is going to be difficult now. Jen lives in Wisconsin. She should know these things. So, he decides to go for it anyway and get out of there. He pushes through the glass doors. He trudges outside. The snow is getting deeper, it's snowing harder, the wind has picked up. And it is still very, very cold. After so long without precipitation of any kind, we get this—a blizzard, he thinks. Yet no one else seems to notice, or care. They're all just strolling to their cars, loading groceries, calling after kids, talking about the cold. And it is cold. Another ho-hum day of sub-zero highs. This, Mitch, realizes, he doesn't miss much at all about Wisconsin, despite how the cold once brought him comfort. He wonders about Bren out in Portland. He'll call her once he gets back to Jen's.

Speaking of cars, where did his go? He can't remember though he seems to recall parking over . . . here. But it's gone. Somewhere amid intermittent, muffled shouts, a bass drum beats, and someone searches out a child with a rising and tumbling whistle. The wheels of his shopping carts twist, snap, rattle, and catch. The handle of the cart he is pushing jams against his wrist while the lower rack of the cart he pulls rides up the back of his ankle, scraping and tearing the skin with a heavy edge. Where, beat, is his, rattle, car? Whiiiiis-tle, beat. Shout. Rattle. My car, Mitch wonders, whistle. Beat. Rattle. Snap. Shout.

The snow is now nearly up to his knees and it's becoming difficult to see. He is almost certain to get stuck if he attempts to drive. But he has to try. The snow takes his breath. He pulls at the two shopping carts, heaped with all kinds of goodies. Frozen pizzas and TV dinners and cupcakes and pails of ice cream and chocolate syrup and pancake mix and tater-tots and frozen hash browns and pounds and pounds of frozen hamburger and huge cans of Spaghetti-Os and several bags of rice and still more bags of beans. Like he knew this storm was coming.

Mitch's car is lost and buried in the snow. The air is noticeably stiffer and colder by the step. Jen is probably coming for him. Maybe he can at least get the groceries loaded into his vehicle before she shows up and stands there, head cocked, hands on hips, frowning like she does.

Where is my fucking car? I resort to my old trick of sounding the car alarm. That's about all that function is good for any longer, anyway—finding your car in some huge snow swamp. The wind is picking up yet again and it's hard to breathe. So, I press the red button on my car key's fob, the Big Red One, I think, and I press it as if launching a flurry of nukes, wipe my face and look around. It's possible I'll hear it, but will still need to see the flashing taillights in order to single it out, there's so much snow and the cars are just smoothed-over mounds of heaped snow and you can't really even get between the cars to open your doors and I can't see anything in this snow. So, I follow the sound of my car's horn and realize that probably at least three other guys got the same idea for finding their cars at the same time I did and suddenly there are four sets of car alarms honking and blurting and blinking all at once all around me in all this snowing snow.

It keeps snowing and snowing. Mitch stumbles and loses one of the carts. It strikes another car, smashes the side-view mirror, and tips onto its side. Groceries spill and break and slide. He's whacked his chin, and he thinks he's bleeding.

I look around. I *am* bleeding. A lot. A tooth has pierced a lip, and I can taste metal pooling around at the front of my mouth. I'm sitting in the parking lot in all this fresh snow and I can see the freezing clumps of steaming blood like a jar of Momma's jam smashed open on the snow by my knee and I check the time on my phone and there's that email again and I leap to my feet to fling the phone as far as I can onto the roof of the store but my heavy winter coat has other ideas and it catches and pulls at my arm and I instead rifle the phone directly into an approaching lady's right eye and she shrieks hysterically and I scream and scream as loud as I can and I try to follow my car's honking but I can't tell which is my car, which is the one doing the honking, it's so loud here now and I am still screaming and can see only white and the lady with my phone in her eye has vanished and there's nothing now but snow until Jen.

She walks with quick, easy strides toward me now, I keep grabbing at my carts, it keeps snowing and *he keeps bleeding and there are groceries on the ground broken all over and* snowing and honking all around. I've fallen, covered in snow and Jen is near? She's walked past me I think but I can only see sideways-falling snow and *he only hears blaring horns and he looks up again and the cars around him spin and weave together beneath the twisting prongs of the parking lot lights above and the ground tilts and Mitch moans and flops onto a side atop the sweet, deep green of the grassy riverbank, twitching and gasping.*

DADS

I first got the idea to drink beer in the morning from my physician. I was something of a fitness freak, and normally such a thing would never have occurred to me. I hadn't been to the doc in over a year, apart from taking my kids in for routine things like ear infections, sore throats, strep checks, and so on. But one day, when I myself showed up with a hyper-extended knee, I was asked to fill out a survey concerning depression.

The form was insulting, but I completed it anyway and promptly disregarded it. Waste of time. I'm a busy guy, and this was stupid. I don't even have a chair in my office, and I chase kids all day long when not pounding away at a keyboard.

The final question did, however, give me pause: *Have you ever had an "eye-opener" morning drink?*

Well, no, I thought. And I answered as much.

A couple days later, I opened the fridge to grab some milk. I tend to prepare meals with four items, no matter the meal. So, on this day, for breakfast it was soft-boiled eggs, oatmeal, pear slices, and toast. Oatmeal is good for warming bellies on cold mornings here. And there inside the fridge lurked a bottle of nice, easy-going lager made from a local brewery. It stared out at me.

Then I remembered that survey.

Oh, well, I thought. What the hell? and reached for the bottle.

It didn't take long for the addiction to take hold. This is the sort of thing that can happen to a widowed dad left to his own devices. The weather didn't help, either. I'll be honest, it had been damn cold here. And soon enough, I'd silently formed the One-by-Eight Club. Membership is easy: Just drink one beer by eight o'clock in the morning while readying the kids and keeping them from killing each other. I imagined a social network of followers sharing in a beer for breakfast with me. However, in my case, the One-by-Eight Club quickly became the Three-by-Nine Club. And after about a month, the Six-by-Noon Club.

Now, the first beer usually makes me vomit, but it does keep my hands from trembling. Sometimes it's the second one. And, oddly, it feels good to drink half a beer and then barf it back up at 7:05. It's an acceptable trade-off for losing the shakes. Throwing up into a snowbank is okay, but the neighbors may see you, and then you have to cover it up at twenty below zero. Kinda like scooping up your dog's poop into a plastic baggie glovey-thingy, but different.

We haven't had a huge snowfall this year, yet we have received a lot of snow. Numerous two-to-three-inch events have given us the waist-high snow in the yard we all seem to remember so fondly from our childhood.

Wait. Hang on. That was *last* year. Dammit. This One-by-Eight Club thing is totally messing with my memory. Yet, as magnificent as it was, that nice, gentle snowy winter featuring me falling down a lot took place a *year* ago. And during this current winter, we have witnessed, in fact, nearly no snowfall, despite the persistent and unyielding clenched fist of cold. A very, very cold winter drought brightened only by gleaming golden fields of wheat and sparkling corn stalks from last October, uniformly bent and arranged into crisp rows, undulating along our rolling terrain. And puke that freezes on impact, if not before. (See Jack London for more.)

So today is a three-by-nine day when I visit my dad. It's late January and negative eighteen degrees with a brisk wind. And, yeah, you'd consider drinking, too: Like thermal underwear, the numbing of the senses can be part of getting through a hard winter.

At the nursing home, Dad yet again swats away the spoon I've offered him. Tells me to go bother someone else. He's ninety-eight years old and suffers from a common case of dementia that's frequently staccatoed with acute spans of delirium. Which boils down to saying he's frequently brusque and not really certain who I am. Sometimes he acts like he should know me—perhaps I'm a cousin, a brother, a priest from up the road, or an old friend. But he doesn't remember me as his son. In his mind it's 1931, over thirty years before I was born, and at least a decade before he met my mother.

If I don't feed him, he won't eat. Or he eats very little. They have staff here, but they've made it clear that they simply cannot feed every single resident by hand. So, about this time every day I request an adult diaper change, please and thank you, then buckle him at the waist into his modified La-Z-Boy recliner-like chair-on-wheels. From there, I steer him through the tiled corridor between his fellow residents, all in chairs like Dad's or tipping into walkers, all frozen mid-reach, mid-lurch, or mid-stride, all hung in suspended animation, seized up mid-somewhere, mid-someplace, far away in another time in their mind. Occasionally, we get in response a flick of their eyes as we pass, or a twitch of the chin, as if for an instant we distract them from wherever it is they're roaming around within their thoughts. Others we catch in the middle of a rant. We greet each with a *good morning* or *good afternoon* on our way down to the cafeteria where I feed him. Or try to feed him at least, and pine for another beer. I'm dehydrated—I could set my watch to the crazy cramps I get in my hands—yet I need more alcohol. I pull out my Starbucks thermos, which I've filled with a bottle of that local lager, to get me through this visit.

After a few minutes, my suit coat is dappled with faux-mashed potatoes, gravy, and peas—but for the most part it works: I raise the fork to his lips and Dad opens his mouth.

It's difficult to see loved ones like this, so incapable of the basics: eating, using the toilet, washing hands, brushing teeth. So many of them here: demented, hysterical, disconnected, confused, displaced, and unplugged. There aren't many coherent thoughts banging around within this building, apart from the staff and visitors. And that's debatable, too, considering the intensity of the work and the burden of the visits. When I hold up a mirror to his face, Dad can't even recognize himself. Honestly, we're kinder to our domesticated animals and livestock than we are to one another. Who would choose to live like this?

And, after spending the better part of a couple of years hanging out in a nursing home, my advice to you is to lose your grudges, resolve your differences, hire a therapist, get over it, and move on. Otherwise, you will rant it all out in a nursing home years later.

Then there's the financial burden: $8,000-plus per month and rising. I'm not complaining, really. I know it's a lot of work to care for the elderly and incapacitated, and Dad indeed receives good, basic, and perpetual care. His hands are clean and his nails are trimmed. They bathe and dress him, and deal with his soupy adult diapers. And I don't have to worry about him eating rotten food and suffering a subsequent bacterial reaction, like when he insisted on living alone a few years ago and he wound up in the ER, and eventually by way of an extended hospital stay, landed in here. But still, month upon month, it adds up.

Across the table from us sits another guy, significantly younger than me, feeding his father as well. He appears to be having just as much luck as I am. The gentleman he's feeding has no idea who's trying to get him to eat, nor why for that matter. The son and I meet eyes wearily.

The window for eating is narrow. When not wheeled out and upright, Dad basically just moans or sleeps. Sometimes both. So, I need to arrive right on time and mentally prepared for him to lose it at any moment. He may stay awake and eat fifty percent of his meal, occasionally as much as eighty, but frequently it's thirty percent or less. He ends each meal by either yelling or falling asleep in his bibs and dribbles.

Today Dad lashes out—the back of his hand striking me high on the cheekbone. I could have easily blocked the shot, but I'm so paralyzed by the idea of what's happening I can't move. *Go bother someone else*, he roars.

Taking the cue, the gentleman across the table stabs his son in the palm with a fork. The gentleman can't talk, and snarls instead. A staffer leaps to restrain him. The son shrieks, bleeding instantly and attempting to remove the fork now buried deep into the meaty flesh of his left hand.

Go away, my father screams, flailing again. This time I stop him, snatching his arm and pressing it, with a thump, back onto the table. Dad spits more peas and potatoes at me. A staffer has come to my aid, meets my eyes and stops abruptly. He blinks. I grab a paper towel from the guy, wipe my face, and turn my eyes back to my father. *Fine. Feed your own fucking self*, I hiss, and walk away. The son across the table utters nearly the same, though he's nicer, despite bleeding all over the tablecloth. He sets the fork onto the table beyond his dad's reach.

We stand outside next to the ashtrays near the drop-off portal, breathing heavily, and when our eyes meet, we burst into tears and hug. Real-deal man-clutch hug. What we're going through is hard, and not many people get it. Apart from our dads, we also have to carry on a real life with kids, families, work, and all that. Staring into each other's eyes, we can tell we've both simply accepted that this is the way it is. Until it ends. I almost ask him to join the One-by-Eight Club. I could use the company.

Following a partial eternity, we release our embrace, wipe our drowning eyes, nod good-bye, and trudge to our cars. It's warmed a bit, and we've now climbed to a balmy—albeit breezy—thirteen degrees below zero. I just now notice that for once it snowed overnight. About a third of an inch. The cars are cold and stiff again, and the knee I hyperextended whenever ago aches. He pulls away first, and I follow him out the parking lot up a long incline to jump onto the Trimbelle Highway. He glides into the left lane at the stop sign, and I the right. We look in each other's direction through our car windows, but only to check traffic. His gap comes and he darts left to head south. A moment later I crank the wheel hard to the right, and stomp on the gas pedal and surge north. I drive, pressing the inflamed flesh around my eye, not checking the rear-view mirror until I've finished my beer just around the first bend, quite certain I smell like mashed potatoes and that boxed gravy. I wonder about the other son, if he checks his mirrors to look back at me easing north, ever distant, pushing the far edge of the frigid gap widening between us, then around that bend.

Inside my freezing-cold car, I wish my father would die.

At home, I change out of the suit I wore while feeding Dad and into something more casual. It's just internal meetings, so I choose a pair of insulated jeans, a long-sleeved merino undershirt, and a heavy boiled-wool sweater. I consider taking a nap but know I should ice my eye, which has already begun to swell purple-blue-black-and-pus shut, though I may have waited too long already—I can feel a sticky seal beginning to form. And I have that meeting to attend in forty minutes. So, I get a move on and start to swap the contents of the slacks I removed to the insulated pants I've just pulled on, and I realize that the other son at the nursing home, during that heavy heart-felt moment we shared outside, our tears freezing in the lash, picked my pocket.

No driver's license, no ID, no credit cards, no debit card, no cash, nothing. All gone. All of it. Weeks of hassle to sort, not to mention no access to funds of any kind. And to top it off, I'm almost out of beer. Shit. I ice my eye and open one of my few remaining lagers. I'm ready to leave for my meeting, but not exactly in the mood. But mood or no mood, there are times a man needs to do what needs doing.

I pull on a thick woolen hat, strap on my helmet and gloves, hop on my bike, and make my way back to the office. My knee feels pretty good now, and I've still got plenty of time before the meeting starts. Crossing at Second Street I decide to bank to the left where I'd normally turn right for work just up the block and take off for the bridge over the St. Croix instead. I'm still a fitness freak, after all, despite my One-by-Eight-Club thing. It's nothing more than a quick jaunt up and back. Maybe the fresh air will clear my head.

Brutal cold is beautiful and necessary. It purifies, clarifies, and purges. You can gauge the air temperature based on the width of the flowing channel of this river. Even at forty below, there always persists a stubborn strip of open running water, refusing to congeal and freeze. About a dozen bald eagles, tall, strong, and unfazed, line the water's edge, heads cocked downward, patiently staring into the current, twitching occasionally. From what I can tell, looking down, it is about nineteen below out here today.

At this point, now farther from the office than intended, I'm going to arrive late for my meeting unless I turn this bike around right now. I'm perched on the highest point of the bridge, above some very thick ice. My nose hurts from the cold, and I consider jumping. That would get me out of the meeting for sure. I hate meetings. I know that *hate* is a strong word, and that I'm choosing to use it to describe a meeting, but that is what I feel. Especially now.

I get off my bike and lean over the railing. About ninety feet straight down. That should do it. From my back pocket I pull out a note I've been carrying around. Not a suicide note, but more of a legacy message that I add vignettes to once in a while, just in case something stupid were to happen. Dread has crept over me for several months now, and I guard this message within a plastic sandwich bag. Perhaps my physician's intuition was correct, and I actually *am* depressed . . . with a capital D. But then again, I don't know much about capital-D depression . . . though I'd take a wild guess that teetering on the brink of a very high bridge, about to release, wouldn't exactly be considered a mentally stable behavior.

L: Your love made me a better man. I'm trying. Please know that I've been trying.

Mom: thanks. You were the definition of grace and kindness.

Dad: What a shame to see you like this. You were a great, strong, man. A war hero who survived raising the likes of me. Thank you for giving me the balls to be a guy who has a pair.

Jimmy: the waitresses at The Club are just doing their job and being nice. they don't like you the way you think. they don't care if you just got a promotion. plus, to them you're like seventy.

Jen, Jen, Jen: What a lovely person you were. What has become of you?

I pull a pen from my back pocket (one is not a man unless he carries a pen at all times) that somehow hasn't frozen solid, press the paper to my thigh, and add:

open frozen fog
across this frozen sheet
creeps up
on bats' wings

It's getting colder out here atop this bridge. Going to be twenty-nine below zero tonight they say, and it seems to be happening fast already this afternoon. The windchill is making my eyes tear up and freeze shut as I place a boot on the railing. This, I'm sure, will be easy. Passing cars are now honking. Just another boot, extend the legs, and let go. Straight down is straight down, at thirty-two feet per second. Then sixty-four feet per second, then ninety-six, then . . . it's just physics.

I blink and consider the sparkling vapor rising from the channel. The frozen vapor beckons, makes me light in the head. To slide through it, to drift amid its mist, would be ethereal on my way down to hitting the ice. I'd strip off my clothes, peel and drop each item behind me on the catwalk, to leave this world just the way I came: Clean, naked, and cold. Embrace the cold. Drink it. Become the cold. Own the cold. Absorb it and pull it in through my pores, through my fingers, up my arms, across my chest, and rotate slowly, naked and going stiff and numb and freezing solid, accelerating to the ice to land full force and let all of me crack wide on that black sheet once and for all.

Man, my eye hurts.

But I decide to leave my clothes on for now. I'm about to release when shaking and trembling take over, and I can't control it. Can't control anything, really. My legs get all jumpy and wiggly and nervy and I can't hold my hands still anymore because now I can't do it. I just can't. I'm scared. Plus, it occurs to me I didn't lock up my bike behind me. Crap. I get off the railing and dig for my keys. But . . . why do I care? After all, someone who needs a decent bike might snap it up. And I'll be dead by then anyway.

I pause and consider the clients I'll hose if they don't have my help today, that they need me. And obviously the kids . . . obviously. And the pain in the ass I'd create for my friends in the local EMS and PD who will have to clean me up once I splat. I've never liked to inconvenience anyone. Plus, I need to plan and prepare dinner for my crazy kiddos.

Then again, if someone wants to die, why not just let them? People leap from this bridge all times of the year. Rescue crews race around frantically and gather volunteers in some weird, selfish, bullshit demonstration of community outpouring, and I wonder ... why? This person doesn't want to be with us any longer. Just let 'em die and save the resources for the actual accidents. We got plenty of those to spare around here.

So, I'm off the railing, pedaling to that dreaded meeting after all, without a wallet. What the hell? Strangers' emotional embrace gone awry. I'm starting to suspect that guy I hugged was an imposter playing the son of a resident. Wouldn't be the first time. Now that I think of it, he didn't look much like his supposed dad ... and wasn't he awfully young to be that old man's son? Grandson? Can't remember now if he called him *Dad* or what. All I know is he'd better hope he doesn't see me again. I never forget anyone.

I can still make it. The temperature is steadily sliding south, and I need to hustle. Besides, I'm also surprisingly hungry, and I wouldn't want to pass into the afterlife on an empty stomach. And I could go for another beer. Or two. Also, I can't have Dad outliving me. Not today, anyway. Man, it's cold.

I press my puffed eye for a moment, now completely frozen shut. Probably totally black, too. I can't even open it to look out over the river any longer. I belch and pump the pedals hard to arrive at the office before the other visiting account reps eat everything. They're loud, gluttonous, inconsiderate, insular, and self-absorbed punks burdened with the liability of a privileged upbringing. They get drunk at strip clubs then later wobble outside onto the street, like swollen sixth graders, to call their wives and blubber into their smartphones.

And I'm drawn to the edge again, where I contemplate making that leap rather than deal with all those happy assholes. To think they run the place now. It's not even clear what it is they do during the day apart from talk about golf and their obsession with current workout du jour. Quote the Holy Bible—one of them is memorizing every chapter and verse—in one breath, then leer at springy interns, indulge in sexual fantasy, and plan the next party one breath later. One foot, two feet, release, let go. Straight down. It's just physics, after all. Just a nose-dive. Onto that vast river. Of solid ice. I'm not a coward, never was, and won't end as one, either. Here, where it will never be cold enough for me, ever.

I turn back, park my bike again, this time remembering to lock it, and leave my helmet, hat, and gloves behind. It's a long way down, but the river's deep ice rushes up to greet me hard, black, and fast.

The eagles are still there, encircled and closer now, pecking and tearing up a fresh catch. I missed the mist, and I understand now that the bike ride did clear my head a bit, and that over the years I've missed a lot of things. Some big, most mostly small. They all add up but eventually work themselves out. Such as forgetting to leave the key for my bike lock up there. Soon enough, though, someone will come along and find it in one of my pockets, I'm sure.

RONNY

Berto figured he hadn't seen Ronny Dolan in over ten years when he got the news about Ronny dying. He sat up from where he worked under a sink and looked at his phone again. *Ron-Don dying,* Kinks wrote. *Full-on organ shutdown. Hours to live.* He blinked, then read, *Yer in da loop, Berto.*

Berto stood up slowly and let out a low whistle. He glanced back under the sink. New basin, new faucet, new disposal. Long blades of a rustic ceiling fan purred in tight, silent circles above. It was a hot July day, but the homeowners had no air conditioning and seemed averse to the use of fans, as well. So, he reminded himself to shut it off now before heading out. He squeezed his phone and looked at Kinks's note again. The drive into town would do him good.

Berto drove. He shut off the radio and looked at the broad fields and dense forests. Tumbling rows of cumulus clouds skimmed the tops of flattened bluffs. He crossed a winding trout stream and slowed. The river was low and clear, amber in the full sun and slick, black, and impenetrable in the shade. And now . . . *Ronny.* A pinched grin speckled with scattered golden caps, an unhittable drop-ball, and a half-crushed can of Bud Light came to mind. And a very faded Minnesota Vikings baseball cap. *Ronny.*

Was that all? He tried to think of something more. Anything more. He shook his head. That was it? Twelve years playing ball with the guy and—

A story of a hundred bucks at a tavern glimmered, and gave Berto hope of further recall as he slowed to a four-way stop. He looked in both directions and he looked behind him. No one, not a soul, apart from him and a red-tailed hawk perched above on a high post. He stared at the radio dial again and checked the miles of empty roads in each direction. He sighed, plunged the truck into Park and stepped out. He felt light-headed and hot and wanted a beer. Or just a glass of cold water. But this seemed like good beer-drinking weather for a good beer-drinking occasion.

He paced around his truck and opened the tailgate loudly and sat down on it. The day was hot and thick yet beautiful, though his thighs felt heavy. Ronny. He caught a whiff of long hot grass, the creek, then something foul, something reminiscent of excreta, something a little too close, a little too nasty, a little too much like . . . he turned at the waist and looked into the back of the truck. It took more than a moment of eye meandering until he saw it. Dog feces. Three loosely tied plastic shopping bags in the back of his truck. He blinked and stood up and closed the tailgate and walked away from it as though walking away from it would make it go away. He opened the passenger door and reached into his cooler for a bottle of water.

The water was cold and he blinked as he drank. He played with alternate spellings of the word *shit*. Hits. This. Tish. Hsit. Wait, that's not a word. Tish was though. Their second baseman was called Tish; funny story there . . . Tish hits this shit. Almost a palindrome, Berto thought, and climbed back into his truck. Almost. Sex at noon taxes.

Someone had thrown bags of dog crap into the bed of his pickup truck. Three of them. This wasn't an accident. Somebody *meant* to do this. This was their *intent*. He started the engine and looked left and looked right and looked behind him. He blinked. Ronny? Still drawing a blank on Ronny. He sighed. He could see the bags of crap in his rearview mirror. He looked up at the motionless hawk and dropped the car into Drive and pulled ahead and drove away. He'd stop at the next picnic area for a waste bin.

Berto drove, attempting to recollect his thoughts about what remained of his afternoon. Ronny. Hardware store. Plumbing parts. Picnic area. Kinks. Dog shit. He wondered about the last time he'd seen Ronny. He could feel his thoughts run more fluidly now, the shock of the shit beginning to fade as the jolt of Ronny began to settle in. When had he seen Ronny last? he wondered.

Almost on cue, his phone throbbed again. *can't remember the last time I talked to that guy, berto. u?*

No, neither could Berto. He had no idea Ronny had been sick nor what could be wrong with him. Organ shutdown? Berto winced and cringed. But that, for better or for worse, had become the norm with the old ball team. So many guys drifted apart once they decided to fold so many years ago when they all got too old or too fat to play, or both. And now the only updates anyone received corresponded to significant life events: a birth, a high school graduate (the right fielder had experienced both just last year), death of a parent, serious illness of a spouse, and so on. But no one from his team had died. Yet. There was one brush with death when the short-stop fell through the ice last winter, but that was it. And he was just being stupid and by all rights he probably should have died anyway. Spared by dumb luck. Swanie lived a charmed life, though, everyone knew. And to learn he'd slipped beneath the surface of a frozen river in March for an extended period of time, and survived—terrifying as it may be to ponder—actually came as no surprise to anyone.

This news about Ronny felt different though. Like it was beyond his control, as though Ronny had been stricken and victimized rather than behaving entirely recklessly. Berto considered this, reluctantly. The judgmental, and easy view would be to find fault with Ronny's lifestyle choices, and picture a scenario in which, like so many guys his own age, Ronny had neglected his health into and beyond middle age and when he finally showed up at the doctor's one day fifty pounds overweight he learned he'd been feeling crappy because he had entered the medical Death Zone, suddenly at the point of no return and dying. Or perhaps the Dolan people just don't live very long to begin with, and they consider any extra years they may get beyond sixty to be borrowed time. A gift. Maybe. Berto didn't know and continued to drive. Sixty? How old is Ronny? he wondered. He scanned for an appropriate location to dispose of the plastic bags filled with dog feces still in the bed of his truck. He sighed. Must have been a rather large dog.

Miles down the road, Berto recalls how Ronny joined the team on extremely short notice when their ace pitcher called in drunk from detox one weekend they played in Wolf Meadows, Wisconsin. Ronny turned in a respectable performance, not walking a single batter, and was key to Berto's team salvaging a third-place payout while Dale dried out.

After the somewhat surprising Wolf Meadows finish, Ronny drank beer and ate grilled chicken and corn on the cob at the ball field deep into the night with the guys and stayed with the team, playing in leagues and traveling to various parts of the country for the occasional amateur tournament, over the course of twelve years. The ball players would bump into Ronny every now and again after he hung up his cleats, but mostly Ronny made himself scarce and kept to himself, his family, and his work. Berto now figures at least ten years have passed since he last saw Ronny and over twenty since he started playing with his team. So, he gives his dying Ronny an age of fifty-eight. One year older than Berto. He squeezes the steering wheel, feeling the need to gasp, to drink down some sky, feeling pressed flat against an inside wall of a freshly sealed Mason jar.

"TOO YOUNG," he mutters to his wife, Marcie, over the phone while driving through Noisy Creek.

"Oh, no!" she exclaims. "Wasn't he . . . about your age? Where are you, anyway?"

"I— Younger, I think." Berto curses under his breath. "In Noisy Creek, heading for some parts now . . ."

"Thought you were in Cylon today? We haven't seen the Dolans in forever. You don't know how old he was?" She cuts away and speaks sharply to a child. There is a short silence, then he hears her breathing resume. "K . . ." she says, distractedly, and hurried. "Uh . . . we need bread."

"How old he *is*," Berto says, almost hissing, emphasizing the present indicative. He softens his tone. "Trying to remember where or when we saw the Dolans last . . ."

They are silent. The busy Noisy Creek streets murmur into Marcie's ear through Berto's mouthpiece as Berto hears a day-care daughter vie with Berto for Marcie's attention, clung, no doubt, to Marcie's waistband back at their home over in Hammond. Berto drives, Marcie inhales and strokes the young girl's earlobe between an index and middle finger. They breathe and hold phones, each idling in the other's background.

After a while, Berto says, "Probably some bonfire at Magnus's place, the Dolans, probably . . . years ago . . . I'll pick up bread."

He blinks and looks out the window as he passes a quiet city park. He scans for a garbage bin.

"Anything else?"

Marcie switches hands with the phone and child clung to her waistband. Her breath connects with Berto's breathing.

"Just you."

Berto's thoughts in his battered truck move on from Ronny to the bakery to Ronny, to some items he needs from the hardware store for tomorrow, to Ron-Don and to Marcie and finally back again to the multiple bags of shit in his truck. The more Berto tries to make sense of that, the more it seems the only sense he can make of it is to assume the worst. How else, after all, should one interpret bags of shit tossed into the back of one's pickup truck? Three of them. It's one thing to *talk* about doing that sort of thing, but what kind of person *does* that? And what kind of person *receives* that? What, Berto wonders, has he done to deserve this? To whom? And when? What, he wonders, will he tell Marcie? And, why didn't he just toss the bags at the four-way stop, located out in the middle of exactly nowhere, while losing a staring contest with a hawk? He didn't know. He didn't know.

What to tell Marcie? Maybe she'll laugh, true. But she may cry. Also true. She may scream or react strongly or she may become very frightened. True again. He himself had been momentarily paralyzed and drove on and on, numbly wondering something about Ronny and getting a bad taste in his mouth. Like burned plastic. He decides there is no good reason to risk causing her to despair anything, driving down the road, trying to picture Ronny's smile and hear his laugh again. And more and more the question in his head becomes not simply *what* to tell Marcie, nor even *when*, but, in fact, *if* he will tell Marcie at all.

BERTO TURNS FROM the hardware store to walk by the bakery for one more attempt. A **BACK IN 5 MINUTES** sign had dangled from the door on his first pass. He walks and recalls a night the team stopped at a regular spot in New Richmond.

Ronny had ordered two pitchers of beer and handed the bartender some cash. The pitchers were filled and the beer passed around and poured into tall lager glasses meanwhile a simmering discussion between Ronny and the bartender commenced. Soon enough bystanders began to take notice. Ronny insisted he had given the barman a one-hundred-dollar bill. The college-age bartender had returned a handful of change for a twenty and was expecting to keep it all as a tip, arms folded defiantly and, Berto recalls, quite arrogantly across his chest.

One hundred dollars was a lot of money to anyone on the ball team back then, but especially to Ronny, whose sleepy scruffiness and overall dishevelment never really gave the impression of being a guy who looked like he'd ever have a hundred dollars on him. Ronny took a deep swallow of beer, then calmly started screaming until the owner finally showed up. Until that moment, the majority of the players had begun to doubt Ronny's story, and quietly agreed with the bartender, who began to yelp about calling the police. Maybe Ronny had made a mistake? And he really did give the barman a twenty instead? Ronny *had* been drinking at the ball field—a traditional fifth inning beer in which the entire team partook—before arriving at the saloon, after all, so . . . But by the time all the team's food orders had been placed, Ronny had become so uncharacteristically furious that the rest of the team stood behind him as one. A front united. One that threatened to never return.

The owner assessed the situation and adamantly re-checked the cash register and then promptly forced the bartender to empty his pockets. Nothing. Still furious and suspecting that up to now the whole exercise had been carried out merely for show, Ronny demanded, in rather colorful fashion, that he check the bartender's socks.

The drinks were on the house the rest of the night.

Yeah, Ronny is definitely alright, Berto says to himself. Hard working, good and grounded, and all that. Is he religious? Maybe. Berto doesn't know and now he's afraid to ask. Where did he grow up? Up North, yes. But where? There's a lot of *there* up there . . . did he go to college? Berto's instinct says no, but he feels awful for leaping to that assumption. Just like the hundred bucks, he thinks, Ronny doesn't exactly look like a college boy, but maybe he was. Or he tried it and didn't like it. Or he's wildly intelligent but due to his towering north woods modesty, he never betrayed more than just what was required to play ball and run from one landscaping or snow-plowing gig to another. There are guys like that all over the North. Berto is pretty sure he is a crew chief, but now he wonders about too many things and all he feels now, walking to the bakery, is dread. He's not sure what he's dreading more: seeing Ronny, Ronny's family, or his teammates, all now surely struggling with sudden attacks of mortality, disbelief, and woe.

He shakes his head. He'll have to say something about Ronny at the funeral. Teammates will expect it. After all, Ronny is the one who had dubbed him, Robert, 'Roberto' in the first place, which by the top of the third morphed into 'Berto.' From there the nickname stuck permanently, and most of the guys still call Robert 'Berto' to this day. Even his wife calls him Berto. So, he could tell the Berto story. And the one-hundred-dollars-all-drinks-will-be-on-the-house-for-tonight-thanks-to-that-snot-nosed-little-shit story, the sight of the puffed up chest of Ronny's stubby frame prancing about the bar all proud and triumphant and satisfied, all cock-of-the-walk. And his invisible, unhittable drop-ball story. The thing came in looking like a misshapen cueball, always somehow at an oblique angle, and dropping out of sight so late that even Kinks behind the plate would get fooled and sometimes bruised by the pitch. That makes three stories. Two quick morsels, one sort of long one. But Berto needs more. Ronny the guy. Ronny the hunterer-gatherer-fisherer. Ronny the husband and Ronny the father. Ronny the human person. Just more *Ronny*. Who the hell is Ronny? And how old is he, for Christ's sake?

Death. Berto imagines slipping into a murky dreamscape, falling, plummeting, as a spinning squiggly dream haze disintegrates and dissipates and evaporates before him. A muted poof, then a nothingness beyond a void, a big room with no walls, a nothingness he could no longer perceive because he, too, is nothing and less, no longer a mere biological vessel for his too-self-aware self, inert, null, and dead. Death.

Berto shakes his head and glances up from the sidewalk, now nearly liquified by the probes of his frantic thoughts, groping for answers. Answers and words. Any words, and any answers would do, among all the edges of all the buildings and sidewalks now jumping out at him like twisted, exposed muscle tissue and sinew, the streets fleshy, and skinned alive with each step. He blinks and sees only the red innerscape of his eyelids. He can smell the sweltering, sweating shit-bags a half block from his truck, and he will smell them half a year from now, too.

A tall, slim young woman with short blue hair slams the tailgate of a pickup truck shut and marches toward the entrance of the Arctic Pelican Bakery. She holds a large wicker basket pinned under one arm as she slides a key into the lock with the opposite hand as Berto approaches.

"Robert," she greets, like a statement, and nods.

"Elspaith," he says, relieved. He exhales loudly. "How goes?"

"Oh, fine." She sighs and runs the back of a hand along the underside of her chin. "Deliveries, ya know." She shrugs and flips around a sign on the door that reads **BACK IN 5 MINUTES** to read **OPEN**. She looks hot. And tired.

"No 'closed'?"

"Eh?" She swings the door wide and gestures for Berto to enter.

"The other side of that sign," he says, pointing. "Does not read 'closed.' Just noticed that."

Elspaith cackles and follows Berto inside. "Ah," she says, "That would be Mom's doing." She shakes her head knowingly. "And, no," she adds, "it most certainly does *not* say 'closed'."

"Never gone more than five minutes, eh?" Berto gives her a mock-accusing look and crosses his arms tight to his chest. He taps his chin suspiciously with a raised index finger. "*Hmmm?*"

She smiles. "Nooks, Robert . . . make you look." She is calm but her eyes seem to flash. She points with her eyes. "A nook! A crease in which *time*," she lowers her voice, "folds," adding, softly, slowly, "and re-loops." She pulls a bright yellow apron over her head, still smiling, now wryly. "It redoubles and renews, all reset, all better. For another five minutes."

Elspaith has finished talking, but she hesitates, sensing something is amiss, hoping it's nothing. This man is Robert to her, 'Berto' to nearly everyone else. He normally comes in once a week or so, and she assumes he has a family based on the amount of bread he buys. *Thank you, Robert,* is about all she's said to him.

She looks at him now, hopeful she's not overstepped but rather relaxed Robert to some degree, by letting down her guard, sharing with him a glimpse of her inner Elspaith. The one she reserves for herself, her friends, the peculiarities that roam about her curious old home.

Berto stares, aware that if Elspaith is anything like her mother, she has a way of knowing something is wrong. Her mother, Zelda. A woman unto herself. A woman who could smell any man's anguish from around the next corner one block away. "Or . . ." he raises his eyebrows, attempts to smile, then stops. He sighs inside, knowing that even on a good day, he couldn't match an eccentricity such as this, if that's even what this is. But he decides he must try. Or not, he rethinks, and pauses again, finally concluding discretion to be the better part of valor. He closes his mouth slowly and looks down.

Elspaith smiles. "Which is to say the sign is always technically valid." She laughs and he raises his eyebrows. "Much like on a molecular level a trout is never, ever, the same length. Ever. Besides," she pauses to slide the basket aside and looks back at Robert, "crazy me is almost mostly always here." She laughs and tosses her head back without inhibition and adjusts a cap that matches her apron and tugs at some fronds of thick blue hair.

Berto knows she's not exaggerating about always being here. Few people work more hours than Berto, and he knows Elspaith may be one of them. He nods and wonders if that's why she's mostly goofy, too. Goofy, with an edge of a real blade she's not shy to bear as required. Elspaith may be a bit of another world, but there's no bullshit there, either.

"So, what can I getcha?"

"Oh, bread . . . I guess."

"OK. Well, you've come to the right place. Take your pick," she says, eyes sparkling, and passes an arm before a sparse collection of loaves resting in a tall wooden rack behind her. "This time of day there's not much . . . but it's all today's. The Bread Fairies said. Promise." She smiles again and nods once, convincingly.

Elspaith washes her hands and snaps on a pair of food-safe gloves. She slices and bags two loaves of honey wheat and rests them upon the counter before Robert seemingly all in one motion.

"Anything else? Something . . . treaty?" She tips an ear toward him, cocking an eyebrow.

It's hot outside, it's hot inside his truck, it's hot on the sidewalk, it's hot at the gas station, hot in the hardware store, hot out on that hawk's perch, hot inside the bags of shit in his truck, hot inside the bakery, it's hot everywhere. Even wherever in the world it's currently snowing. Yet a ball of ice tightens inside his chest like a fist slowly clutching his windpipe. Berto makes a dry, tight throat noise and vacillates.

"Yes?" she asks into her apron, grinning, as she wipes her hands. She looks up at his pause and catches his eye. Her face goes slack. "Oh," she says, allowing her mouth to hang slightly open. She holds his gaze until he looks down at the counter. A moment later, he begins to toy with the bread bags. "Ooooh," she repeats, in a fading voice, and licks her lips.

Berto sighs and feels his shoulders sag. He rolls his tongue behind his teeth. He'd believed joking with her about the sign had given cover. Wrong. He blinks and wonders what to tell her. And he must tell her something. If he couldn't match her weirdness, he must give her something now. But what? Ronny, and not knowing anything of substance, anything at all, about the man he apparently wasn't much of a friend to. His swollen ball-team buddies, by now all hysterical that someone on the team is dying and wondering if they'll be next, hearts practically exploding in their chests any minute. And the plastic bags of fecal matter out in his pickup. He also needs some allergy pills. Getting to be that time of year.

"Allerg—" he says, then stops. He starts to speak, again. His breath is icy and his voice catches, hard. His head wags side to side unconsciously. "Sorry, Elsp—"

She nods and raises her eyebrows slowly and dips her chin. She hasn't moved.

"An old frien . . ." Berto says. He pulls his eyes away to look down to fiddle with the sacks of bread again. He struggles to breathe.

Elspaith eyes him steadily, draws in a deliberate breath through her nose. She turns and opens a small refrigerator and removes a pitcher of water and pours a clear, glittering stream into a wide drinking glass and slices a lemon with smooth strokes. She gives a slice a slight squeeze before dropping it into the water.

She moves quietly around the counter and extends a hand to Berto. He hesitates but finds himself pulled into her dark, mossy eyes. She closes her fingers around his forearm and guides him to a bench near the front window display and hands him the glass, the skin on his arm suddenly fresh, alive, and spry. Then, just as quickly, the flesh where her hand had held him goes chill and clammy, as if dying, when she releases. She sits next to him and she feels his shoulders slump and he pitches slightly as the old bench sags beneath her weight. She offers Berto a crust of bread plucked from an apron pocket.

He cocks his head and twitches his brow.

"Here," she says softly, raising her eyebrows. Her face still looks tired but her eyes are clear as a child's. She smells of bakery and something verdant that's been soaking up the sun all day long. "It's a crust of bread from a loaf I sliced earlier today. An end piece. Some customers don't like them . . . But you do, I can tell. Here," she says again, offering. "You just got some truly . . . sad . . . news."

Berto takes the small, crusty loaf heel from the palm of Elspaith's hand. She stands slowly but effortlessly and motions to the water glass. "I'll be right back."

He watches her slip behind the counter and through a swinging door that leads to the ovens. What do you call the room with the ovens in a bakery? he wonders, tracing a finger into the fog that's formed on the side of the cool glass. Bakery kitchen?

He looks up again but doesn't see Elspaith. He drinks. The water is cold, light, and lemony, and Berto realizes just how thirsty he is. And he now knows she is right: All of everything had sunk in during the moment in which she bagged the bread, and now he needs to sit down. He feels weighty and clumsy like wet sod.

He thinks about Ronny as he chews the crusty end-piece of a dark wheat. It is delicious. Late afternoon, and it's still steamy and bright outside, though Berto can sense the bakery settling in for the day, the way an old house gently pops and knocks at bedtime. All that's missing from this drowsy moment is the yawn of buttery sunshine streaming through the front windows onto the floorboards.

Ronny. What does he really know, really, about Ronny apart from the news that he was about to die? This was a man he completely depended on more than once in order to play. A man he fought and laughed with. A man, in the end, he used. Merely because he could pitch, and pitch well enough to keep his team in most games. His mental fatigue continues to scramble while his teeth chew, rhythmically, at a lip. Nothing. Absolutely nothing.

The intensity of the occasion of this void, the magnitude of the realization of this absence of anything, obliterates all consciousness of the man he played beside for twelve years, as well as a part of himself. So many innings on ballfields, all that time on airplanes and in airports, so many drinks after games, nights in hotels, Packer-Viking ribbing, road trips, camping, and Berto doesn't even know if Ronny went to college or if he believes in God or Bigfoot and UFOs or even how the hell old he is for sure. An utter chasm of nothingness beyond the context of a ball diamond. He sighs, light-headed and unable to stand, wondering only what he'd been doing all that time. What had happened?

Elspaith slips out from beyond the silent kitchen doors and pours more cold, clear water and cuts another broad slice from the bright lemon. She looks over at Robert, reclined on the old church pew, tailbone slid forward, and legs straight in front of him, boots out.

She crosses over to him, renewed bakery aromas trailing like a veil in her wake. She hands him the fresh glass and takes the empty one, his fingers uncurling slowly as she pulls it from his grasp. His fingers recoil as he releases, then open again to receive the cold, new glass Elspaith slips into his hand.

The old bench sags and dips again as she sits beside Robert. Silently, Elspaith reaches into his empty glass resting on her lap and with her long fingers plucks out the lemon slice and eats it in two bites. Berto allows a small snigger to escape his nose, smiling sadly, looking straight ahead with Elspaith at some point just above the floor in front of a glass case. At some point in space. But he doesn't know. He is focused on a mid-air nothing and doesn't seem to know anything. Elspaith continues to look straight ahead with Berto. Ronny. Is he a misunderstood man? An under-appreciated one? Berto could be convinced of that, but now he just doesn't know. And knowing nothing allows for becoming convinced of anything.

The depth of this void makes him feel shallow. And making matters worse, apparently the process involved in becoming so tragically vapid also results in dramatic aging: Not so very long ago, possibly even just last week, it seems, Berto would have never given a second thought to bags of crap flung into his pickup truck. Kids ... He'd have written the whole thing off to some kids. Just some goddamned kids. He'd have picked up the bags of shit and tossed them into a garbage can or a ditch and moved on, done, wondering in the next thought about what was for lunch. Things were different today, though, the way it seized him. This rebuke of his existence, this commentary on his personhood, this condemnation of Berto himself, his Berto-ness.

He closes his eyes to view the replay of himself, donning a pair of work gloves before lifting each sweating, dripping, leaking, reeking bag gingerly from his truck and carrying them oh-so carefully to drop them into the burnables under dark cover of the shade at Creekside Park across town, so careful as though they'd explode right there in his face. Had that truly been him, today, not even a few hours ago? Berto.

A plumber, wounded and made queasy by a pile of poop. And now the sudden news of Ronny whom he clearly doesn't know at all beyond the context of how he had played ball years ago.

His thighs ache and feel hollow. It occurs to him that he will be an old man for a very long time.

A new message throbs noisily in his pocket. He doesn't want to look. It throbs again after unknown moments of staring outward and occasional blinks next to Elspaith, seated here in this porous, in-between space of an elongated moment. And when he finally does look, his eyes confirm Ronny now lives on only beyond the margins of his own story. He looks at his phone again and from the bakery feels Kinks's remote groan.

oh, berto . . .

Beyond the clear display of his phone, Berto becomes aware of a faint, hesitant reflection in the glass case across the neatly swept floorboards. His eye catches, and he's struck to discover he is seeing his own reflection looking back at him. He turns his head in slow double-take to view his profile, just to be certain. Elspaith materializes beside him in the glass, casting her eyes into his. She stirs slightly, as if she had been waiting for him to see himself for himself, finally and for once, but she says nothing. He picks at a thumbnail, then raises his eyes to glance at his face again. It's the distant face he washes and shaves and hurries away from every morning. The face he avoids and now seems to know less and less of.

Bags of shit. Getting old. Dying and dead friends of convenience. Berto just doesn't know. And he decides about all he really knows for sure about Ronny is that even though Ronny doesn't look like a college boy or a guy with a hundred bucks on him, Ronny probably wouldn't flee from his own face. Ronny wouldn't run from what he sees while washing up in the morning because Ronny was not the kind of guy who wound up with bags of shit thrown at his truck.

Berto sets his phone down on the bench next to his leg. Elspaith feels the back of the bench give beneath his gentle sniffle, and he senses her swallow and stir beside him. He shifts and her reflected eyes are soft and lustrous, and she nods minutely. There's what appears to be the slightest hint of a smile, but it could be the light, too. He swallows what's left of his end piece of bread. The icy fist clutching at the insides of his chest and neck warms and loosens. He will tell his Ronny stories. He will. They're good stories. And they're real stories. About a real person. And he will also tell Marcie about the three bags of dog shit after all, and she will laugh. Of course she'll laugh. It's funny.

Elspaith hands Berto another end-piece. He takes it and she raises one of her own to her open mouth.

REMEMORYING TOMORROW

I just told my son to please go away. And to leave me alone. I was nice about it, I think. Though after last year's extended blackout, I will always wonder about these small things. Small gestures made and turns-of-phrase uttered, small things that over time can add baggage to a childhood and surface later in life as big things. Was I nice? I will forever wonder. They will always be with me, now, these things. These blurry things. Small things good, and small things bad.

Speaking of small, bad things, I am currently standing between the bane of my enlightenment that is my garage, filled with thousands of tiny nightmarey things that are of my own doing, of which I have zero memory, and an enormous dumpster, newly arrived and itching to be filled.

After a while, Coyle, my oldest and same son I just told to please go away, comes back.

"So, what are you doing?" he asks, the gap between his eyebrows closing quickly. He looks up at me, but only slightly, with his mother's sable eyes. These days he only has to incline his head a touch in order for our eyes to directly connect. Coyle is fourteen now and grew nearly four inches while I spent much of the last year groping around, blacked out. At times when I catch a glimpse of him in my present fugue-free state, I find myself startled and awed, struck with the thought: Who is this . . . *guy?*

"Tomorrow," I say, absently, and pull off a work glove. The evening air is heavy and sticky from the hot afternoon, newly steamed up by a late thundershower quickly whisked away and replaced by a couple hours of additional sunshine. Along the horizon the sky murmurs orange and pink, as the tall evergreens and hardwoods blot, in swipes and dabs, at the spot where the sun just rolled off the edge of the earth. Behind us, early evening gives way reluctantly to an infinity of stars, climbing and dripping, freshly applied by a fine brush to a darkening canvas.

"Ask me again tomorrow," I say, and smile back at him, whites of his eyes as bright as a lone birch in a deep forest. He turns and stands next to me to look beyond the tree-tops at the wine-stained sky where the sun has disappeared. He's not sure what to think, I can tell.

This *tomorrow* thing is part of my personal Project Rememorying. It's a mentality I've adopted since recovering from a wicked experience with PTSD my shrink calls *dissociative fugue*, or *dissociation* for short. With dissociation, an individual who becomes mentally detached can partake in erratic, paranoid, and potentially unsafe behaviors all while functioning in a dazed blur-state of survival mode. Memory recall once the fugue has passed is minimal. And in my case, the post-dissociative-fugue state comprises something of an otherworldly, out-of-body experience you instinctively know better than to talk about among casual company. Sorta like speaking openly about your alien abduction. You just don't do it. But it nonetheless eventually needs to be talked about, and in the unfortunate event you find yourself coming upon the term *dissociation* the hard way, you will doubtless find yourself in the position of having at least a little explaining to do.

My advice to you on that one would be to explain it to a licensed someone you need to pay to hear it before you try it out on one of your friends. Yet another lesson I learned the hard way. Ironic, and cruel, like so many ironies, really, that the people who need to hear it most are the least able to really *hear* it.

I declined a glass of wine at a party one night not long ago, wide awake and fugue-free, and a friend, whom I don't recall seeing since before my fugue, gave me a long look from across the room. A wave of satisfied understanding washed over her face. She raised her chin slowly, mouth slack. *Ah, of course*, the arched lines above her eyebrows said. *Mitch was boozing it up. That explains everything.*

So badly did I want to scream out *If only!* above all the heads between us, that I invited her to coffee the next day. She said that Ja, would be so great to catch up, Mitch. Amy is a nurse and I thought she'd get it, what happened to me. But all she got was bored and condescended the story of my experience down to nothing more than stress.

"And we all get stressed out from time to time, Mitch." She sipped her coffee. "PTSD?" she said, incredulous and smiling at me from over the edge of her cup. "You? Oh, please." Then she dug around, head down, in her gigantic purse while I thanked her for the chat and left.

I DISAPPEARED INTO MY FUGUE on the most beautiful autumn afternoon two years ago. Sunny and warm with a gentle breeze. Full fall coloration. I saw a guy walking along with a kid about the same age as one of my boys, about the same age as me when Todd first took me. He grabbed the kid and said something, darkly . . . I think. Next thing I knew it was spring. It was as though I stepped directly from autumn inside my office building into a spring day out in my yard. Thanksgiving? Christmas? New Years? Winter? Gone, all of it.

Memories from that time do come back now, in glimmers. Scarce flickers hover, surge, and burst. Fireworks muffled and veiled. But for the most part, memory of that time is like the afterlife of a mammal or insect. Nothing. The memories that do survive are like faces of people looking out through a square of light on a glimpsed subway car, all trying to communicate something to you as the train speeds by. But you can't really hear or see them. And the order they come in is incorrect, too, you're pretty sure. None of it is clear, and what is there, this amorphous distortion, disappears before you can process it. Maybe this is a good thing. The memories I can reconstruct aren't pretty. Such as me moving myself into the basement of our home, where I was eventually arrested for trespassing and vagrancy.

Apparently, I actually reported myself to the cops, telling them some homeless man was living in my basement, and I watched them arrest me, and saw myself tell them how glad I was they finally got the guy outta there, and watched them drag me up the steps. They're everywhere, those homeless, I said, there present in the moment, watching it all happen to myself as it happened, then asked, desperate for someone to take me seriously, while seeing myself get stuffed into the back of a cop car, if it's a crime to be homeless for Chrissakes.

So as a part of that personal mental repair path, I moved back into our bedroom with Bren and took care of the small things around the house. Things that had gotten so much worse within an environment of neglect. Repairing window screens. Fixing light fixtures. Shampooing carpets. Cleaning drapes. Digging up that sad and overrun landscaping. Tasks with tangible results.

And now's it's finally time to tackle that albatross of mine, the garage. Would be nice to one day do something crazy like, say, park a car in there again. And in there I decide to start with—*shudder*—the apple fridge. At one point while so totally out of it, I lost track of all the food I'd kept inside the apple fridge, my annual two bushels of Haralsons included. Properly stored, Haralson apples will remain crisp, crunchy, and delicious until February. Beautiful. But then my fugue came barreling over the North Pole and leveled me. And all of my psyche, like the contents of that fridge, all those beautiful red apples, withered and rotted and occupied a tremendous amount of the garage. And now clearing out the fridge means clearing away a path through the heaps of non-me memories, those piles that are mine, but belong to someone else, in order to get the refrigerator out into the yard near the reach of a hose for cleaning.

I don't know entirely just what happened, what I did in my altered state, and how often. It's a hard thing to accept, that giant rip in my past. And my present day awkwardness about it. But I need to overcome it, become me again. I miss the calm and confident guy I was. And I need to bring him back. Enter *rememorying:* to avoid future fugue plummets and to process reality in a way that sticks. Avoid evaporating into the ether mid-sentence while sharing a nice moment with Coyle, for example. Remain grounded and attached to the Earth. If not for me then for Bren and the kids. I'd die for it. I'd even redo the T part of the PTSD for it. I would.

GUYS ARE WEIRD ABOUT THEIR GARAGES. You probably have a garage weirdo living near you, too. Mine is named Randy. Lives next door. He compensates for his personal relationship deficiency disorder (PRDD?) with a dry-walled, carpeted garage complete with satellite TV and wet-bar. Tools hang on pegboard walls, pinned safely within bold borders obediently drawn in blue, black, or red marker with the duty of a child inscribing RIGHT and LEFT onto the toe of each shoe, presumably to prevent himself from mistakenly hanging a pipe wrench where a claw hammer or rip saw belongs.

I turn to open my garage door to the sound of Coyle's deep new voice echoing in the background. And a vision of the bank of a creek, with low-hung boughs presses upon my consciousness. A tall man's feet slip from his shoes, and there's the sound of his belt unbuckling . . .

I shake my head. I need to open that wide, slate-gray door and bare the ugliness of my psyche to the planet if for no other reason than to let in some light and better see the "me" mess and focus on what I'm doing. Just a garage door. And all I gotta do is raise it.

Delphine lives across the street. Like Coyle, she changed dramatically during my fugue, too. Coyle, by virtue of his pituitary gland. Del, thanks to a plastic surgeon's very motivated and busy knives. She also quit her job as a corporate comptroller and now works as a fitness consultant and sells skin-care products out of her house.

"Oh, Mitchy-yoo-hoo!" she yodels. There is nothing new about this. Yodel has always been her second language.

She has a large head that seems to be mostly face, the majority of which she occupies with a tall, wooden smile. Delphine strides up the driveway, purposefully, pumping her arms in a manner intent on burning calories and defining delts. She's yoga clad, surgically tight, completely made up, and I can smell her sandalwood spritz from forty feet away.

"Afternoon, Del," I nod.

She eyes the dumpster carefully, slowing as she pumps her arms past, as if assessing just how much of her living room she could cram in there once she's shoved my bothersome items aside.

"A dumpster!" she calls out, as though I'd chosen Door Number 3 on *Let's Make a Deal*. Could have just as easily been a goat or a trip to Tahiti.

I nod. This won't take long. Delphine generally gets right to the point. She'll ask about tossing a few things inside and then I'll be stuck. Stuck because I'm supposed to be a nice neighbor and not say no to a person who should really know better than to ask. Stuck because not immediately saying yes could convey that I remain the aloof asshole she and everyone, according to Bren, observed while carrying on in fugue-me mode. So, I need to show her that I'm fine now. That the fugue is gone, and that she and everyone else we have in common can drop the shun game, stop continuing to find reasons why, for example, their kids are always unavailable to play with ours. Reasons that come fluidly and easily because they're well-practiced and have been at the ready for a long time now. I've probably already heard some of them. I just don't remember. And if I say *no* or *we'll see*, her shit probably will end up in my dumpster in the middle of the night anyway. So, I may as well admit she's got me and say yes outright. But I can't resist the urge to make her squirm, even if only a little.

"Yep. Big feller's a dumpster alright," I say, patting the thing on the side, like a horse. She stares at me, apprehensive and uneasy now. She has a habit of looking at me as if I could be teetering on the verge of spontaneous combustion. Recently, she's kept her visits short, the way you're supposed to respect a mother and newborn. I haven't even considered explaining to her in any detail about anything. And here today wouldn't be the place anyway.

"Thinking of sending it back, though."

She gasps. "What!?" She snaps her head from me to the dumpster, and back. "Seriously?!" she yelps. "But . . . It *just* got here!"

"Ja." I look around and shake my head solemnly. "Wrong color, Del. I asked for green and," I smile on one side of my mouth, "the bastards send me—"

"Oh!" she exclaims, appalled, yet relieved.

She turns toward the house, then back at me with an appreciative look up and down. "You've lost weight."

I run a hand along my side where I broke the ribs and where I've shed some flab. In the end, the pounds may go away. But these ribs . . .

"Maybe," I say, though fully aware I've lost twenty-one point three pounds exactly, right to the tenth of a pound, since waking up a fat, broken, parallel me. Each pound lost equaling another step to full recovery. And I'm almost there. "Just a few more pounds to go," I say, and rub my side again and smile like you're supposed to when pretending to be bad at taking a compliment. But I'm also glad she's noticed. It hasn't come easy. Lots of time at the gym and a serious change in diet. Turns out there is no Fat Fairy, though my arms can now magically swing through a new gap at my sides without bumping. I glance toward the house. No sign of Bren. Now that Del has made her presence known, Bren will remain indefinitely unseen. She can't stand Delphine.

"Skank," Bren scoffed one morning. "Does nothing but butt crunches and talks about what she *doesn't* eat. Or what new thing she's onto. Now it's seeds. All kinds of roasted high-end protein-rich bullshit you buy at Whole Paycheck. Miracle of miracles I'll live to see my forties," she said, then bent and hoisted Carlie.

"Skunk?" Carlie said, twisting up her face.

Bren smiled. "Yes, sweetie," she murmured into Carlie's ear. "A big black one with a white-striped tail."

Bren is gorgeous.

Randy comes to life next door. Can't believe it took him this long. He moseys over, as if he just now happened to notice the *Exxon Valdez* parked in my drive. He pauses to pick up a small piece of litter, and when he straightens there's something about the way he turns that reminds me a bit too much of my father. My father, who I could never tell what was going on with me when Todd took me fishing so often. Though Dad did wonder. One thing he did know *wasn't* happening was me catching fish.

"He's bad luck," Dad said. I asked what he meant, but I knew. "You used to bring home all kinds of trout. Now ya come home skunked."

And a nauseated, sick mess.

I was eight or nine when Dad said this, and Todd's persona far too respected and solemn in the public eye for me to say what it was Todd was actually interested in, rather than trout fishing, that is, forcing me to say something like, "He walks heavy by the crick and spooks all the keepers." I recall saying that last bit, actually. And also that later that night when I looked up and prayed in blood for it all to end, I added asking God forgiveness for that particular lie.

Over the years, nothing substantive happened as far as making it all end was concerned, though I somehow managed to take solace in the possibility of God forgiving the white lies I told my father. Maybe God wasn't capable of stopping some of the big and horrible things of His own awesomeness, His own creation. Yet maybe a god capable of creating such a powerful, evil force could find it within His powers to forgive a boy's coerced white false witnessing borne unto his father.

Anyway, the guy walking at me now is not my father. It is Randy. Lonely man from next door with the satellite TV system and wet-bar in his carpeted garage.

"Mitch-*ell*!" he booms, with a falling glissando. His customary greeting.

"Randy," I say.

"What's happenin?"

I lean a plump garbage bag against the dumpster as he wanders over. The bag, tightly tied, looks innocent enough at first glance, though I can assure you its contents are not for the faint of heart. This one garbage bag equals the end result of hours of scraping pungent, vile food slops from my garage floor. Very old food slops of the sort not even Templeton of *Charlotte's Web* fame would touch. The molded food I just let fall and rot out or ooze and dribble from the fridge, then freeze, sort of, all over the floor in there. Seemed to take hours just to get the smell off my hands. Later, I jammed the clothes I wore for the job into yet another garbage bag along with other such nasty slops that didn't fit into this one. I steady this bag with my knee and decide to wait until he and Del have gone to hoist it and its trembling contents into Mr. Dumpster here.

"Oh, ya know."

"Doin some remodeling?"

I start to shake my head, but he's not paying attention. He's only here because Del is here, and he's likely got a dumpster story to share, or a remodeling one, much the same way folks share personal accounts of broken limbs should you show up at work in a cast.

"Ja. Good idea. Your place could sure use some work." He glances at Delphine for agreement, his eyes slowly making their way up from her buttocks to rest somewhere scarcely north of her breasts. "That overhang there has been miserable since we moved in ... what? Six years ago?" he asks, seeking confirmation of timeline from Delphine's ass.

Randy moved in a few years after Delphine and Max, who moved in a year after Bren and me. One look at the future lady-neighbors-to-be and he likely paid cash on the spot for his place.

Delphine places a hand on a hip and shakes her head. "Dunno, Rand-eye," she says. "Sounds right."

Randy wanders over to a set of boxes I've set aside in what I'm calling a *keep* pile. As though having my garage door open and a dumpster in the drive gives license to start picking through my things. The box he's looking at contains a combination of hard-cover and paperback novels. He grabs the one on the top of a stack and squints at the title.

"*Driftless?*" he says, suspiciously.

Of course, the only book in the pile Randy would pick up would happen to be the book I'm currently reading. It's gotten me through some critical downtimes when my brain could have otherwise wandered off to less productive pursuits, but also finishing books I start to read is yet another road-to-recovery checklist item. And I'm less than one chapter away on this one. Will be done later today or tomorrow.

"I think I've heard of this. David Rhodes. Name is familiar… mind if I borrow it?"

Look, I want to say. *I'm nearly done with that goddamn book. I really need to finish it. I'm beggin ya. It could save my life.*

"Go ahead," I say to Randy, and gesture for him to take it. I sigh inaudibly as he tucks my novel way up and into a probably soggy armpit. While suppressing a shudder, I will them away. But it's no use, their brains incapable of the telepathy required to hear me screaming at the top of my lungs inside my head for them to please go away. Now.

"And no," I finally say. "Not remodeling. Just getting ready for winter is all."

"Oh, of course!" Del shouts, and here I've just given her an in. And an out. "So am *I! I* have been tearing through *all* sorts of …" and I stop listening, sort of. I drift away as Randy steps between Del and me, my softcover novel wedged solidly in his left armpit, and joins in the *Winter is coming* chatter. I backpedal toward the garage, step by step, and consider what to take on next when Del raises her voice to me. "And I was thinking, uh, Mitch, wondering, really, if you wouldn't, uh, mind if …"

SO, THE DUMPSTER IS HERE, further committing me to the task at hand. Yet a dumpster needs to be filled. And I only have it for a limited time—five days. Monday afternoon drop, Saturday noon pickup. Timelines have been very difficult for me since snapping out of my fugue, though. Goes along with my powerful apathy, an overwhelming inertia which I wear like a lei of thorns, and yet I figured having the dumpster in the drive would force my hand. Turns out it has. I'm here now, Del and Randy have left me alone, Bren's behind me one hundred percent on this one, and I am indeed filling it, right now.

Rememorying. I said it for the first time about a month ago while at our YMCA, working that fat-fairy magic. I'm not certain why. I only knew that I had to come up with a new approach, a way to stay on this current track, and avoid any future slides into that horrifying abyss that is my fugue state. God only knows what fugue-me will attempt next. Or worse, in what he'll succeed.

My shrink bailed on me to write a book about *a certain remarkable patient* of his who happened to suffer dissociation for an insanely long span of time and managed only to break five or six ribs while it lasted. How the patient didn't commit suicide, or more seriously injure himself or anyone else, remained beyond the good doctor's comprehension. He regarded me with concurrent confusion, disappointment, and delight. He played the sabbatical card, leaving me to follow through with a listing of bullet points he'd handed over. I showed it to my sister, Jen, who promptly tore it to shreds, tossed it all over her head like confetti, and took my hands into hers.

Problem is, while rememorying may be a cool name, and while I know its purpose, I don't entirely know how to accomplish it. But clearing out the tangible and the bad— such as this garage—is a start.

One thing the shrink did leave me with, though, on that list of things Jen tore to pieces, is a blueprint for Eye Movement Desensitization Reprocessing therapy, or EMDR. You flick your eyes back and forth, as if following the motion of a metronome, when you sense an encroaching fugue-slip or trauma attack. So, it's back and forth with your eyes; meanwhile you picture a moment of your traumatic duress. Then shift to a moment when you broke free or came away stronger than when you entered, all the while you keep rhythmically flicking your eyes side to side. And you feel yourself succeed from a position of strength and control.

I'm not there yet, but apparently this process will become second nature, and I'll start doing it involuntarily. Part of the trick is convincing yourself that it's not complete and utter bullshit. But I'm getting better at it and can now foresee a day when I can cast a healing spell smoothly and silently and without my even knowing it. It always ends with that moment of me dancing away across slippery rocks to the other side of that creek, and up and over the opposite riverbank while Todd snoozes.

I GOT UP EARLY THIS MORNING, even before the kids, to get a jump on the garage before Randy could start in on me. Del would likely leave me alone, but no doubt Randy would again be astounded I had no interest in whatever could be on his mind today, that somehow my interests were not his. But that is Randy. And I am me, and I am no one else, moving forward.

At one time, I considered clearing this place piecemeal, chunking out the problem into manageable segments, sneaking away piece by piece in the back of my car when I ran errands, like a convict burrowing out of Shawshank, tunneling a pathway to mental freedom, one teaspoon of dirt at a time until one day breaking out and splashing down into a river, and flinging the garage door open to reveal a suddenly highly organized, non-embarrassing garage.

My son—that sudden *guy* walking around here—even offered to help. I refused. This, I said, was mine. My mental mess. And I alone have to fix it.

An old radio buzzes fuzzy atop a shelf beyond the distorted air shimmering around that apple fridge. A cultured public radio voice purrs: *NPR will be there to guide you every step of the way through all the bullshit.* Gradually the disaster moves from within the dark garage to the open air of the expanse of driveway and front yard.

Days later, I've managed to move the fridge outside the garage. Took around four hours to clean and remove all the mold and hardened food deposits. Still not perfect—this is a forty-year-old fridge, after all—but far, far better, and aligned with my overall expectations of most things as they come these days. Del only checked on me once, and that was just to make sure I wasn't "stabbing at it with an icepick." I move the unit back into the garage at nightfall, plug it in, set a plate of coffee grounds inside, and close the door.

The plan is that the coffee grounds will magically absorb all remaining fridge odors, but the next morning I am greeted by a fridge so hot and sultry and reeking on the inside I'm nervous to touch it again without first unplugging the thing. So much for the coffee grounds. I press a fingertip to an eyelid that has begun to twitch. Merely a minor setback, I tell myself.

Now on dumpster Day Five, with the majority of my garage funk as well as Del's contributions located here inside the dumpster, I am sweeping an open area when the truck from the appliance store beeps its way backwards up my driveway. Two young blueprint-blue work shirts hop out and roll a tall, rectangular box down a slide-out ramp. That'd be the new fridge I ordered. They make quick work of it all, and by the time I look up again they've got the old fridge part way up the same ramp. I grab the refrigerator door from beside the dumpster and lean it against the truck for them to haul away, then continue to sweep and organize piles. I don't know where anyone else is. Bren, the others. It's just me, a cleaner floor, and the fuzzy buzzing radio atop the new fridge, now located in the exact place as its predecessor, humming away. I stand there looking at its newness amid the clean empty darkness of my garage, no longer ashamed to have this gash in my past flung open to the world.

I edge closer to my non-me memory bin, that big orange dumpster in the driveway. So many loose and random items here in which I unknowingly played a part. It occurs to me I'm saying goodbye to things I never knew. One nugget is a graduation announcement for the daughter of a good friend of ours. It's one simple photo of the now-graduate during a birthday party about ten years ago. Hers was a home where paper streamers, hats, and ice cream with syrup were completely allowed—*inside the house*—and probably expected. A home in which it was ok to straddle the arms of chairs or, on the occasion of this photo, swing from the cedar rafters once in a while, the latter most likely even encouraged. Beyond the knobby knees of the girl's dangling frame, behind the wadded up wrapping papers tossed onto the floor, rises a column of color-coded markings to track her and her siblings' growth upward along the edge of a doorway starting, it would seem, at a very young age. The girl's shrieking smile blurs in my hands and summons a memory of the stark walls, the mercilessly scrubbed floors, and the spans of hostile silence of Momma's house where Jen and I grew up.

I flip the card over, and back again. I don't remember receiving it, seeing it, writing out the graduation congratulations card, nor the requisite check. Going to the party, interacting at the party, coming home. None of it. All gone. And yet, I was there. There with Bren. Not so very long ago. She later told me how I was, and how I was not.

"You don't know," Bren said, eyes red and dry and all cried out. "You don't remember yourself."

I grimaced and stared and imagined those eyes opening at first light every morning while I was dark and deep in the fugue.

I looked at the floor. "I . . . don't."

My lips went cold. Normal people would cry. I just got thinning, cold lips.

"You don't remember what you were like," she said again. She spoke so slowly, every word weighed and measured, each with equal emphasis. "Just sat there. In that old Badgers sweatshirt, muttering the same story about some homeless guy living in our basement. His long fingernails, hairy hands, what he probably eats." She glanced away, cupped some hair from her forehead. "Ya picked yer nose ... farted ... scratched where it itched." She winced. "Stared either at something on your own nose, or ... Miles and years away from here, then mumbling, all of a sudden—sometimes shouting—the same story over and over again to whoever was around. Oh, God, Mitch," she moaned, biting back at the memory.

I'd heard much of this before, this time it was a graduation party instead of a wedding reception or a school fundraiser. The latter being an annual event we weren't invited back to this year. And I drove us there and back to all of these things. Yet recall none of it.

I look at the invite again as a now-familiar tension squirms inside my chest and I recall how a few days ago, despite how much I dreaded its arrival, this dumpster couldn't get here soon enough.

Rememorying. How is it possible I've lost so much from the past year, yet from my childhood I've lost nearly nothing? Remember too much, too clearly and in wildly vivid detail. In time and place, color and taste. Rememorying is the process by which I attempt to overwrite all the horror with some of the good, for now. Days, weeks, years from now. EMDR deals with symptoms and prevents future into-fugue plummets. Which is great. But then you need to do concurrent hard work in the present to forge a decent future past to look back on. One I can remember and will want to remember. Surely there exists a way to do this. If the brain is so incredibly capable of protecting itself with mechanisms such as dissociation and cognitive vapor lock, why is it not able to self-mend, to self-cure as well? And with the same instant ease? Also, backing up . . . why does the brain self-protect so poorly in the first place? *i.e.*, with mostly incapacitating results to the host system? Knocking the likes of me, Mitchell McGannis, so totally off the rails?

I need a drink.

Of water.

Alcohol has been out of my life since snapping out of it, for some reason. Like a post-hypnotic suggestion, almost, I've lost all taste for it and even find myself repelled when I come near it, in any form. Beer, wine, whiskey. Doesn't matter. So interesting. Not long ago I served up a fine tap beer for Bren at a party and spilled a goodly amount on my hand. I wandered around searching for a towel rather than licking it off, as a neighbor, Wade, suggested. Lick, he said, with a knowing look. More for you, Mitch, he winked.

Lick it up, he said, suggestively.

Lick it up, Todd demanded.

I looked at Wade, commanding myself to smile, desperately forcing myself to focus on other things. The color of his hair. The means for measuring the height of mountains in the 1890s. The yellowed and tired whites of Wade's imbibed eyes. How high an elephant can jump. Anything. Keep licking, I heard Todd say, and I could smell nettles and berry blossoms and wet grass of the creek bottoms. Noisy Creek. Wade nodded at my wet wrist as Todd grasped the back of my neck, huge adult-man hands wrapping and clutching and pulling. Right there, Wade says, pointing, in tandem with Todd, Right . . . *there* . . . Mitch. A towel will do, I told Wade, hearing Todd say he had a clean towel in his duffel for when we were finished. Your loss Wade said, and smirked and in one motion tipped his head back to drink. I'll just wash up quick, I told Wade. I heard Todd tell me to do the same in the creek. I watched the bulge in Wade's throat pump and squeeze the beer down.

A gnawed walnut pit, stripped of its husk by a squirrel or chipmunk, feels like a split golf ball as I roll it under my boot. I tap it toward the dumpster, where it ricochets off and spins in place, like a top, whirling up to become my son as he sits upright on a daybed during a bright, sunny afternoon years ago. He looks at a peach at rest on a wide saucer he's placed upon his lap. He is five, still two years younger than I was when Todd first took me. First of countless times, year after blinding year, years of me praying for spring never to come, ending each night's prayers with *And a winter without end. Amen.* Years and years of summers that included forced coy posing each and every time. Years I can still taste.

Still in my memory, I remind Coyle, five, not to eat out on the daybed, that the peach, once bitten, will stain Gramma's quilts and pillows. He replies that he's not going to eat the peach at all, but rather he's just enjoying looking at the "peach's flames in the glowy light" near the window. I sit behind him as he presses his back up to rest against my chest and he traces a fingertip along each red and orange streak of the furry, honey skin, like caressing his someday child's cheek. We breathe. His chest rises and falls with mine.

Coyle, the fourteen-year-old one, steps out of the house to retrieve something, and for a moment, I long to take a photograph in order to burn an image—any image—into my forever memory. But that's not necessary and I realize, too, that I don't want to. I ache, but I know. As psychologically powerful as the photo of that girl's birthday may be, it's just a photo. A flattened version of a moment. And I don't want to fold this moment into two dimensions and dull my memory of all this multi-dimensional nowness. Feels too much like a dead thing Randy's got in his garage, killed, gutted, stuffed, and nailed to a wall. This moment is not a prize, not a trophy.

Coyle turns to look up at me again from the piece of fruit, then rises from the daybed and crosses the yard to stride into the present at my side and watch the truck drive away.

"Sup?" he asks.

I look into his eyes, my stomach squirming, yet ever remembering. A voice on the radio mews atop the new apple fridge awaiting apples.

Coyle looks into the garage, then back at me appreciatively, with Bren's sable eyes, his gaze holding mine. And the weight of this moment unfolds.

"Tomorrow," I breathe, and pull off a work glove. I want to reach out and hold his eyes. Hold them in memory. A coil in my gut rolls over, heavy and slow.

"Ask me again," I say, and feel the air between us begin to haze, like clouding cataracts. Walls disappear. Sound goes weightless and loses its bottom beneath my feet. I open my mouth to finish but can't.

"Tomorrow," Coyle says, cooly, and nods, eyes still locked on mine through panels of haze. My eyes flick back and forth, back and forth. I can see the slippery river rocks, and that far river bank I'm about to scale yet again when Coyle says, "I'll ask ya again tomorrow," and takes my hand.

TURNS OUT THERE IS NO FAT FAIRY. Yet there are certain ways of brains. And sometimes a lot of what you pack in there isn't you, not your doing. But how you unpack it is.

1931

A woman named Jen is yelling in the small room next to the one I am seated in at the nursing home. I know that's her name because I hear her shout it out every time she arrives and needs to tell her mother who she is. I'm the same way. Except for me, it's my dad. I've never spoken with her nor introduced myself. In fact, apart from the occasional glimpse of Jen from behind while leaning over her mother, I don't even know what she looks like, really. We trade off, Jen and I, via our tacit arrangement, politely screaming at our parents in turn. Just one adult child at a time raising their voice to one elder parent at a time. There's always this pause in the air, a suspended vacancy that hangs like that moment of rest between the throbs of another person's pulse beneath your fingertips. A rare instant of nursing-home silence opened by the tail-end of what one of us has to say that tacitly urges the other to the effect, *Okay, now you go.* But she's way better at sensing when it's about to be her turn to talk again than I am at figuring out when it's mine. Jen just seems to know, almost as if she can see how the paragraph I'm yelling out ends while I'm still in the process of shouting it out.

So, I know her name is Jen and I can now say with confidence that she's more than aware of my name, too. And she likely wonders, as do I, if all of this shouting at our marginally responsive, very demented parents is doing them any good. I know what the visits are like for us. Our voices drip with drawn-out, prolonged fatigue. But what are these visits like for our petrified loved ones, trapped within these beds, chairs, walls, and . . . bodies? Surely this Jen person wonders the same.

Jen has been trying to bring Momma back to the present by way of the past. This bit is very interesting, and at times I can't help but listen more closely to the detail of her screaming about the person the body before her once was.

She gives me ideas, and I try them out on Dad. So far though, nothing. In his mind it's 1931 or so, and to him I persist as a persona-shifter: a brother or cousin one day, a buddy from Yankton the next, and now and again that one priest with surprisingly good English for a Finn. But never his son. I'm not even a flicker in his libido yet back here in '31, a full decade-plus before he met the love of his life, my mother, and set off for the war in Europe.

1931 sucks. It's heartbreaking to be here with him during this part of his life, despite his good spirits about it all. He knew no better, of course. The endless dirt drifts resulting from swarming soil storms on the farms, the hammering sun in record-breaking summer after summer end-capped by unyielding winters he spent thawing ice and snow for coffee, meals, and laundry while frigid blasts whistled through knotholes and cracks in the walls of his farmstead home. This was the Great Depression, and that explains why I haven't brought in any photos of this era. *They're depressing.*

The photos and stories Jen brings seem to be as much for Jen as her mother, to remind them both of a life once lived. I wonder about them, and the ones I'd use for my father. Way back before my mom. Way back when men built and taught themselves how to fly airplanes on their farms in South Dakota. Way back when men rolled up their sleeves and faced the teeth of the shitty weather, the dirt drifts, the blinding blizzards, the economic disasters, all the hardship and the frozen beds of the Great Depression. Way back when it meant something to be a man.

I think the photos I'd bring would be from mid-war 1940s, right around the time Dad was about to marry Mom. I glance over at him, wondering if, like me, his focus now falls upon Mom, or perhaps that group of men he served with. If he's made the trip to wartime with me now, he'd be standing as always alongside his uniformed buddies, most of them not assholes, he alone clad in a bright white V-neck undershirt, always with a fighter or two in the background, always the snazzy baggy khakis, during an always sunny and bright day streaked with high cirrus clouds. This is who he was, with new lives and a nation that he and the uniformed men on each side of him were about to put back into working order. And happily. Or, without complaining, at least. And it was with that untenable optimism of his generation—an optimism, determination, and innocence that my generation seems to have left behind back about 1975—that they did the big, energetic things we now take for granted. Like build the massive highway system that allows me to visit him as often as I do.

Jen next door has paused, and it's my turn to yell again. The pause extends while I'm adrift, brain spinning amid the next few things on my list once I leave. A reduction sauce of work, bills, kids.

I'm staring out the window past Dad, who has fallen back asleep, when Jen begins to yell again. It's hard not to notice she has a rather nice voice. Provides good accompaniment to my attempts to clear my head while Dad sleeps. As futile as it may seem, visiting my dad often proves to be a good break from the hectic life I constantly race around and around in, playing catch-up. And there's always some *thing* somewhere someplace, lurking. No matter how close you come to actually being caught up, no matter how you creatively free up that future block of time, some *thing* unexpected, unplanned, and unaccounted for will head you off to pre-consume it all for you. So, not to worry, that chunk of future free time is already gnawed up and gone. The endless busy regenerated permutations of cycles of life simply do not stop. Ever. If anything, they multiply, spinning off increasingly tinier, ad infinitum concentric cycles, that gain mass, momentum, and volume at a bewildering rate.

Outside, majestic oaks and hemlocks play a hypnotic game of catch with the breeze, and I tell my brain that I am just tired. It's a tough trick to turn sometimes, to convince your brain that no one else out there knows, and no one cares about your tiny little life, your puny and mundane accomplishments, concerns, and woes. And to call them mundane would be a compliment. They're all out there though, all these people, all these infinite threads of existence, all living equally important little lives, all carrying out similarly minute yet important tasks, standing in lines at bus stops and metros, waiting for tickets and trains, elbowing in for coffee, idling in piles at drive-thrus, all placing orders, all wanting things, all wasting things, all waiting for things, all connected to others wanting, talking, teaching, waiting, learning, gardening, crying, delivering, consuming, producing, growing, shoveling, hollering, caring for—and neglecting—countless other things. All concurrent, all buzzing, all everything, all the time, all around you, all always everything all.

ONCE UPON A TIME, I was quite the athlete. Baseball, football, hockey. Especially baseball. Which is probably what, in part, led me to becoming something of a fitness freak today, now that my days of varsity sports are long behind me. But one thing that was true then and remains true today is that injuries don't become me. Not that injuries really become anyone, of course. But my body functions like a well-oiled, high-performance engine hitting on all cylinders when it's "on," though. It does. Yet take away any one cog and it rapidly falls apart into uselessness. It's not age—well, that may be part of it now—but this all-or-nothing tendency is the way I was wired from the start. When I was on, I posed a fearsome force on the mound, in the outfield, in the batter's box, on the base paths. When not on though, be it an iffy ankle or a sore back, you could find yourself scratching your head wondering how I'd made varsity.

Speaking of baseball, most recently, I hurt my knee while doing just that—playing baseball with my kids. My two-year-old daughter cut in front of me as I chased down a fly ball over at the park. In an effort not to trample her, I planted my left foot hard to pivot over and around her.

My foot planted all right, but right in the middle of a rut, and my "pivot" wound up executing a contorted backwards ostrich-like fold of my knee. My nine-year-old, who'd hit the fly ball in the first place, said he could hear the crunch of the joint while running the bases. I lay on my back on the dry outfield grass, reluctant to move, asking my little Laurie if she was OK. But she was chasing down the ball at the moment, good girl, and it wasn't until I had my knee propped up and under ice that I learned she'd survived that divot-pivot without a scratch.

THE NURSE WALKS into the examining room for my scheduled knee check, and after exchanging some cordial conversation, hands me a form clasped to a clipboard by a heavy wire and spring. It takes a minute to read between the lines, but it's a questionnaire regarding Depression. Depression, with a capital D. I scan the page again and look up at the nurse, confused.

"What—"

"Standard protocol," she says, and sighs. "Just fill it out, please."

"But—"

In a semi-casual manner, Nurse Anne and I go way back and know each other socially, out in the wilds beyond this clinic. Can make for some interesting moments at parties or local gatherings, such as bumping into her at a happy hour the same day she removed a deer tick embedded deep in my nether regions, but we manage to keep our two selves where they belong. That's usually how it works.

Today, though, I can see she comes to me as the person I know out there, and rests the back of a hand holding a pen on her hip. "It's standard procedure now," she says again, like she's been trained to say, but conveying with her eyes that maybe it's not, and hands me her pen. "For insurance." She pauses and exhales and takes in a deep breath and says, "What with all these new healthcare laws . . . it's just a box on the forms for us to check for Corporate." She sighs yet again and locks eyes with me. "Just do it, Cyp." She cocks her head into a twisted frown, adjusts her glasses, then allows a look of concern to groove her brow.

Anne can tell I'm not buying it, that I know there's something else, and she lowers her voice to close in on me like a friend. "And, it can't hurt . . ."

"What?"

"Well," she says, and edges even closer. "It's been a year and a half or so, after all, so, maybe as long as you're here for the knee—"

"A year and a half?" I say, startled.

Anne nods, and I shrug, silently pleading ignorance and suddenly lost, but not entirely. My ears start to ring. So loudly I can't believe she herself doesn't glance around to locate the source of the noise. I'm looking up and around the room, wondering, sort of, what she could possibly be talking about. My vision blurs and I begin to sweat. I'm missing something big here, something pressing up against me, and then I understand she's reaching out to me now, and touches the thick wedding band on my hand. I adjust it unconsciously with my thumb and feel a chill.

Our eyes lock again. "I know," she says. "I mean—I can't ... *know*. But ..." She nudges my wedding ring again. "I know." She sighs, smiles sadly, lets her arms dangle at her sides. Her shoulders go round, and she turns on a heel and leaves, head down. She doesn't look back.

I breathe in the stillness of the air as my vision comes back into focus in expanding chunks, and finally I move on, just to keep my day in motion and not skew the timing of the rest of the day leading up to dinner. I shrug and fill out the form. Some of the questions make me laugh, they're so sad and, well, *depressing*. Do these things actually work, these surveys? Catch people who've got real problems? Do the survey-takers with real-deal issues truly answer them honestly? I always thought the psychotic and so on were far too smart for their own good, capable of outwitting tests as simple and base as this. Depression. As if. My life may currently be depressing, surely, I suppose, but that doesn't mean I *suffer from* Depression, the capital-D kind. I'm just tired. And busy. And run down. People with Depression sleep all day long and are listless and static and mope about when they finally do make it out of bed. So, whatever. I check a bunch of boxes, flex my bad knee, and wait for the doc.

I'M LIMPING MORE NOTICEABLY today as I move through the nursing home, passing Jen's shouts, and plunk into the chair next to Dad's bed. The combination of my knee and standing desk at work means that it feels good to sit down again. I cause a little commotion, bumping and sliding a chair loudly, but Dad hasn't moved. Doesn't know I'm here yet. I take advantage of the moment to relax and stretch my leg once I pop off the brace.

"Here, Momma, is a Fourth of July," Jen is yelling next door. "That's me . . . there! And Mitchell." She giggles. "Look at him," she says, voice filled with nostalgia and love.

I can't see the scene from my chair, but that Fourth of July photo is certain to include a small Main Street complete with a marching band, a court of teen beauty queens on a float, waving, palms out, elbows up, clean armpits freshly shaved for all to see. There are fire trucks cooling off shoulder-to-shoulder crowds, ice cream dripping from kids' wrists and elbows, a heavily used Port-o-Potty or two, a child here and there frightened by a siren, the smell of hot tar and warm potato salad.

I'm somewhat surprised I don't know Jen. This is a small town, after all, and you'd think I'd have seen her around. Though I don't think she's really from here in the sense that she's lived here for the majority of her adult life. Seems she's from the area, though. Grown up in the same small town, the same nowhere as me, just somewhere else. But I get the sense based on her purposeful walk, her manner of speaking—an accent and cadence of speech that come off as blend of upper-Midwest tinged with East Coast—that it's been a long time since she's lived here. But some of the way she speaks could just be what it sounds like given the need to holler down a black hole in her mother's head in order to be heard.

What she's engaged in, though, is familiar. I can tell just by the way she's sitting in there as I walk by. And some days it's as though I can feel something from her. Perhaps it's the commonness of our experience. Or maybe it's something else. I'm not sure what, but it's there and it isn't all at once. Some days I picture it romantically in my fatigue that in some sublime and Zen way this connected commonness simply *is*.

My eyes are watering and I can smell the food prep wafting up the hallway from the cafeteria. There's always a certain food-in-the-making smell around here that would turn your stomach and remind you—no matter if you were a hot-luncher or a cold-luncher—of grade school. Though the nuance here changes from meal to meal. Now it's the baked chicken, faux mashed potatoes and gravy, warmed frozen peas and carrots. Gravy is the strongest today. Yesterday it was fish sticks and baked beans. And, sadly, even during the height of the abundance of our growing season, everything in this nursing home that winds up on a plate hails from a box, can, or freezer.

But it's solid food, and as an institution they, too, have forms to fill out, boxes to check, and the middle to serve and conform to. So the pre-packaged, pre-processed, sometimes pre-cooked off-truck-and-in-the-box goodies it is. Once out of the box, success in the food prep mostly hinges on clean hands and clean kitchen habits.

I often stay to feed him, but today I can't, which hurts. The window for feeding is narrow and difficult, and spare hands are at a premium here at the home. And if I'm not around to lift the spoon or fork to his lips, he may not eat at all. It's not the staff's fault, really. I'd like for them to prod him to eat more, but they've made it clear that *feeding*—the act of forking food into residents' mouths—falls squarely upon the auspices of *volunteers*. That generally translates to visitors like me, though once in a while I do hear of a group of church do-gooders or whatever coming in to bestow their benevolence upon the residents.

Anyway, it's a bit different now with my dad. I feel good and terrible and revolted all at once. Good because I'm visiting—so few here receive regular visits. I've seen folks show up who haven't been around since the last set of holidays, wandering around the facility in search of their loved ones, wherever they've put him or her now depending on their current state of decline—some residents are relocated to an entirely different wing of the building. The staff take certain smug delight in informing guests that their mother/father/

brother/sister/uncle/aunt has been in their new location for a surprisingly long time now.

The terrible side of how I feel comes from a sense of feeling good for visiting. As if I'm visiting to prop up my own self-righteousness to some extent, e.g., See, I went to see my poor, lonely father today. You?

But I manage to shake that feeling once it's my turn to yell again. And I usually feel better once it's over.

Today my eyes get wet because I'm tearing up again. There are days when I can walk in here, yell and scream for a half-hour to forty-five minutes in turn with Jen, and walk out covered in peas and potatoes completely unfazed. I stroke his cheek, call out that I love him, kiss his forehead, and go back to tearing it up at my keyboard and interfacing with entitled frat-boy account reps as if nothing happened.

But today I'm sunk with that hollow-boned emptiness of the loss of an entire evaporated existence all dried up and blown away, absorbed by the insidious sponge of dementia. My dad: a man, husband, father. A war hero now rendered sawdust and whisked aside by this disease. I shrug and wonder if Jen is thinking the same things I am right now. For all the yelling the two of us do, we frequently share a powerful silence, breathing in turn, suspended in something of a misty daydream, perhaps moments of drawing strength from each other, or of times of shared despair now gradually bending into apathy.

I close my eyes: she's over there, quiet now, crouched in running skins, the long fingers of one hand touch her mother's side, the other forearm at rest across a lean thigh, fingers dangling between her legs, her fine profile blinking at Momma, waiting. Like me, she knows that somewhere in there inside our parent's head, everything makes sense on some level. It has to. It does. Just because they're confused on the outside doesn't mean it's not all clear to them—wherever it is they are, and whatever it is they are doing—on the inside. They just can't tell us about it right now. Which must be really fucking frustrating. And as they wane and die, so do we, Jen and me.

This is overwhelming. I can feel all of this pulling at me, pulling me down and under, and I should just go. Leave. Limp outta here and just get out. It's getting harder by the day, by the hour, and it's starting to seem I leave his side feeling like this more than not these days. I don't hate him, but I hate what dementia has left me with. Left of him for me, and how the most recent past—he's now become more prone to flailing outbursts and bizarre rants and hurtful verbal attacks—can cloud out the entire lifetime of good he and I shared. I remind myself that this is not him, that I love him. But it's gotten hard to remember what he was like before here.

My phone rings. My brother. I can tell by the loudly quacking-duck ringtone I set for him. Not sure why I picked that for him, but it fits. Apart from his impeccable timing, he only calls when he wants something. *Needs something*, as he puts it. Always never small, never not time-consuming. And yet I always answer, always, sometimes for no other reason than to make the quacking stop plus the fact that the quacking will start up all over again, somehow more insistent and obnoxious, minutes later when he calls back.

Soon the rapid advent of a predictable and involuntary drowsiness his voice invokes overcomes me. It's a trained response at this point. Decades of hearing his authority, his reasoning, his diatribes, fostered within me, the younger brother, a spontaneous sleep reflex defense mechanism.

Brother's voice in my ear, my mind wanders, but knowing that everything he's telling me, somehow none of it his fault, is a lie. And I wonder, barely awake now, how deep, my brother, is the hole you've dug yourself this time?

I take Dad's forearm into my hands, and give a firm and gentle squeeze. Then I reattach my knee brace, kiss him above each eyebrow again, and get up to leave, albeit slowly, knowing Jen's left me in the dust.

The roadway back to my office winds and eases through a lush river valley, primed to burst into Midwest fall glory. The saffron- and crimson-dappled treetops and rolling hillsides, like day one of a Monet, suggesting it won't be much longer. It's one of those afternoons that reminds you why you live here and put up with nine months of winter, and that winter is coming. Winter is always coming. Winter that some years won't leave.

JEN HAS STOPPED HOLLERING.

That's because Jen has stopped coming.

That's because Momma's dead.

It happened yesterday and I missed it. Traffic accident closed the road.

And so I missed Jen. And now she's gone.

I ask the staff here about Momma. A newbie nurse's aide raises her brows earnestly, then pokes her wide eyes into the now-empty room, as if to make sure what I'm saying could be true. She doesn't seem to know, entirely, what I'm talking about, though she's promised to totally absolutely help me out in any way totally possible. She skips away, ponytail bouncing along behind her.

On my way out of Dad's, I step inside Momma's room, now so empty, now so quiet, now so newly enormous, the air tinged with a disinfectant. I didn't realize how loud Jen yelled until now that she's no longer here to do so. The bare walls gleam with scrubbed semi-gloss, photos and personal effects have vanished from the ledge near the bed where she lay, the cork board just above plucked perfectly clean. Not even a thumbtack, nor a dustball beneath the bed. So empty everywhere. As though Jen and Momma never happened.

As I turn around, staff wearing gloves push through with a welcome kit and cart piled with fresh linens to finish preparing the room for the next resident. Of course. There's a long waiting list to get into this place, after all. And I'm now a bit surprised it's taken this long for them to swoop in. I leave and they start.

DAD IS SITTING UP TODAY, eyes bright. Like a dog you've been planning to put down that wakes up all frisky the day of.

It's days like this I'm convinced he's still in there. But then I come back to myself and realize it's just another previous, pre-me him he's speaking to. Asking me—Henry today, a new one—to rig up the "timber blade" for cutting up all the broken-tree havoc "from that last tornado." So, we're back in 1931 again. A tornado has just gashed southern South Dakota, completely scrubbing a small one-street village from the map. Entire community disintegrated. Outlying homes split in half into the next county. And a many-miles-long zipper of uprooted trees zig-zags along the Missouri River. Surviving residents there moved away without any attempt to rebuild. To this day, what's left of that town is mere overgrowth. Oaks, maples, lilacs, and daisies sprout forth from wandering cracks in the broken tar that used to be Main Street.

The "timber blade" refers to a round metal blade the size of a tractor tire used to cut wood. The blade is placed upon the rear axle of a tractor once the tire has been removed and the tractor hoisted from the ground. Once bolted on you fire up the tractor and presto! One foot on the gas gives you a wicked and enormous circular saw. Breathtakingly powerful and incredibly dangerous. Any fear of chainsaws you have would immediately pale in comparison to what feelings the sight and sound of this horrible beast in action would stir within you. This was a time before the advent of safety goggles and possibly lead work gloves and aprons, and it was shared lore out in the prairie states for the huge, wobbling blades to snap and peel apart mid-rip, often with disfiguring and frequently fatal results. Makes me shudder every time I think about it, and I tell him I'm not so keen on cutting wood today. He's having none of it, of course. After all, there's work to be done, a mess that isn't about to get cleaned up all by itself.

I bang around Dad's small room, glance out the window at the well-kept gardens, the expensively manicured shrubbery and trees pruned in berserk angles and shapes, still contemplating the realities of ferocious tractor-axle circular saws biting into fresh timber.

Holy crap.

Dad grunts, his detached gaze drifting away, then above me with who knows how many questions there just inside wherever it is he just now went. What year is it in there now? Where are you? What are you doing? And, pray tell me, who am I this time?

I tell Dad it's lunchtime now and we'll deal with all the downfall and broken limbs once we've had a bite. He gurgles something in German, now no idea what I'm talking about. Little did I know that time travel not only transplants the traveler from one given time to another, it also resets the brain, *click*, resets one's default mother tongue should one exist, as in Dad's case, *click*, and sometimes the appetite, *click*. It can even refill or, incredibly, empty one's bladder, *click*.

But it's often up and around like this in his room to simulate activity. To mimic the doing of something. The umpteenth time the horses got out of the corral, frozen pump handle, the propeller on the wing of an airplane burning out—the AM radio station coming in fuzzy over Nashville and messing up in-flight St. Louis-to-Boston navigation. The latter was back when pilots used radio broadcasts to gauge their relative location and route. Apparently that technique worked fairly well: Dad obviously made it out to tell me about it. In all cases I get up and move around to feign searching for livestock or working on a mechanical problem or resolving whatever it is that is the current matter now nestled in the locale of his mind.

Dad's already seated in his heavily padded wheelchair, something like a La-Z-Boy recliner on wheels, so I just need to strap him in. He always fights me with the straps, whacking at my forearms. I laugh. Can't say I blame him.

From his room it's then a slow slalom down the corridor dotted with wandering, weaving, and moaning residents, many frozen mid-lurch. They're mostly like Dad, all trapped somewhere in some place in another time inside their heads, their current-day physical outer selves now leaning into walkers or propped up into adapted wheelchairs like Dad. Can be a lot to witness. Then he lashes out at me again, pulling me back into the moment. It's going to be hard work to feed him today.

SLEPT ABOUT THREE HOURS LAST NIGHT. Laurie was all over me for most of it, has been ever since Silvy. And that's pretty much become standard routine at this point: Laurie hops into bed with me at around 1:30 and I wake up because she's pressing her ice-cold feet against the bare skin of my back. She then kicks and elbows—sound asleep—for fifteen or twenty minutes until finally settling in and I lay there as motionless as possible either trying to return to my slumber, or waiting until I need to get up to use the bathroom, at which point I cart her to her own bed, where she'll stay until around 4:00 or 4:30, and the icy feet and pointy elbows start all over again.

But sweet Laurie aside, I did sleep some, though it was one of those sleeps that tire you out as the small hours deepen until you finally wake up exhausted and you realize that it's time to start yet another two-decade day. Sometimes I wake up feeling like this after having slept an unusually long time—six, seven hours, say—and mentally I don't take note of the extra rest until a couple of days later when I find myself churning along out there in the wild, running on Empty, wondering how I've managed to get so far along on fumes alone.

Today though, a beautiful, thick, and dewy mid-fall morning scrolls up in to view as I raise the blind here alongside my kitchen table. Sweet, cold air seeps in through the screens. All kids asleep, coffee hot, dawn yawns and shimmers, slowly lighting up the trees to my left, daytime oozing across the deep green bluff. These moments, this time of day, when you can exist there at ease, timelessly at the base of a crease along a shallow fold in time, truly are a gift. The opportunity to think in consecutive paragraphs without interruption, then potentially a few more. Even my knee doesn't hurt as much.

I need to keep moving though. Always moving. I raise my cup and look up at the clock, then the bluff. Soaring bald eagles glide and stitch the deep sky, tracing lazy exes and wyes above the treetops, none dipping, none rising. Just idling: one dappled juvenile without the gleaming white head and tail feathers, beside two magnificent mature adults flashing in the sun.

Kids will wake soon enough, too. Their circadian rhythm reflex requires no less than ten minutes of morning daylight to kick in. Need to stretch out my leg anyway. Take the front stairs, I remind myself, not the winding back ones today with my knee unsteady like this. My mind wanders from Jen to my knee to winter to Jen and again to that last doctor visit. Last night I dreamt Jen walked into Dad's photo, took one of his Air Force buddies by the hand, and marched away to a middlin' life out in Arizona off Route 66 someplace. Still no face: just the tip of her fine nose poking out beyond the graced curve of her cheek and easy coils of that honey hair. Or, whose hand was it she took? Part of me thinks it could have been mine, but it likely belonged to someone else I don't yet know. And yet, there was something familiar about the guy she led away by the hand. Dreams are silly to make sense of. But at least I'm dreaming again. Or remembering my dreams, anyway.

More coffee.

I hear my eldest drop a blunt object, possibly a brother, on the floor upstairs. I'm assuming it's him doing the dropping, but by now it could be one of the Middle Ones dropping another. For sure not the youngest. Her biological clock has been skewed since the funeral, and won't move today until I lift her out of my bed, wrench off her pull-up, then peel her, clung quick round my neck like a marsupial, from my person and plunk her onto the toilet. (Note to self: remember the 'ear plugs' option today. Vegas's odds makers currently have Imminent, Deafening Shrieking opening at 3-1. Also: print off today's *NYT* crossword.) But it doesn't matter. That thud from above is my cue to start breakfast and poke the Others.

I begin to hope they don't wake Silvy. Then I remember.

I remember I keep forgetting for brief and sometimes extended spans that there is no Silvy anymore, though beneath all this crap clicked to the fridge with magnets there is a photo of her buried and lost in the flurry of life ever since. Somewhere. My ears begin to ring like an approaching siren. Somehow I have managed to live these past eighteen months—I think that's what Anne said—like one continuous day broken up by interspersed naps, going through the motions all this time blanking out she's not coming back from that last trip she took. Ever. That some drunk didn't nod off and meander over the center line in his giant-ass Hot Wheels pickup and flatten her one night.

She was on her way home from the airport out on County Road N. On her way back to us. On her way back to our kids. Back to me. And pulsing within my subconscious lingers this kernel of belief that she's still coming back, that she's still here among us, still out there somewhere treading along in some ether just biding her time or feeling her way along the cracks in the darkness. I've managed all this by carrying on as though she will someday do just that: step right back into the picture frame of the photo someone has snapped of my present. My planned present. My planned future present. I can even see the void in the photo next to me where she belongs, where she should be standing, see my arm around her and my hand on her shoulder. I can smell it. But the photographer is long gone now, and she's now well beyond my picture frame, someplace, having been ended by a stranger that night just a few miles away. I know the exact arc of her timeline, where it is drawn, how far it goes, the color of the line, and where it stops.

Stopped.

The shrieks coming from above snip that particular thread of thought, though, and it's back to matters at hand: my twenty minutes are officially up, the day cracking and splitting open, the rising and speeding sun now gathering brighter green across that bluff. The eagles have moved on. And like everything else, the present won't wait. And if it does wait, it waits within a perpetual-motion mayhem machine.

I open the fridge with designs on breakfast. Unconsciously, I make nearly all meals in four parts, no matter the meal. Silvy always points this peculiarity out to me, and—

Anyway. Today I am thinking: oatmeal, bacon, fruit, and toast. Well, maybe yogurt instead of toast. Toaster probably needs to be cleaned again—found a dead mouse in it over the weekend when I took the thing outside and unhinged the bottom trap-door to shake out crumbs. Mouse hit the ground like a singed hockey puck. Everyone on the patio— including me—screamed and jumped back a good three feet as the thing landed, rolled onto a side, and stopped, paws up. So, there's that, I guess: no toast today.

Brown sugar and butter for the oatmeal, and a glass of juice once my gang of four all get enough water in them. I scan the fridge: yellow mustard, sliced pickles, Polish and

Bavarian sauerkraut, brown mustard. Milk, orange juice, baby dills. Beside the juice in the door a bottle of an easy-going local lager bats its eyes, and stares out at me. And here emerges Jen, leading some happy asshole out of Dad's picture frame to a new apartment complex soaring up from midtown Manhattan a decade later. All she's left me with is her name. I can't picture her anymore, her voice, those easy coils of honey-colored hair, an image of what I'd imagined she may look like, now slowly eased away like how the sea gradually fills, erodes, and finally drowns a deep footprint on a beach. All gone. Just a name now, and the small mark left behind.

Silvy still not out there anywhere.

Upstairs, the din of kids. Down here, I twist the wedding ring on my finger, and place a hand on the open door of the fridge. I raise my free hand to rub the corner of an eye. I'm not sure which hand, nor which eye. Jen, beyond earshot, now faded and small. Too small, even, to breathe. Two shouts and a yelp from above. Behind me, the rapidly evaporating dew and bluff gaining green, then the muffled quacking of a loud duck from my back pocket. The beer blinks out at me again.

And for once I ignore the quacks and reach into the fridge.

THESE ARE MY PEOPLE

Seventeen-year-old Jeremy Baxell leans against his side of the counter at the Arctic Pelican Bakery in Noisy Creek, Wisconsin, holding high a fresh loaf of honey-wheat bread before an agitated customer in an ankle-length cotton dress.

"What no one understands," the woman yells, "is that in 1791, the Haitian government dedicated itself to Satan!"

"No kidding," Jeremy says. He wags the loaf with easy twists of the wrist. He smiles. "You want this sliced, then, Pauline?" he says.

"Yes, thank you," she says, disarmed. She glances around and lowers her voice. "*Aaand* . . . in 2003, they made it legal for Voodoo priests to perform marriages and baptisms!"

"Well," Jeremy says, "priests will do what priests will do, won't they, now?"

"But in the name of Satan?!" she yells. "When *men* reject *God* . . ."

Jeremy tilts his head to a side, and slips the sliced loaf of bread into a fresh paper bag.

"Anything else for ya today there, then, Pauline?"

"Yes! Do your research, Jeremy! Satan is the prince of lies! And when he is in charge, no one should wonder why their land is so riddled with murder, mayhem, illiteracy, and disease!"

She snatches the paper bag from Jeremy's hand and spins on a heel and stomps out of the shop.

Jeremy raises his eyebrows to Elspaith, the bakery owner across the floor.

"*These*," he says, smiling broadly and waving in the direction of the woman's departure, "*These* . . . are my people!"

Elspaith looks up from where she slices a fresh lemon. She is tall with a willowy build. Slim fronds of short dark-blue hair frame a face graced with a relaxed and natural smile. She glances at the photograph of her mother, Zelda, recently nailed to the wall, and puffs air up beneath her blue bangs. She drops a lemon slice into a fresh glass of cold water and hands it to Jeremy. The two look around the quiet bakery.

Jeremy clears his throat. "Day after tomorrow," he says.

"Whazzat?"

"My wake. Goes down the day after tomorrow—Mom just told me—so I'm calling in dead now."

Elspaith blinks and fills a drinking glass with cold water and returns the pitcher to the small fridge behind the counter.

He clears his throat again. "Care to come?"

She swallows. "Okay."

"Thanks. I'm only doing this for my family," he says. "The wake."

"Okay."

"And," he says, "gonna need tomorrow off. To rest up for all that Renata pressure."

Elspaith recalls her first encounter with Renata. She bristles, and looks back at Jeremy. "Renata . . . your mom?"

"Ja. This wake . . . may well kill me before I can."

He's really going to do it, Elspaith thinks. First Mom, and now Jeremy.

"Els?"

"Of course," she says, and blinks. "Of course."

TWO DAYS LATER, the Arctic Pelican Bakery is quiet, and so is Elspaith. She hesitates before the bench on the front sidewalk, and walks back inside to load a basket with rolls and breads. She wipes sweat from her brow with the back of a hand and flips around the **OPEN** sign on the front door to read **BACK IN 5 MINUTES** and inserts a key into the lock.

Inside her old pick-up truck, Elspaith thinks of just listening to the air, then turns on the radio, but soon flips it off to listen to nothing again. Just her, the air flowing through the truck, the gently bent trees clipping by, her open windows, and the fact that today marks exactly one month since her mother died her strange and brutal death. Elspaith drives and breathes.

Two delivery stops to make. Rolls at Counter Intuitive, baguettes and rolls for Elephants. Then Jeremy's wake. Three stops, she corrects herself. Three stops assuming she decides to go to the third. She drives, windows down. One's been stuck in the rolled-down position for two years and the other cranked down because that's the way she likes it, cranked all the way down.

She thinks about Jeremy calling in dead. He told her again this morning, that all was going according to plan. She repeated his secret was safe with her.

ELSPAITH PARKS AND WALKS the block and a half from The Ledge Like White Elephants Café and Patisserie to the Counter Intuitive Café wearing her signature saffron baker gear, complete with matching cap and apron. Her slender arm flexes and presses a stout wicker basket loaded with rolls against her hip. A dark-haired waitress with a gray cowlick greets her on the sidewalk outside the café. She nods and smiles.

"Els," she says.

"Heids," Elspaith says.

"Whacha got? Heard you were runnin late."

"Rolls."

"Ah. Justa get us through dinner, eh?"

"Ja."

Elspaith hesitates.

"Els?"

Elspaith shakes her head. "Nuthin. I just—"

Her friend, quickly serious, pulls the long salt-and-pepper frond of hair from her eye and wraps it behind her left ear. She lowers her hand and reaches for Elspaith.

"Els? What gives, kid?"

Elspaith raises her eyelids. "Jer," she says. "Jeremy. Gotta go to his wake after this, Heidi."

"After *this?*" Heidi asks, looking around. "What're ya talkin bout? The kid in yer shop? When'd he die?"

"He hasn't," Elspaith says. "Not yet, anyway." She takes a deep breath and continues. "His living wake. He invited me. Doesn't die until tonight."

"What?"

"Ja. He's been plannin his suicide since he heard the words *stage four.* His family doesn't know . . ."

Elspaith senses these devastating words, now finally uttered, echo and muffle inside her head. She turns to Heidi, feeling pressed against the inside edge of a dangling cube of ice that creaks and sways beneath the hammering afternoon sun. Heidi pushes through the front doors of the noisy café.

"Shee-yit," Heidi sighs loudly, looking back. "Where's the wake, then?"

"Shepherd-Collier Club," Elspaith says, in an official voice, following Heidi inside. She smiles weakly, and they laugh awkwardly.

"Rich white-guy stogie place, right?" Heidi says. "Golfers in ascots?"

"You got it."

"Jeremy."

"Yes . . . Apparently Jeremy."

"Ida never guessed."

"Me neither."

Elspaith lowers her eyelids. After a while, she's first to speak.

"Anyway. Back in the mornin, Heids."

"Not me. Off tomorrow. Good thing—Got a test Friday and I'm totally hosed."

"Bah. You? Please . . . besides, summer session is sposed tuh be easy."

"Hardly. Full semester of Hegel and Kierkegaard jammed inta six weeks. Six. Friggin. Weeks, Elsie."

Elspaith caws, quietly. "Ironic, doncha think?"

"What?"

"So much existentialism . . . so little time."

"Never thought of it that way!"

Elspaith sets the basket filled with rolls on the counter next to Heidi. A man emerges from the kitchen, nods, and disappears with the basket. Elspaith and Heidi smile and twitch as if about to embrace when an elderly woman with billowing copper hair raps a coin on the counter several stools away.

"Honey!" she hollers.

The man from the kitchen emerges and sets the empty basket next to Elspaith. He winks.

"Shit," Heidi says. She looks back to Elspaith. "Gotta go. Look, I'll swing by with some beers Friday post-Kierke-hegelgaard. Hang in there till then, though, okay Sweetie?"

Elspaith nods vacantly and hoists her basket and turns and leaves. She hesitates at the corner, recalls the location of her old pick-up truck, and crosses the street, walking but not feeling her feet.

ELSPAITH EASES HER TRUCK through the security check-point of the Shepherd-Collier Club. The long driveway winds through a heavily wooded forest which opens up to reveal an expansive clubhouse estate.

She meanders the dark foyer, allowing time for her eyes to adjust. A thin gentleman with gray-streaked hair combed wetly back raises the long beak of his nose to point her, with a sniff, in the direction of the Ladies' locker room. She walks, looking at the artwork, the ancient trophies, the framed member photos spanning generations of Shepherds and Colliers striking golf poses along a corridor of polished black walnut walls atop red velvet carpeting. Mahogany lockers buffed to a high sheen complete with engraved copper name plates line the walls of the locker room. Porcelain and brass bathroom fixtures. She uses an ample toilet stall, washes her hands with a European soap, dries them on a combed Turkish (probably) cotton hand-towel, and applies a Japanese emollient, mostly out of curiosity. Smells of late-summer lawn clippings and jasmine. She blows her nose into a silky facial tissue, tightens her yellow cap down over her short blue hair, and straightens the sleeves and collar of her saffron baker's garb. A quick intake of breath, and a small smile and a nod for the tall mirror. Her reflection nods back.

The gentleman in the tuxedo regards her curiously, surprised she hasn't changed into a different outfit, probably. Reluctant to call it a wake, she asks for the Baxell reception. He points the tip of his long nose in the opposite direction as before, and sniffs again.

Reception, she thinks. Perhaps these people are of a class not to call this event a benefit, but that's what this is. A silent auction and fundraiser to benefit the Baxell family, whose son is eighteen months terminally ill and about to die very soon. There just happen to be hors d'oeuvres and champagne, stationed and butlered.

Elspaith folds a twenty-dollar bill and slips it into the donations box near the registration desk. *Elspaith Stoltz,* she writes in the guest book, adding *Noisy Creek, Wisconsin* beneath other important-sounding locales: Stockholm, New York, Wilmington, Marquette, Ithaca.

A man in his mid-thirties looks over from where he writes in his checkbook.

"Is this tax-deductible?" he asks, loudly, to no one in particular. A fellow standing nearby blinks a partial eye-roll and smirks. His eyes bug wide as he lifts and lowers a shoulder.

"Well . . . ?" the man with the checkbook says aloud. His face sags into disbelief as he looks down and resumes writing the check, shaking his head.

Not a familiar face in sight. Just rich skin and dark dresses and glowing pearls. Her eyes scan beyond the tops of the coiffed heads for Jeremy, whom she imagines muttering his new mantra: *These are my people.* He borrowed the phrase from the title of an online photo gallery that had gone viral, a series of snapshots of trash scattered along the shoulder of a highway out in the Oregon wilderness. Striking images of litter clung to hardy strands of native flora, bending and swaying in snapshot breezes beneath sepia skies and charred hills. And the poem—that poem!—introducing it all:

> On the roadside
> > Of a lonesome nation
> My people
> Wash ashore.

Jeremy repeats the phrase whenever bemused, amused, irritated, or saddened by a particular interaction with a local: *These are my people.*

The lighting glares off the framed art and photographs under blasts of over-conditioned air, beneath which Jeremy no doubt finds himself freezing.

Her pulse quickens as she can't find him, finding instead only curious looks and abruptly halted conversations upon first sight of her. More than once she is asked to fetch more hors d'oeuvres or a fresh round of drinks. One fellow, approximately her age, asks if she's a member.

She's uncertain how to respond. A lacquered Shepherd-Collier ID swings from a lanyard. DAVID, she reads, upside-down and backwards. Am I a member? she asks herself silently. Is this a come-on? Or a snub?

She stands up straight and levels her eyes with the young man's.

"No. I'm here for Jeremy."

"Who?" He swivels his head around.

"Jeremy Baxell," she says, continuing to scan the room. "About seventeen? He's my . . . friend."

The young man shakes his head and smiles in vague disbelief. He leans to maintain eye contact, blocking Elspaith's line of sight. She frowns and steps around him.

A different man's self-important voice rises above the buzz. "Well, this has to be Elara's decision," he says. "Obviously I'd prefer she attend Williams . . . but Tufts is fine, too," he sighs.

The throat of a woman across from him rattles. "At least it's not *Smith*," she says with a sniff, suppressing a smirked nostril laugh.

"Right!" another woman cries quietly, and guiltily, and they all chortle polite wake chortles.

These people. Apart from Jeremy's soft hands and clear skin, she'd have never guessed that he came from this sort of money, that these people are his people.

Renata, Jeremy's mother, approaches. She is a painfully thin, self-starved woman, with wavy grayish hair she grabs at intermittently, as though she's never been happy with how it lays. She wears a tight gray-and-white herring-bone skirt with a wide black leather belt and chrome buckle. A dark, loosely hung sweater covers a cream blouse rung with large beads. She greets Elspaith with an anodyne smile.

"Elspaith," she says, breathless and pressing a palm to her breast. "So *kind* of you to come. But you *shouldn't* have . . ." She nods, slipping a bony arm through Elspaith's elbow to link forearms, her cool and lucid skin pressing gently against Elspaith's warmth. She pats Elspaith's wrist with her free hand as she speaks.

"Of course," Elspaith says, quietly. "Honored to be here, though I must apologize for my late arrival. Got delayed at a delivery—"

"Oh, yes. Well, no bother, dear. This," she says, still breath-less and stretching her matchstick arms about the hall, "was all so very last minute. You're here *now*, aren't you? That's all that really matters, dear."

"Thank you."

"Have you had a chance to scan the auction items?" She gives Elspaith a slow and intrigued look.

"Not yet, no," Elspaith says, wondering what there could possibly be to bid on. Tickets to the Masters' in Georgia?

"Well, maybe something will catch your eye, dear." She pats Elspaith's hand, already beginning to disregard her, tipping away.

"Do excuse me, Elspaith."

"Yes, of course. Thank you."

"It really was so thoughtful of you to come, dear," she says.

Elspaith smiles, tips her hat, and turns to Jeremy.

He leans heavily on a round cocktail table, his head cleanly shaved a stark cancer white, in the midst of the crowd of dark suit-jackets and bronzed skin. He licks his cracked lips with a papery tongue, then takes a small swallow of water and looks at Elspaith and nods.

"Hi," he says.

Elspaith nods. "Tonight?" she breathes.

"Tonight," he says. He nods and says, "Tonight they get what they want." He touches his dry tongue to his even drier lips again and takes a breath. He seems more wooden than sad, and overall appears more sick here than in the bakery, where he merely looked like he didn't get enough sun.

"It's . . ." he says. "Time to put an end to . . . their impatience." He folds his hands. "They're avoiding me," he says. "Didn't even tell me about this thing till coupla days ago. But you knew that."

Elspaith nods again. "Of course."

"And now they're avoiding me. Don't wanna get sneezed on . . . yet making damn sure they're all seen."

"Jeremy, they—"

"You saw it, Els. I know you did. Way worse than Facebook or Caring Bridge. Which is why I never even look at my pages. Empty gestures, here just done in person. I'd rather they stayed home and click on a heart beneath whatever status Kat posts and tell me how fucking blessed I am."

He coughs like a muted goose.

"Aw, Christ," he moans, looking around at the crowd now closed together and grown solemn, hands interlaced. "Now they'll fucking pray," he says.

Elspaith's mouth opens in a soundless gasp.

"Oh, fuck me, yes," he groans, pitching his head to a side.

She places a hand on Jeremy's forearm. They stand together, alone in the center of the room, quietly watching the family receive greetings and condolences pressed forth in murmurs and shrugs.

His parents separate to make the rounds. His younger sister reclines upon a sofa, batting her eyes at a smartphone. Older sister Kat presses her smartphone to an ear beneath a cascade of shoulder-length golden hair, and paces about near the donations table. Her bright teeth flash and a free hand waves, the lush glow of her supple, opaline skin nearly obscene. Elspaith looks at Jeremy, fading, and speaks again.

"It's all karma, Jer. *Good* karma. People don't always know what to say, and often say what they say poorly. They just have no training in expressing actual empathy. So they end up repeating clichés. They're trying to tell you they're thinking about you—"

"Feels more like checkin sumthin offa list."

A pause for prayer arrives. Elspaith and Jeremy turn to the solemn voice calling for silence. A quick amen, then resumption of chit-chat, laughter, and drinks pouring.

Elspaith turns to Jeremy, alone on a stool in the middle of the room. She nods, kisses him, holding her lips to his bony cheek. She squeezes his thin hand, and walks out.

Once out of eyeshot, she shoves herself down the long corridors to the exit, breath catching. The man at the entrance with the wet hair and long beak of a nose nods and sniffs and closes his eyes respectfully. Elspaith pushes through the thick doors into the muggy late afternoon. Heavy clouds sag and roil in wet-gray relief against a cobalt sky, gearing up for early-evening storms.

Elspaith starts her truck and rolls down the window then rolls it back up and turns on the radio and rolls down the window and turns the radio off. She tilts her head back and Zelda materializes, starving and dying, in recurring night-mare fashion, from the storm clouds beyond the clubhouse. Dying slowly and somehow not screaming. Starving herself to death.

By the time Elspaith stopped by for a visit and discovered what her mother had been up to, it was too late. Her body had reached the point of no return. Without water, Zelda would have lasted less than two days. But she drank water, which her body craved and she rapidly pissed out, each flush removing minerals and salts lost forever.

Elspaith coughs herself awake inside her pick-up truck as if awakened by the sharp squalor where Zelda slept and starved and evacuated until she died six days after Elspaith found her.

A thunderhead presses down upon the glacier-flattened bluffs outside the truck's open windows. Elspaith could never open enough windows at her mother's. She blinks slowly, eyelids sticky, pulls up Jeremy's Caring Bridge page on her phone.

The Baxell Reception for Jeremy was announced in May via a Kat posting. Her stomach swirls as reedy Renata's breathless words replay in her head: *This had all been so very last minute . . .*

Jeremy was informed scarcely a day before the event was to take place. In July. Elspaith wonders if Renata kept the news of the living wake from Jeremy for the sake of his sanity, but also to prevent her from coming. She looks at the expensive cars surrounding her truck. Maybe Renata didn't want the blue-haired, flour-covered bohemian artsy weirdo commoner tainting her event? Maybe. She sighs. Friday and Heidi and those beers can't get here soon enough.

She scrolls through the comments about Jeremy's most recent clinic visit, then the history of comments and posts, in reverse chronological order all the way to the start, when Jeremy first walked in to the clinic with a painful cough. It's all there, the rhythm of the disease and melody of his demise. She scrolls forward through time again as the prayers gain momentum and exclamation marks, all the heavy punctuation and emoticons through to Jeremy's first remission, the declarations of proof of the power of prayer, then shifting to more pressing prayer requests, then quickly ratcheting up to urgent pleas for prayer once the cancer revived itself and came on full throttle during his relapse to the present day, to the point where the disease has nearly completely run its course and about all anyone really prays for now is comfort through to The End.

Elspaith scans the brewing storm. Back home, Zelda rests in a marble urn. She looks down at her phone. A blank text area awaits.

IT SEEMS EVEN HOTTER when Elspaith makes the final corner for the bakery. She wants to keep driving. Just drive and drive and drive and drive and not stop. Drive with the windows rolled down until she falls asleep. But she can't. Her mother a month dead and Jeremy soon to join her and there's work to do tonight for tomorrow's bread. Elspaith and her perpetual kitchen and ovens, mixing, kneading, rolling, baking, rolling, kneading, mixing, baking, mixing, *never*, rolling, *really*, kneading, *ever*, baking, *sleeping*. And there may be customers. Customers—her mother used to say—not an interruption of our work, but the reason we open our doors.

She stops her truck in front of the bakery—*her* bakery, she reminds herself, again—and thuds the gears into Park. Ahead of her on the sidewalk she spots a man walking slowly, staring intently at the concrete beneath his feet, as if it's about to liquefy before he can complete another step. Something is very wrong. She can sense it even before she gets out of the truck. She walks around to the back of her vehicle and opens the tailgate and grabs her basket and slams the gate shut, watching the man hesitate midstride.

"Elspaith," he says, nearly yelping. He looks exhausted and off-kilter. She knows the man, Robert, only as a customer who buys bread for his family.

"Robert," Elspaith says, with a smile.

She presses the empty basket under an arm and savors the heat of the day before walking to the door of the bakery. She swings it wide to allow Robert to enter.

He orders two of the remaining loaves of honey wheat, and chokes up when Elspaith offers him a treat. He apologizes, says he has just received some bad news about a friend. *A dear friend* is all she can get out of him. She guesses the friend has either just now died or will very soon be dead.

Elspaith looks at the portrait of Zelda hung near the doorway to the ovens and wonders if she may know this friend of Robert's.

She pours a glass of cold water and plops a fresh lemon slice into the glass. She walks around the counter and leads Robert by the arm and sits him down on an old church pew across the room.

He sits clumsily, like a rag-doll plunked into a corner. She sits beside Robert and feels the bench move slightly as he shifts his weight.

Her slender fingers pluck a crispy bread-end from an apron pocket. She explains she can tell the sort of person who likes bread loaf end pieces, and the sort who does not. Robert is a bread-ender, she can tell.

He eats the crispy bread crust and watches her slim figure glide away and around the counter and through the swinging doors of the kitchen.

An echo of Jeremy's mantra in her head: *These are my people*, followed by her mother's voice. She'd turned her head on the pillow to Elspaith, spoke in a frail whisper through a sad smile.

"Oh, my Els," she said. "Turns out we don't live a very long time, we don't."

Elspaith stands staring mid-air. Bread dough rises behind her.

Her mother.

Jeremy.

Robert, over there, stunned and staring at nothing, too, in unblinking shock, needs another glass of cold water. She sniffs and reaches for the glass pitcher and slices lemon with precise strokes.

Elspaith will pull the wet glass from Robert's thick hand, and feel the glass release from his fingers into hers as she eases a fresh glass of lemon sparkle back into his free hand, and his heavy fingers wrap and clutch cold in all this heat. And she will sit with Robert, eating crusty bread ends on the old church pew in her quiet bakery, listening to him breathe, for as long as he needs. Robert. Alone and washed ashore. Robert. One of hers, one of these, her people.

S P A C E S

Robert parked his pickup truck across the street from the Counter Intuitive Café on the University of Wisconsin-Noisy Creek campus and walked inside and sat down at the counter. New place, and he thought he'd take a break and check it out.

Warm kitchen aromas and a young and dark-haired waitress with smart black eyes greeted him. Next to Robert sat a cordial man who introduced himself as Phillip. He extended a chapped hand and they shook politely.

The black-eyed waitress sported a long and light-gray frond of hair that looped over an eye down near the tip of her nose. A distraction and attraction both. She glanced at Robert's name, sewn in a careful red script below a company logo, *Rupe and Pine's Plumbing,* on the breast pocket of his clay-colored work shirt.

"I'll call ya Rob, if ya don't mind."

"Fine," Robert said, shaking off the cold. Seventeen below outside.

"Figured it beats *Bert.*"

Robert laughed. "What should I call you?"

"Heidi. Go easy on me, though. Supposed to be studyin for a test now, but they got me workin a double."

"Ope."

"Yep. Been here since four-thirty. Marge was a no-show, so I'm flying solo til some new someone named Jaime comes."

"Gotcha."

The long frond fell across her nose again, and caught Robert's eye. "I was born with this . . . mostly," she said, crossing her eyes and twisting the subject of his unasked question between a thumb and forefinger. "It's been a white and gray swirl since my hair finally came in. About age three. Until then my mother was convinced I'd be bald forever. Like one of those butt-heads in that one episode of *Star Trek*."

Robert nodded.

"Got hot coffee and fresh pies, though, Rob."

"Sounds good." He looked at his hands and flexed and massaged a knuckle. "Coffee, please," he said, and looked up. "Smells great in here, by the way." He blinked and glanced around at the art-studded walls, then at her. "What kind of pie?" He was suddenly starving.

"I'll get ya a menu," she said, and pulled out a Monet-themed coffee cup—*Woman in a Garden*—and matching saucer. "So how's yer day been goin, then?" she asked, and began to pour and speak with a certain rhythm and cadence that bordered on singing. "Drivin round . . . windows rolled down . . . arm hangin out . . . enjoyin that crisp valley air . . ." The strands of her grayish whorl pulled free from the top of her ear, and uncoiled to partially cover an eye again. "Cream?"

"Truck, yes. Windows rolled down? Uhmn, *Nooo*. Another time." He smiled with his eyes. "Cream—Yes, please."

"What?" Heidi giggled. "You don't got your windows rolled down, man?"

"Nope." They both smiled. Phillip squirmed, brow rumpled.

"Rob!" she scolded, mockingly serious. She slid a porcelain creamer in his direction and nodded at Phillip. "Oh, yeah, man!" she said, and raised her outstretched arms. "Wind . . . in your hair . . . Shiftin and driftin," she sang, and shook her dark hair lightly. "If yer not drivin around with your windows rolled down . . ." she sighed and gestured outside and shook her head slowly. "You're just drivin around." She let her arms go slack at her sides and glided away to the next group of diners, speaking in a dreamy and distant voice, "Just *driiiivin* around."

Robert raised his eyebrows in a *Well okay, then* way, and drank coffee and set the cup onto its matching saucer. He rotated the saucer to see the painting open before him. With a small smile he wondered if Claude Monet had ever seen weather quite like this. He turned the saucer another quarter turn to view the *Woman* in her white petticoat and parasol scoot beyond the far edge of his rotating cup, giving way to reveal more bright summer sunshine, sharply defined shadows, and lush green hues.

"Heh, *Rob*," Phillip, on the stool beside Robert, sniggered.

Robert looked up from the Monet-in-a-saucer gardens, and blinked, back in Wisconsin, back in winter, again. He shook his head. "What?"

"She," Phillip said, pointing to a space behind the counter until a moment ago occupied by Heidi. "*She* calls *me* 'Trig,'" he said, and cast his smug eyes to scanning about the café. Robert suspected "Trig" to be the sort who would hang out at the counter here all day if he could.

"Well, *Phillip*," Robert said, tugging at the name embroidered into his shirt for Trig to see. "My name *is* Robert. So . . .'Rob's' not much of a stretch."

"No, it is not," Trig agreed. He looked at him sideways. "But for *me* she chose something *totally* original." He sniffed. "And that lady over there," he said in a lower voice, and tipped his head in the direction of an older woman down the counter, "is named Harriet. But Heidi calls her 'Lucy.'"

He folded his arms in apparent victory.

Robert was tired. His insides groaned and he sighed. "She must like you more, I guess."

Trig laughed and drank coffee. Heidi slipped Robert a pie menu and asked with her eyes if he wanted more coffee. Robert responded no, thank you, silently, and she moved down the counter to take an order.

"See? She barely talks to *you*," Trig snorted. "So ha-ha, *Rob*."

Robert rolled his eyes in exaggerated fashion, and Trig laughed again.

Robert's calves and thighs ached with the cold. He exhaled slowly. Beside him, Trig sipped from a unique cup and saucer of his own, themed after a scene from *A Streetcar Named Desire*, in which the wide-eyed Stella assures a skeptical Blanche that she and Stanley are fine, *juuust fine*. Robert smiled, wondering what other drama—possibly within a Stanley context—could lurk on the other side of Trig's cup.

Trig was probably ten years older than Heidi, yet there was a certain fleshiness about him that made taking an accurate stab at his age somewhat difficult. A pale blue dress shirt, probably tucked smartly into his dark dress pants earlier this morning, had freed most of itself from the clutches of a tight leather belt that strained against his waist and exposed a clean white undershirt beneath. Trig continued to savor his slice of pie, shirt-cuffs and sleeves unbuttoned and pushed up over his elbows, raising his head expectantly whenever the kitchen doors swung open. A clean and completely untouched linen napkin rested on his thigh and made Robert smile and think of his kids, who without fail eschewed napkins in favor of the back of a hand, a sleeve, or a pant leg.

Robert tasted his coffee and stretched and looked around at the artwork on the walls, all varied, all local, all somewhat dark and esoteric in scope. But pulled together into this space it worked, and encapsulated a neat, edgy, yet welcoming atmosphere. Even the gloomy *Bemoaning Lisa* screwed into the opposite wall, which portrayed a haggard and emaciated Leonardo da Vinci weeping on his muddied knees before a freshly etched gravestone, worked. He glanced again at Heidi. Fit and trim and dressed in black, she seemed to be cast for this place, too.

He sighed and tried to relax, mentally beating back his habitual resistance to giving in to the need for rest. A sensation common to borderline workaholics. Manifested in this case as self-accusatory blame that coming here was a mistake, that he should be doing bookwork or writing up estimates. Or it creeped upon him like the blooms of Catholic guilt—the excesses of coffee and pie consumption, for example, which an inner voice admonished as an indulgent behavior. Then, once the initial wave of Catholic guilt subsided, he would be overcome with a nagging suspicion that he was either forgetting something or he was somehow selfishly putting off going straight home. He should be speeding home to help with the kids. Or to tear the clothes off his very beautiful wife, for example. He should be—

In the end, what Robert really feared was now that he'd finally sat down for a minute, he'd never manage to get up again.

His spirits perked up when he scanned the pie listings, though. And he smiled once he noticed the café's music from the UW-NC student radio station—a Duran Duran selection. He nudged the menu away with the tips of his fingers and nodded up at Heidi.

"Yo, Rob," she said, and walked over. "Pie slice for ya today there, then?"

"Yes, please." He found it hard not to smile. Trig stared.

"What'll it be, then?"

"Uh. Trying to decide here . . ." His eyes scrolled the list one more time. Camus's Raisin Cream. Poe's Blackberry Woe. "I'll go for a slice of the Kvothe's Apple," he said.

Heidi gasped. "Yes!" she sang. "*Naaaaailed* it!"

Robert blinked and leaned back, startled. Trig's eyes widened. "Pardon me?" Robert said.

"You pronounced it right," Heidi said, excited. "I told the baker—Manuel—'no way anyone gets this one,' when I saw it on his menu this morning. And you did it! You got it!" She beamed and scribbled and walked away quickly but just as quickly spun around on a heel and came back at them. "That pie comes with a wedge of sharp cheddar, by the way. Today's is kinda crumbly, but yer game for that, right, Rob?" She nodded and looked up from her notepad, still bright and giddy.

Robert smiled. He'd have apple pie served no other way. "Of course." He nodded and she vanished.

"Huh?" Trig asked, and wiped his nose. "What the hell was that?"

"The pie." Robert laughed quietly. "Kvothe is the main character in a book called—"

"*Name of the Wind,*" Heidi interrupted, already breezing past them again. "Love that book," she said, and continued along to another group at the end of the counter.

"Yeah." Robert said. "Really good. Even better the second read. My friend who lent it to me said Rothfuss could write about something as mundane as buying groceries, and she'd probably read it."

Heidi strode past them again, nodding, then leaned into the kitchen and hollered something in Spanish.

"Never heard of it," Trig snorted. "And grocery shopping is *anything* but mundane."

"Of course," Robert said, and smiled at Heidi. "Well, good stuff. I hadn't heard of the book, either." He scratched deliberately at the stubble along his jawline. He caught a fingernail, and paused to examine it. Robert looked straight ahead in the direction of the wall beyond the counter, but his vision blurred at a point in space about four feet in front of his nose as he spoke. "I was stuck in a bit of a reading rut. My mom had passed, and—"

"Oh! I'm so sorry," Trig said.

"Oh, don't be, please . . . I—Well . . ." Robert smiled uncomfortably and swallowed more coffee. He paused and explained, almost by rote, that his mother's passing wasn't exactly tragic, that he wasn't utterly devastated by the passing of a woman who had enjoyed good health and had nearly hit ninety. Yet devastation seemed to be what people expected, and, on a certain level, craved.

"But thanks. She was actually eighty-nine!" Robert said fondly. "Got sick one day and boom! She was dead and in the ground six days later. No suffering, really." Robert cleared his throat. "Very quick, but she gave us enough time to wrap our brains around what was about to happen." Robert paused again for more coffee, eyes making one sweep up the counter and back for Heidi before his thoughts folded into memories of his mother, and her legacy. Did not showing constant and overt dismay make him a bad son? As a mother who broke her back for her family, did she not at the very least deserve to have distraught kids left behind in her wake?

Robert crossed his legs at the ankles thought about his workaholism again. A mere cover to mask his feelings and numb his ability to process anything beyond what's for supper? Did workaholism suppress depression? It's been known to, he knew that. But in his case? Maybe, maybe not. He sighed and thought of his beautiful wife and his family and his pretty good little life and all the other little lives he gets to peek into daily for his work, how he alone is allowed intimate glimpses—their dire plumbing needs often playing out as a backdrop to their wailing kids, partially cooked meals, or brutal loneliness. He glanced outside through the iced-over window panes and considered the span of these short yet continuous golden sunsets, now glinting off rooftops and windows. He sipped his coffee. All these little lives, all these places, like this café, drawn together like metal filings to a magnet. He sipped again and swallowed.

"Left behind no regrets, I don't think," Robert said. "What more could you ask, right?"

Trig nodded and glanced down at a distressed Stella on the side of his coffee cup, poor Stella's mouth opened wide in the shape of a long O.

Robert cleared his throat.

"Anyway," he continued, "for some reason I fell into reading lots of history and biographies. Then heavier stuff like Hitchens and Harris." Trig straightened up as if to interrupt, but politely fell back into his slouch. "Then one day I asked an old friend if she could recommend something really different. She's always reading something cool." He took another sip of coffee. "'Maybe some Fantasy,' she said, and dropped off two books couple days later." He cleared his throat and glanced around for a clock. "*Name of the Wind* was one of them."

"Huh." Trig paused as if wondering about the last time a friend had lent him a book. He wrinkled his brow. "May I ask what was the other book?"

"*IQ84.*" Robert blinked, recalling the opening sections. "I'm only about fifty pages in. A longer read, but I hear it's definitely worth the time." He smiled. "I'm told it's kinda 'out there.' Author is Japanese . . ." He folded his arms and spoke through a stretch of his legs. "It came from her," he said, "so that's enough for me."

HEIDI EMERGED from the kitchen, scanned the diner, and leaned a hip against the counter across from the loud, older woman she'd dubbed Lucy. She had billowing copper-colored hair and strong eyes and steady hands. She spoke fluidly and intently to Heidi, who made a remark about *the inherent tic* of the local accent.

"Friend of mine here from Arizona hasn't noticed it," Heidi said.

"Well," Lucy said, gesturing with bony fingers. She opened and closed her hands when she spoke. "Everyone probably still sounds alike to her! It's a subtle thing, and I didn't notice it when I first moved here from Raleigh, either."

ROBERT LOOKED UP at the ceiling. Colorful, florid beer mats from around the world studded decorative metal ceiling tiles painted galvanized gray. He felt the ache in his thighs subside, and he now believed he'd made the correct choice in taking a break.

"*IQ84*," Trig said, glancing up to see what Robert was looking at. "Cool. Now *there's* a book I've heard of." He nodded with authority. "But I have to admit . . . I haven't read it." He paused. "And," he said, "you'll have to excuse me now." Trig straightened himself with a certain amount of effort. "Gotta get back to work." He stood, rolled down and buttoned his sleeves, dropped a few loose bills onto the countertop, and turned and steered himself toward the coat rack. "See ya around . . . *Rob*." He smiled, then swung around in Heidi's direction. "Thanks, Heidi," he called out. "Good luck on that test tomorrow." He walked toward the exit with a wink and a nod to Robert, and stepped out, closing the door quickly behind him. A sharp burst of frigid air rushed inside.

HEIDI LOOKED UP from her conversation with Lucy to wave. "Bye, Trig. And, thanks!" She returned, with attentive eyes, to Lucy's story. She crouched to a knee, leaned an elbow on the counter, and rested her chin on the back of a hand.

"At least it's freezing cold out," Lucy continued, speaking freely and easily. "So mercifully cold . . . So they won't stink up the place." She glanced around.

"No kidding," Heidi said. "But certainly you can't wait until spring to bury them all, can you?" She gestured at the woman's Elvis Presley cup. "More?"

"Please," she said. "And, no. But those cats! They keep coming—about two or three a week—to die out there in the back." She gestured over her shoulder in the direction of a yellow house across the street.

Heidi leaned slightly to the woman's left to look across the street, then back to meet her eyes squarely. "How many?"

She slurped from a spot next to Elvis's ear. "Not sure, honey. They're all frozen together in rings." She blinked and seemed to ponder something very far away and entirely different, then returned to Heidi. "Nineteen? Twenty, maybe." She set her cup down onto its matching saucer.

Heidi gasped. "*Twenty?*" She snapped her head up and squinted across the street at the woman's house. "Jesus Christ," she breathed.

They shared a lingering, locked look. Heidi shook her head and finally mouthed the word *wow*. Lucy nodded and shooed her away with the back of a hand. *Maybe call a vet?* Heidi wondered. *Holy—*

"YOU GOT A TEST TOMORROW?" Robert asked as Heidi approached. He smiled through a bite of pie. "What in?"

She put the frozen dead cats out of her mind for the moment and coiled the salt-and-pepper frond of hair over an ear. "PHIL 452," she replied, mechanically. "Metaphysics." She mocked a yawn.

"452? Sounds advanced."

"Doctoral, actually," she said, and rolled her eyes.

"Whoa. Impressive." He thought for a moment. "Wait—" Robert narrowed his eyes and raised the cheddar wedge to his mouth. "Metaphysics . . . Nature of evil, right?"

"Well, sort of." She grinned as he chewed and she poured. "It's a branch of philosophy that studies the essence of one's being. Of cause and identity. How's the pie?"

"Pie is amazing, actually. And the crust . . . ! But, don't tell my wife I said so." He winked, pretending to duck for cover, then straightened back up, shyly. "That other stuff you said?" He shook his head and shrugged. "Over my head. Never did like Ortega y Gasset." He scratched at an eyebrow. Heidi eyed his battered knuckles briefly.

"Oh!" Heidi said, quietly surprised. "So you *do* know!"

Robert shook his head. "No, not really. Had to read him—them?—once in college during a previous life. Could never get more than a few pages in."

"Oh." Heidi stared for a moment, nodding. "And Ortega y Gasset is just the one guy—José." She smiled.

"Name rolls off your tongue easy enough."

"My father is Chilean."

"Ah." He paused to consider this. "And your mother?"

"Brazilian."

Robert raised his eyebrows. "Really?" Images of a steamy rainforest and pink fresh-water dolphins panned before his eyes. "That's quite the combination."

Heidi hesitated. "It was at first," she said, with a wry smile that waned. She broke eye contact to survey the counter quickly, then returned her eyes to meet his. "They moved to Wisconsin before I was born. They split once I started college. One of those we-stayed-together-for-the-kids sorta deals."

"Ah," he said, with a nod of understanding. "I see."

"Ja. Can't say I'd recommend it for everyone." Her eyes wandered to the front windows and what remained of a thumbprint she'd pressed into the iced-over glass a few hours before. "Sometimes kids would rather their parents just be happy and apart rather than together and at each others' throats." She shook her head. "Anyway. Ortega y Gasset." She smiled vacantly, paused, and took note of his hands again for a moment. "You didn't care for poor ol' José, eh?"

"Just wasn't my thing at age eighteen is all." He took another bite and wiped his mouth and fingered the remaining lump of sharp cheddar. "Always thinking the writer was two people made me feel like I was being ganged up on."

Heidi eyed him at length now, though really only for a moment, and imagined Robert back in that previous life, this unassuming, hard-working man with those thick, weathered hands, broken fingernails, and a gentle resting smiling face, who could say 'Kvothe' without a hitch, all fresh and sweet with a head full of hair, skin still smooth, waking up to pain-free mornings and wandering about a leafy college campus somewhere, tomes of Ortega y Gasset foisted upon him.

"You were just too young is all. No one should have to deal with metaphysics at that age. Especially from *him*—very heavy dude." She nodded and turned to who was calling out for her attention down the counter. Multiple groups were now asking to settle their tabs and she wiped her hands on a towel and met their eyes. "Anyway," she said, and looked back at Robert and patted her hands dry as she drifted away, "some pretty seriously deep shit for just outta high school."

Robert raised his chin. "True enough." He smiled and relaxed, now fully convinced he'd made the correct decision to stop in for a short break, despite all the 'should-be-doings' on his invisible mental list, and could feel some long-departed mental energy begin to make a welcome return.

Heidi coasted back a few minutes later to check his coffee and tend to the small group beyond Robert.

"So what's the essence of metaphysics in terms a plumber can understand?" he asked, playfully, as she passed.

Heidi glanced at the embroidered script on his work shirt, *Robert,* tapped her lips with the fingertips of her right hand and adjusted the whorl with her left. She looked at the layers of ice coating the windows. She considered searing another opening in the ice, this time with her nose. She looked down the counter and raised a finger to Robert, indicating that he should hold that thought, that she'd be right back.

BY THE TIME HEIDI GOT within comfortable earshot of Robert again, his pie plate was empty and clean, and he was all business on his cellphone. She blinked at him slowly. He held her look for a moment as he listened to whatever it was being said into his earpiece. She longed for a less wonderfully and perpetually connected planet.

"Yep," Robert said, now serious. "Oakdale. I'll pick ya up." The voice spoke intermittently, sharing a story of its own.

Robert's question gnawed at her. She pictured the next day's exam she was supposed to be studying for with friends. The midterm exam she would be writing in eighteen hours. Metaphysics can run deep and vague pretentious all at once. Like dark matter. She thought about the hole she'd burned into the iced-over window with her thumb, the new one she wanted to make with her nose, and sensed the look, feel, and smell of tomorrow's blue exam booklet resting on a desk before her.

Consider for a moment, Rob, Heidi thought, imagining her trusty Bic ballpoint pen in her hand, *that your mind is made up of atoms which are microscopic, and are very sparse. This sparseness is filled with empty spaces we call 'dark matter.' It is the null essence that fills the entirety of our universe. Dark matter makes this infinite universe a concept that lies within our finite grasp. It's in your eyes, in your hairs, in your toenails. It's in the DNA of Trig's sniffles and it binds the Cholula sauce you dump on your eggs.*

"A simple job, really," Robert said.

The nutmeg in your pie and the bacteria in your cheddar and the foam on tonight's glass of Schlitz.

"A p-trap and who knows what else. Bathroom sink out in the burbs. A hairball, maybe?" Robert laughed. "Should be easy."

This dark matter flows through your veins and fills your lungs with life, Rob. Your heart pumps dark matter all around your body.

There was a pause and a grin split Robert's face. Heidi could hear the man on the other end chuckle, then exhale a knowing and amused sigh. A sigh of the sort shared between close friends.

Consider, she thought, looking at Robert from farther down the counter, *your entire being is filled with the sparseness of the atoms that flow and inflate and give you shape. Even your so-called being, your metaphorical heart, your fleshy notion of time, of self, consists mostly of empty spaces.*

Robert caught her attention, pointed at his clean plate and gave Heidi a thumbs-up. She stepped over and removed the plate and fork and topped off his coffee. Robert touched the back of her hand. "Gotta go," he mouthed, and pointed over his shoulder with his free hand. He pulled a twenty-dollar bill from his wallet and edged it across the counter. Heidi looked at the spot where he touched her hand, then nodded and reached for the bill and left to make change.

Your fingertips slice through these spaces, Rob. Dark spaces they slice, and dark spaces they touch. We are in fact more 'dark space' than we are matter. All darkness all fused together so tightly to formulate the beings we are and everything we see, touch, breathe, create, love, hate, desire, and destroy.

Heidi returned with Robert's change and wandered down to the last group seated at the far end of the counter. She heard Robert's voice lift slightly above the chatter of the remaining café crowd beyond.

All microscopic, from the sweet smell of a newborn's scalp to the sounds of its dear, tiny cries, pushing and spreading these unctuous spaces around us, filling our noses, pressing in on our eardrums, all around all of us. We are defined by the sum of our voids.

"... home in time for dinner," Robert was saying, and paused as an unruly multimedia piece of art pegged to the wall above the cash register caught his eye. He grabbed his jacket, gloves and heavy cap, and stepped through the iced-over door back into the attacking, ferocious outside air.

Already starting to get cold again, Heidi thought. *And dark.* The waning mid-afternoon sun, slipping in the deepening winter indigo sky, pressed and stretched shadows and glowing gold lines up around edges of houses across the street. The buildings now becoming dark outlines of shapes below thin ribbons of clouds already blushing an evening purple, stars primed to poke through. And the quick bursts of cold air into the café smelled of early nightfall. *We are the spaces that surround and contract around us and freeze solid and melt and swirl in the wind. The spaces are the wind and we are the spaces. Farts and roses, Rob, on a microscopic, granular, atomic level. Roses and farts, man.*

"I'M ON MY WAY NOW," Robert said, then skipped through a gap in traffic on Vinny Street. "Besides," he puffed, once across the street, "I could use the company."

He hung up and removed a wad of keys from a jacket pocket and climbed into his pickup truck.

HEIDI STARED AT HER THUMBPRINT on the front window, now fully iced over again like a thick and misshapen scab. A gray delivery truck eased in front of the café and filled the windows beyond, hazard lights blinking and clacking cold and stiff echoes. Other customers bundled up and pushed outside, angling up the street or down the sidewalk toward the creek, bent and crouched into the wind. She looked back across the street above the mark left by her thumb. By the time the delivery truck slipped away, Robert was gone. Not an instant later another vehicle swept into the open parking space probably left behind by Robert. Heidi laughed and yawned and shook her head. *Spaces where we park our vehicles.* She cocked her head to a side.

The steady flow of cars on Vinny Street stretched, slowed, and jolted back and forth in distorted bursts, front and back, on the other side of the windows' icy veil.

Heidi set the coffee pot aside and yawned again and leaned back against the pie case, pressing her tired shoulder blades into the spaces of its warm, welcoming glass. She blinked slowly. Marge remained at large. Only another hour. *Or whenever this 'Jaime' person gets here. Then meet for Group. Test tomorrow at nine.*

She crossed her feet at the ankles, looked outside at the passing vehicles rippling and slowly popping in and out of view beyond the frosted front of the café. Lucy's curious yellow house trembled and seemed to lean slightly to one side beyond the glass, up and across the street, like a winter mirage.

Outside more locals pushed along in the cold, some pausing to peer into the new café, wide eyes distorted by the iced-over windows, attempting to stare inside like land-locked humans getting their first-ever glimpse into a saltwater aquarium, seemingly deciding whether to take the plunge and head inside to have a closer look around. Maybe warm up for a bit. Another couple seated near the door stood to leave and anchored a handful of cash onto their table with a coffee cup, pointed, waved, bundled up, and shot outside. Heidi brushed her bangs aside, lifted her eyebrows, and nodded.

Everyone who slipped in and out of this place formed a part of this town's being, this small space, this special little place with a university out in the middle of somewhere on the very edge of nowhere. Maybe her new friend from Arizona would come walking in to her café one day and tell her how the maddening tic of the local accent had finally gotten under her skin, too. Or maybe she still hadn't noticed. Or maybe her friend the Arizonan had picked up the accent herself, and began to use it unknowingly, and at length. Maybe she'd grown to like it.

The accent, the creek, the plumbing, the metaphysics. She could see the entire town flowing through here, eventually.

Not all at once, but gradually Counter Intuitive would gather, and hold, just for a short while, the entire vibe of this town in the space of the palm of its hand one cup of coffee, one BLT, one mug of soup, one slice of pie, and one wedge of cheese at a time.

Heidi closed her dark eyes and sniffed the ends of her thick swirl of hair deeply, then coiled it slowly around her left ear. Her eyes opened and scrolled the length of the counter in languid blinks. The quiet and empty counter, save for Lucy and all her glorious, everywhere copper hair, and the mystery of her rings of dead cats.

Robert was gone. The delivery truck's flashing and clacking had stopped, the truck's bangs and echoes rumbling off and fading away and disintegrating over the Noisy Creek bridge. The cold continued to squeeze the remaining droplets of daylight from the darkening sky. And Heidi realized she never did answer his question about the essence of metaphysics in terms a plumber could understand, at least not out loud. But it didn't really matter, and a better question would have been *What is the essence of plumbing in terms a doctoral student can understand?*

EPILOGUE – OUTTAKES

Editor's note: Several characters appearing in this collection of stories submitted a request to leave closing statements, remarks, etc., particularly those written about in third-person or whose presence remained off the page. Ed. staff agreed but requested each character keep their remarks brief. Their submissions follow. Some items have been edited for clarity.

—Ed.

* * *

So while telling you about Joyce and Roger I mentioned that I finally lost some weight. Thirty pounds exactly! My family is amazed, and like everyone else, wants to know how I did it.

I discovered a crazy diet plan. It's called eat less, read more. Seriously. But, actually, it's:

Decrease/eliminate:
  cheese
  beer
  sausage
  baked goods
  candy

Increase/add:
  morning reading (30 min)
  afternoon reading (30 min)
  evening reading (30 min)
  1 hour of sleep/night[1]

The first ten days were very hard.

How did I manage so much extra reading and how did reading help me lose weight? Well, for one, I bought a cross-trainer. One of those elliptical models that tracks calories burned with a digital display. For another, I live alone and have few other actual responsibilities beyond my job (actuary at UW-NC). So I finally just made myself do it. And, I love to read. So I just read while "cross-training" and following the food-items-to-avoid list above. That was it.

This is totally unrelated, but after a while I noticed that I burned more calories while reading certain authors than others, and I started to pay closer attention. At first I did so casually, just happening to observe that Madonna was always consistently higher than McCarthy, for example. Then I started to write them down at which point it became a bit of a game, which prompted me to read more and more and thus burn more and more calories. It was exciting. I could see myself losing weight and making progress through my reading backlog. Win-win!

Here are my numbers on avg cal burned/.5 hr/author, rounded to nearest 5 cal. Your results and choice of author/s may vary. And these numbers are by no means an endorsement nor reprimand of any of these writers, as wonderful as they may be. Remember, I went from being a person of zero physical activity to 90 min/day. So anything other than what I had been doing would seemingly equal a 100% increase in physical exertion. Add to that skipping the foods listed above, and something was about to give! *poof* Thirty pounds.

Tom Perrotta: 295
Madonna: 300
Sam Harris:: 275
Robert Heinlein: 240
Bette Adriaanse: 290
Paula Fox: 285
Cormac McCarthy: 280
Salmon Rushdie: 295
Danielle Steele: 275 (I know, I know!)
Stephanie Meyer: 265

And the surprise (or not) winner: Shirley Jackson at 320 avg cal/.5 hr! Not even close! I have no idea if a scientific study of author to calories burned exists, but this is really interesting.

Also, and this totally has nothing to do with Shirley Jackson, but there's a place near Luck called Straight Lake State Park. I'm pretty sure I have to go there, just because.

—**Phillip Nelson Stephenson** *('Trig'—ed.)*

End-note/s:

1. How does one extra hour of sleep per night help with weight-loss? Not certain. It just sort of happened in some weird reward loop. I'd always heard that one who wishes to lose weight should sleep more, but it all seemed rather counter-intuitive to me. I mean, how could laying around more, idling immobile, prompt weight loss??

But the reality seems to be this:

First, exercising more tired me out, thereby causing me to require more rest. Especially at first. I was soooo out of shape. I had zero muscle-tone and I was heavier than I'd ever been in my life, which meant that not only did I have more bulk to heft about, I possessed my flimsiest muscle-mass ever with which to transport it. That is bad.

Second, extra sleep meant less time available to eat the things I needed to avoid. A lot of how you look and feel is connected to what you eat. And this bit, less time for indulging in those tempting sausages or malt beverages, for example, certainly helped. Very simple. Sleeping = not eating/drinking crap.

And finally, the extra sleep, combined with a new/better diet, meant I was more rested and thus more able to hit that cross-trainer with more vigor three times per day. So I exercised harder, burning more calories, which tired me out and required that extra hour of sleep my body came to crave so as to allow me to cross-train more energetically (you should have seen me the first ten-fourteen days. Uuuugly!). Also, a well-rested mind has more self-control, more will-power, and seems more disciplined and less prone to cave to the yearning supplications of bakery sweets or whatever. And within a month I'd hit a certain self-sustaining eating-and-reading rhythm, and I'm pretty sure I couldn't have done any of it without that extra hour of sleep per night. Hence that weird reward loop.

* * *

I never wanted any part ever of any of this. And, as such, I abstain.

—**Elenor L. McGannis** *("Momma"—Ed.)*

* * *

I dint get any words in here, but no biggie, really. I don't say much. Not that kinda bartender. Not gonna hear and solve all yer problems and all that. I don't got the stomach for it anyhow.

This is a bar you come to to clear your head, not your conscience. Do that somewhere else. Then come back for the happy hour taco's 5–7 pm Friday's.

—Ernie

* * *

Empathy isn't the 'spirit world.' We empaths certainly have greater access to it, and we do tend to come and go in and out of that realm from time to time. But we don't <u>live</u> there.

The spirit world isn't really all that extraordinary or interesting, anyway. It's just another realm. This, despite the surprisingly high number of spirit-world tourists and wistful wannabes, all migrants rushing at it for permanent residency and practically causing a spirit-world refugee crisis.

So, stop. The spirit world can be, and often is, just as industrial, mechanical, boring, and burdened with dread, doldrums, and the common cold as this world. The glittering New Age candles, incense, tinkling bells, music, robes, gowns, and all that are bullshit. If it doesn't make any sort of sense here, what on earth would make you think it does there? And I don't know why anyone would want to trade for that world when they're already from a perfectly good one to begin with.

Houses hold memories. There's an old yellow one here on Vinny I trot by on my run depending on the day's route. It feels as though it tips to the right no matter which way you come at it. The windows are very wide, and more rhomboid than rectangular. Everything about it echoes charm and a sorrow dripping wet with a sweet gentleness. And goofy. Because of its age, and the strong older woman who lives there alone, people say it's haunted. Nooo. Charmed, maybe. But not haunted.

Damnedest thing, though. Cinnamon and pickling spice and stewed tomatoes. Warmed clove candy canes. Fudge on a gas stove in a steel pot every time I run by there. I've never felt anything quite like its draw. It's as though it's running <u>at me</u> as I approach. I always feel so backward after running past it, like it's trying to pull something that's inside me to the outside, in a neither good nor bad way.

—Jen

* * *

I am a twenty-eight year old orphan, and I've been a pick-pocket most of my life. That's my dark secret while I live the life of a marginally alcoholic theater major at UW-NC.

Anyway, that guy at the nursing home was my last job. I'd supposedly quit, but he, some kinda pickled, blue-nosed drunk, made it a bit too easy for me. So I got back to my apartment, pasted his ID into the mosaic of IDs I'd collected from all the pockets I'd picked, and called the mosaic done. I leaned back and decided it was time to move on.

Heidi, who finally agreed to meet me out for a drink, got wind of my wall project and decided to move on, too.

—James

* * *

Emmet was such a dear. He hated Christmas. He wanted me to think he hated it for me, but I knew better. He hated it all on his own without having to try to please me. He'd put up a tree and lights early every December and insist on taking it down right after the New Year. This was a passion, to avoid the tacky. And to keep Christmas stuffed in a box in the upstairs closet.

Emmet and I were only married for fifteen years, though going back to our childhood, we were together for thirty-eight. Which is why once in a while I am asked the secret to a long and happy marriage. And I think the key to any happy marriage may well be to marry young and die first.

One day someone different will be looking out the mirror at you. Will you be ready?

Live like there is no afterlife. Live true to yourself, not to fear. You will find eternal life right here in everyone around you. You will live on in them just as you lived within yourself.

—Harriet

* * *

Probably the worst feeling in the world, Dad said, is piloting an airplane with iced-over wings. Once the ice hits critical mass you're basically flying a bank safe.

Straight down is straight down, and you start grabbing around fast. And at that point, he said you may as well have just jumped straight away and have done with it.

—Cyp

* * *

Now is as good a time as any to re-discover Led Zeppelin and Peter Tosh.

—Heidi

* * *

No vaccine exists.

—Mitch

* * *

Another man came into the bakery a few minutes after Robert left the day he told me about his dying friend. The man asked about mice. He said it like he had information suggesting I had mice in my bakery.

He said he asks everyone the same question.

I laughed, imagining the man going all over town asking, "Got mice?" and I explained that there are no mice in my bakery. He said, "Oh, is that so?" and I said, "Yes, that is so because I grew up in a house without a cat, and I therefore had to get really good at catching the mice."

The man gave me a curious look.

So I shared a tale of my mother standing on a kitchen chair while I crouched down and sprang and snatched a mouse as it scooted along the floorboards. Then I walked to the creek out back and tossed it by the tail into the long grass on the opposite bank. I told the man that I always wondered how long it took that little guy to eventually make its way back into our house because I'm pretty sure that over the years I kept springing and snatching up the same mouse.

This seemed to satisfy the man, and he asked for a glass of water. It was a hot day, and he drank it down in one swallow. But I didn't offer him a bread-end because he wasn't a bread-ender, I could tell.

—Elspaith

*　*　*

About that twenty-five-minute at-bat. Ball two should have been called strike three. Like that one kiss I never risked, it was there. Right on the corner.

—Robert

ACKNOWLEDGMENTS

Gratefully acknowledged are the following publications, where stories first appeared in earlier versions:

"Ronny" first appeared in *Midwest Review* and was selected as the fiction winner of the Great Midwest Writing Contest by Liam Callanan.

"These Are My People" first appeared in *Barstow & Grand*.

*   *   *

It bears repeating: *Writing is hard.*

This, despite all the other true things that writing is—necessary, fun, joyous, a struggle, therapy. Also true: Once you start, you'll never be the same. Yet in the end, what remains is that writing is hard, and most certainly cannot be done alone. And in my case the people to thank for getting me out the other end is too lengthy to list and can't possibly include everyone. So instead I'll give it a go in semi-broad strokes.

—My wife, Stephanie, who shouldered too much.

—My siblings, Kathy, Mary, and Rick, and their families, who, like Stephanie, watched me write my way out of a very bad place;

—Our children, Samuel, Elliot, and Leo, whose love and wit and charm keep me sharp and alive.

—My parents who, while never encouraging me directly to be a writer, provided a stability that allows a child to take so much for granted and imagine looping such things as being a writer within his possible futures.

—Virginia Wilcox, eighth-grade English teacher who told me to never stop writing—even if it was always about getting eaten by bears.

—The erudite Pen and Think Writers, who patiently read through so many initial drafts of these and many other stories: Jim Guhl, Carmen Pinkerton, Gary Jader, Charles Ladd, Jan Dunn, Anne Hollenbach, Jim Swanson, Bev Larson, Paul Hambleton, and Manfred Gabriel.

—The very clever and damn good members of the Black Dog Writers a.k.a., Erin Lunde, Marcia Williams, Jacob Wrich, and Michelle King.

—Kim Suhr, Director of Red Oak Writing, who told me I was ready, and also kindly blurbed this and my previous book, *Sometimes Creek*.

—The Wisconsin Writers Association.

—The #WritingCommunity of pre-Elon Twitter.

—Brad Nelson, Peter Siavelis, Molly Ramsay, Bridget O'Meara, Heidi Metro, Carmen Martines, Ansley Kolinsnyk, and Shannon Rutngamlug for so many early, brutal reads.

—Dr. Ross Tangedal of Cornerstone Press for giving my prose a chance in the first place, Cornerstone Editorial Director Brett Hill and his close-reading team of crack editors who took on this book, Lillian Kulbeck, Kim Janesch, Gwen Goetter, and Karlie Harpold, as well as cover art designers Samantha Bjork and Scott Miller.

—Tim Storm, founder of Storm Writing School, for developmental and inline edits, patient back-and-forth emails and video calls, needed doses of reality, and meals at Himal Chuli.

—The Larsen Public Library of Webster, Wisconsin.

—Tricia Christiansen for website design and *The Name of the Wind.*

This book would absolutely not be possible without the insight, expertise, and encouragement of writer, coach, and mentor Allison Wyss.

The kind and thoughtful writers out and about who took time to read through and/or blurb this book, Amy Cipolla Barnes, Kimberly King Parsons, Matt Cashion, Sean Little, Jeff Esterholm, Manfred Gabriel, Carol Dunbar, Wendy Wimmer, Ghassan Zeineddine, Richard Thomas, Michael Hopkins, Kim Suhr, Nikki Kallio, Barry Wightman, Richard Mirabella, Dave Rank, Alice Kaltman, Rebecca McKenna, Jim Landwehr, and Amber Sparks.

Finally, I'd be remiss if I did not extend a certain gratitude to all of these, my people, of Wisconsin. Thank you for being you.

STEVE FOX is the award-winning author of *Sometimes Creek* (Cornerstone Press 2023), winner of an American BookFest Best Book Award, finalist for the Chicago Writers Association Book of the Year, and longlisted for the Edna Ferber Book Award. He is also the recipient of the Rick Bass Montana Prize for Fiction and the Zona Gale Award for Short Fiction. He lives in Wisconsin with his wife, three sons, and one dog.